Magic Touch

A.S. Fenichel

ALL RIGHTS RESERVED

Copyright © 2022 A.S. Fenichel

No part of this book may be reproduced in any form or by any electronic or mechanical means, including information storage and retrieval systems, without written permission from the author, except for the use of brief quotations in a book review.

Edited by Penny Barber

Cover by LoveTheCover.com

Images from Depositphotos, Design Cuts

First Electronic Book Publication April 2022

First Print Book Publication April 2022

ESME

I never dreamed my small curatives shop in Windsor, England would attract the attention of war hero Sir William Meriwether. My feminine heart is aflutter when he enters. But I'm a witch and a healer, and he's a man in pain, so I heal him. Desperate to do him a good service, I stretch my powers to the limit—or perhaps beyond. Somehow, in curing his ailing leg, I unleash powers inside William. At a loss to stop what's begun, I'm forced to seek assistance from the coven I've sworn never to join. I dread the encounter, but for William's sake, I put my family's hatred aside. Getting to spend more time with William is an added enticement.

WILLIAM

I'm mesmerized by Esme O'Dwyer from the moment I lay eyes on her. Despite our different stations in society, I want something more personal than any restorative tea she might offer. As a gentleman, I contain those baser needs and accept her assistance to ease the pain in my leg. When the alluring witch's touch bestows me with magic of my own, I want no part of it. But the coven's leaders insist magic never makes mistakes, and for this to have happened, I must be needed. I've never been one to shy away from duty, and being secluded for training with Esme is magical in more ways than one.

ESME

Trouble is coming to Windsor. The signs are all there. The race is on to train William as a witch before his power is needed, but our growing attraction is as undeniable as the battle that lies ahead.

ACKNOWLEDGMENTS

Special thanks to my writerly friends who constantly encourage and stand by me, even when my story ideas are unusual. Maybe that's what you love best about them. I love you all so much. Thank you to Gemma and Juliette for helping me get this book started with a fabulous writing retreat. Thanks to my dearest friend, Karla Doyle. Your support all these years has meant everything. xoxo

This book is dedicated to the real Simon. He came to us starving and alone on a cold January day. We had plans to find him a good home, but he won our hearts in a few days. We loved him and babied him as best we could, but he wasn't long for this world. As wonderful and full of life as he was, he was only two when we lost him. In such a short time, he filled our lives with love and joy. We miss our sweet boy every day.

And, to Dave, who brought magic back to my life when I believed it had left me forever.

CHAPTER ONE

WILLIAM

I never should have told my driver Samuel that I would walk the last five blocks, but the carriage was delayed by an overturned cart, and the afternoon is waning into evening. Foolish as it might be, I hope the healer will be able to give me some relief. The idea of waiting another day depresses me.

Shooting pain screams up my leg. If the healer says she needs to cut the damned thing off, I won't argue. I exaggerate, of course. The surgeon in France wanted to do just that, and I threatened to gouge out his eyes, even as my blood-soaked the table.

I check the address on the parchment again. Mr. Preston, the apothecary I visited yesterday, said Miss O'Dwyer, a healer, had a shop on this street, but he didn't know the name of the establishment.

A grocer, a book shop, and a door with no marking at all line the street, but nothing says "healer." Of course, Mr.

Preston had hesitated before calling her a healer, and I swear he'd muttered *witch* under his breath.

My disappointment turns to anger as I turn back up the street. The awkward movement shoots a bolt of pain through my thigh as if a hot poker were stabbing the bone. Biting my cheek prevents me from crying out and drawing the attention of people going about their day.

As the wave passes, I take a deep breath.

From the door with no sign, a bell tinkles.

A woman of middle years with blonde hair poking out from her cap creeps from the door. Eyes wide, she looks down the street in both directions before she hurries off.

Perhaps the healer doesn't need a sign in this part of town. I go to the door and step inside, causing the bell to tinkle once again.

"Did you forget something, Mrs. Cauly?" a woman calls.

Lavender and frankincense fill the air. As my vision adjusts to the dimness, I find myself surrounded by shelf after shelf of bottles, jars, and packets.

At the far end of the narrow shop, a counter stands with bowls of herbs and earthy scented powders.

At eye level to my right, a soft-pink skirt moves. Perched on a ladder, a woman with moss-green eyes surrounded by thick dark lashes stares down at me.

"I beg your pardon, sir. I thought my last customer had returned." She scurries down the ladder and faces me with a kind smile. Her dark hair is swept up in a loose bun, and soft curls frame her face. Lips meant to be kissed long and hard distract me utterly.

In fact, I can't seem to remember anything. I'm sure if anyone asks my name at this moment, I will stumble for the answer.

Her curved brows rise, and she cocks her head. "Are you lost, sir?"

Perhaps I am, but that isn't the right response. Shaking off my fascination with her unmatched beauty, I say, "That depends, madam. Are you Esme O'Dwyer?"

A wider smile pulls at those maddening lips, and my brain fogs over again. "I am she. How can I help?"

It takes me several long moments, while I likely look like a dimwit, before I can put a sentence together. Damn those lips. "Mr. Preston, the apothecary, said you might have something for pain. I've exhausted all my options, and laudanum muddles the brain too much. It's not to my liking. I was hoping you might have a tea." I prattle on while she stares with those pouty lips and sympathetic eyes. "I've tried peppermint and clove, but they didn't help enough. You see, it's been some time since I've had a night's sleep, and what my physician gives me is effective but makes waking rather difficult."

I order myself to stop talking. Why did I tell her all of that? *I need a tea for pain* would have been sufficient. Lord, I'd die happy if I could kiss her. What? No. I've clearly lost my mind.

Her cheeks flush briefly. She strides behind the counter. "I will try to help. What kind of pain do you suffer from, sir?"

"It's my leg. You see, I was wounded in France." Unsure what else to say, I force myself to remain quiet.

She nods as if she'd expected as much, but instead of gathering items for tea, she stares at me a long while, her gaze so intense it makes me feel as if I'm under scrutiny for more than a painful gait.

Unable to decide if I should leave, stay, speak, or grab her and kiss every thought from her beautiful head, all I can do is wait. As if frozen in place, I stare back while heat climbs up my neck and blood rushes to my manhood at an alarming rate. When she finally speaks, I have to clear my head to make it out.

"If you will trust me, Sir William, I think I can help you far more than any tea. Though, a good curative tea is not without merit. If you had a recurring headache, I would make you a tea. This, however, may need more than herbs."

Moving to the counter, I bite back against the searing pain. I've almost gotten used to living with the reminder of my time at war. Almost. Between the leg and my growing arousal, I stumble slightly and have to catch myself against the wood. I regain my balance and look at her, my face entirely too close. "I apologize, madam, I don't know what you mean, nor did I realize you knew me."

Color infuses her creamy cheeks again. "Pardon me. I read about you in *The Herald* last year. A few months ago, I saw a portrait hanging in the Royal Museum. It seemed rude to mention it when you first walked in. Perhaps it's still rude."

"Not at all, Miss O'Dwyer. It's easier to be honest in my experience." I loathe that damned painting the king requested. I can hardly stroll down the street without some stranger calling out or wanting to hear about my time at war. Annoying and invasive, it is as much a part of my life now as the pain. However, Esme O'Dwyer's recognition doesn't offend me at all. That's something to examine later.

"Indeed." She pauses, looking down at her hands, which are fidgeting on the counter. "Would you like me to try to remove your pain?"

This stunning woman could certainly make me forget my leg for a while, but I'm sure that isn't what she's offering. "I'm afraid I still don't understand."

Her lips pull up in the most alluring smile. "Did Mr. Preston not tell you what I am?"

"A healer."

Searching my face, she cocks her head. "I'm a witch, Sir William."

"I don't believe in such things," I remark automatically even though part of me feels bewitched by her already.

Her low laugh shoots lust directly to my groin. "Your belief in a thing does not discount its existence. I am here. I am real. And I am most certainly a witch. However, I'm happy to brew you a nice tea that should ease your pain for a time. I can also mix a sleeping draught if you like."

Yes, that's exactly what I'm here for, but I don't want the encounter to end so quickly. "What other treatment did you have in mind?"

"I might be able to heal you."

"Heal me?" I can't wrap my head around what she's telling me. I've been to dozens of surgeons and doctors, and none would even attempt going back into my leg. Managing my pain is all anyone offers.

Hands on her hips, she laughs again. "I would put my hands on your leg and try to draw the injury out and heal whatever damage was done."

Her hands on me? The idea is so wickedly appealing that it takes all my wits to process the rest of what she's saying. "You wish to touch me?"

Shaking her head, she rounds the counter, marches to the door, and throws the bolt. She returns to me. "Follow me, please."

What else can I do, but as I'm told? We leave behind the shelves and remedies with their earthy scents and follow into a brightly lit kitchen with a large window and yellow roses in a vase on a wooden table.

It's small but bright and cheerful as opposed to the mysterious darkness of her shop. I find myself nonsensically afraid to touch anything and hold my hat in both hands in front of me.

"Please sit, Sir William." She points to one of two wooden chairs by the table.

I admire the roses and do as instructed while she stokes the fire smoldering in the cooking hearth and heats a teakettle. At the wooden counter, she takes bits of this and that from different canisters and puts them in two teacups. The water boils, and she pours the tea and brings me a cup.

"You said tea would not help me." I stare into the cup as the water turns darker.

Sitting in front of me, she sighs. "Sometimes a cup of tea is simply a cup of tea. I thought it might put you at ease."

"Oh." I'm a fool. "Thank you." I sip the tea, and it's quite nice. Far better than I would have expected from someone who lives in this part of town. As an apothecary of sorts, I suppose she has more opportunity to buy finer leaves.

Her grin is like a reward for good behavior. "Is it your right leg?"

"How did you know that?" My heart thrums wildly. What have I gotten myself into? Yet, being near this beautiful woman is like a drug and far better than the laudanum on my bed stand. If she wishes to touch me, I cannot deny it, and perhaps I can still leave with a curative that may help me sleep.

Eyebrows high, she says, "It is the leg you favor when you walk."

Closing my eyes, I take a long breath. "I'm not usually this much of an idiot." It shouldn't matter if she thinks I'm a fool, but it does.

"May I touch your leg, sir?" Her moss-green gaze bores into mine.

"It's unseemly." My words can't do justice to my thoughts. I want her to touch me. I want all of her touching me, and that is not at all gentlemanly. In fact, such base thoughts about a woman I've just met are completely out of character.

She nods. "May I do it anyway? I promise I shall do no harm. It is our most sacred rule."

"Witches?" It may be nonsense, but I can't help the rush of curiosity. My heart beats a bit faster and my skin tingles pleasantly.

"Yes."

While I'm sitting, my pain dulls to only an ache. I stretch my leg out in front of me to provide her better access, and the pain sharpens.

With graceful fingers, she opens the four buttons at my knee. A small silver ring around her pinky glints in the sunlight as she unties my garter and rolls down my stocking. After exposing my calf, she places her soft hand on my outer thigh.

Her touch isn't much different from that of my physician, but hers sets my body on fire. I should tell her to desist, but it's the last thing I want. Soon the evidence of my arousal will be obvious, but I can do nothing about that, short of storming out. And I long to be near her.

She stops at the scar a third of the way up my thigh. Strange heat and tingling encase the old wound. Her hands glow a shimmering sky blue. My instinct is to pull away.

"Wait, William. Do not move yet." Her voice is like a balm, soft yet commanding. Masses would follow this woman to their death if she asked it of them. Of this, I am certain as I remain in her kitchen with her capable and delicate hands on my bare skin.

The tingling intensifies. Pain follows, but it's muffled. Something moves inside my leg. It must be my imagination. Then I feel it again, and my knee jerks of its own accord.

My pulse thunders, and my leg heats as if on fire, but still the pain is tolerable. She has no knife or sharp object in her hand, but it's as if my skin is coming apart. There should be more pain. I know it on the deepest level, but everything I see and feel is strange and impossible.

Her full lips pull into a thin line, and her eyes meet mine

and glow like stars on a clear night. Sweat beads on her forehead and upper lip, and her cheeks have gone pale. "I've nearly got it, William, just a bit more."

"Are you injuring yourself, Esme?" I have no right to use her given name, but she has her hand inside my breeches, and it seems some liberties should be allowed.

A slow smile pulls at her lips, which look rosier with her color drained from her face. "I thank you for your concern, but I will be fine."

She's lying, and I tug my leg back, but her grip is firm, and her eyes glow brighter. A low mutter stills me as she sings, "Goddess sure and true, of this I ask, strength of will and power now to heal a hero good and proud. Let his pains be lifted. Let this need be gifted. Pledging willing vessel me, as I will so mote it be."

Light fills the kitchen, obscuring my vision. Fire swallows my leg from the inside, as if branding me with a hot iron.

The room returns to normal light, and I blink to adjust my sight. Warmth fills me.

Esme's hand remains on my leg. Then she draws a long breath and pulls away. She puts a bullet fragment on the table and leans back in her chair. Her skin is so pale she looks near death, and red rims her eyes. "It seems—" she draws a breath, "your surgeon—" another breath, "missed part of the bullet."

Staring at the bit of metal, I have no words for what I just saw. Magic is a thing of fantasies and children's stories. Yet it's hard to deny the evidence before me.

I look from the shrapnel to her sickly face. I have seen that same pasty look on the faces of dying soldiers on the battlefield. "Esme, what have you done?"

"I will recover." There is no confidence in her assurance, and as she attempts to stand, her legs collapse, landing her back in the chair.

Rising, I lift her from the chair. Even my worry can't completely shadow how soft and warm she is in my arms. "Where are your rooms?"

Eyes wide, she swallows hard. "The door there leads to stairs. I live above."

I follow her gaze to the dark wood door in the corner, then carry her up to a neat set of rooms with a sofa and two chairs. Another door ahead probably leads to her bedroom.

"Shall I put you in bed?" My heart pounds at the idea of being in her bedroom, but she is in need, and I want to help.

"Here in the sitting room will be fine." She points to the sofa.

Placing her on the cushion as if she might break in two, I'm filled with sorrow when I release her. "Can I get anyone for you?"

She shakes her head. "There is no one. If you would be kind enough to pour me some of that wine, I will be fine."

On a table at the far side of the room is a decanter and two small crystal glasses. Rushing to help however I can, I do as she asks and bring her the wine. It smells of something I don't recognize, and I suspect it is more than just wine. Some witches brew, perhaps.

As she sips, the color returns to her heart-shaped face. "How is your leg, sir?"

My concern for her is so all-encompassing, I didn't even notice that I carried her up a steep flight of stairs without pain. But in her cozy little sitting room, I flex my muscles, and only an echo of pain remains.

Elation floods me, and a blue light surrounds me. I'm glowing the same color as her hands when she had them on my leg. Inside my chest, something familiar rises like a bird trying to escape its cage.

Esme's eyes widen as she stares. Her voice is breathy and perhaps fearful. "William, please sit."

Not wishing to be the object of her trepidation, I sit in one of the two gold-and-brown striped chairs and examine my glowing hands. *Not possible.* I close my eyes and know it will be gone when I open them. "What is happening?"

"I'm not certain. I've healed many people but never has the magic remained after the healing. Perhaps I overextended, and this effect will fade." She sounds doubtful.

I force myself to look again, and the glowing fades. I should excuse myself and leave her. Instead, I pull up my stocking and button my breeches at the knee. My leg offers no resistance to movement. I stand and sit several times, and still there is no pain beyond stiffness and a very dull ache. It's as if I was never wounded. "Do your healing activities often leave you so drained?"

"No." Already looking stronger, she sips her wine.

"How was this different?" I should ask how any of this is possible. I should deny everything I have seen, but I'm not a man to lie to myself. She healed me with her hands, and there is no doubt about it. Somehow, with some power I can't possibly fathom, she coaxed a bit of metal out of my leg, and healed the wound. My suffering is a shadow of what it has been. Even now, the remaining discomfort continues to wane.

She shakes her head. "I'm not entirely sure. Perhaps it was moving the object from flesh and bone. Perhaps it is my own fault for wishing to help you more than was objective."

My pulse quickens. Could my desire be shared? *Don't be a fool.* I lean forward to bridge the distance between us. "I don't think I understand."

Those eyes I so admire shine with passion and ferocity. "I am attracted to you, William. I know you and I are not part of the same circle, and I have no designs or desire to quit my sphere, but attraction is part of being alive, and I'll not be shamed over it."

"Shamed?" It's impossible for my heart to beat any faster, or for that organ to withstand the joy flooding it. "I certainly would not wish you to feel shame."

Her chest rises and falls faster, and her cheeks pinken. "You should go now, Sir William. I'm sorry to have been a burden, and I'm pleased I was able to help you."

Obviously dismissed, I stand. "What is the fee for your services, madam?"

"A healing is one sixpence."

"May I ask how you did it, or is it some mystical secret?"

She tilts her perfect face and those green eyes smile up at me. "It's not, but it is very hard to explain to someone who has no frame of reference."

"Will you try?" I'm stalling, but also curious.

"As a healer, I can see the broken parts in a person or animal. I can use my magic to reach them, and will the body to heal."

I am mesmerized by her lips as she speaks and can't look away as they close on her last word. If anyone can wield magic, it must be Esme. She has me completely under her spell.

I don't want to leave her. There is no expression of thanks that will do justice to what she has done for me, and her admitting her attraction is a balm to my soul. I dig two shillings out of my purse and place them on the table near the door. She will likely be angry to find I paid four times her fee, but I'll be long gone. "Thanking you hardly seems enough, madam. You have done for me what I was told could not be done. I am in your debt. If you are ever in need, you should come to me, and I will do all I can to help you."

"I'm glad you are well again, sir." Her voice is tight, but her gaze is direct.

How I would love to have those eyes on me while bringing her pleasure. She is a dream. Nodding, I open the door. "Esme?"

"Yes, William?"

"I'm attracted to you as well."

She nods. "Yes, I know."

Smiling, I plod down the steps. I collect the shrapnel from the table and put it in my pocket before walking through the shop to the door. The bolt is thrown, and I realize it won't be possible to lock it from the outside without a key. I exit through the kitchen and secure the door behind me.

As I exit the alley, Samuel jumps down from my waiting carriage and opens the door.

Taking one last look at the shop, I climb up and think of moss-green eyes and the most kissable lips I've ever seen.

CHAPTER
TWO

ESME

The moment Sir William Meriwether walked into my shop last evening, my heart soared. It was some kind of strange dream come true. Except, he came for help, and I nearly drained myself to give him what he needed. It was a foolish mistake. If he'd not been so kind, I might have lost consciousness in my kitchen and lain there for hours with who knows what consequences.

Luckily for me, he is a good and kind man, and I had an elixir recently brewed in my rooms. He paid too much for the healing. I will send a note around to his home with the overage.

I shall never admit this out loud, but I have been smitten with him from the moment I read his story in the paper. When I saw his solemn portrait hanging in the Royal Museum, I stared for an hour. I couldn't look away.

In person, his eyes are more passionate than sorrowful. While he said he didn't believe in witchcraft, he must have had an idea he was coming to a witch for help. The apothecary knows what I am. That showed both desperation and open-mindedness. Never has my magic made someone glow as it did William. Perhaps I gave him too much, too fast, but the fragment had woven its way into muscle near the bone. Removing it took more out of me than expected.

The last thing I wanted was to hurt him, but I felt desperate to take away his pain.

I've thought of nothing but him since. I spent my workday in a fog of memories. Touching him and knowing my touch aroused him was a constant distraction. Of course, many men would grow hard from a woman touching their leg so intimately. It's foolish for me to believe there is anything special in my touch.

Nearly time to close, the bell over the door rings and Mrs. Bates enters. "Miss O'Dwyer, I'm in need of more of that cream for my face if you have any."

Smiling, I hand her the cream in an envelope of waxed paper and say, "I keep it just for you, madam. I'm glad it's been working well."

Mrs. Bates puts her coin on the counter. "You have never failed in keeping my skin soft."

"How is your son's rash?" I ask. The babe was suffering from a terrible diaper rash last time she was in.

"Right as rain." She smiles. "Do you think that salve will keep for the next time?"

"You've put it in the cool larder?" I wrap up her purchase.

She nods.

"It should keep for three months without any problem." I thank her for her business, and she bustles out, checking the street to make sure no one sees her leave.

Many of the neighborhood people frequent my shop, but few admit it. I'm a witch, a fact of common knowledge, and yet still a secret. I clarified it with William, more to remind myself that he is not for me. Any childish notions I might have about the knighted landowner are silly at best.

As I take Mrs. Bates' money to the back room, the bell tinkles again.

Planning to lock the door as this will be my last customer, I turn back to the shop.

Cloaked in black, William stands in the middle of the shop, hands on his hips. He peers out from under a hood, and surrounding his sky-blue eyes is a blue glow, which is my magic, no doubt.

"Oh, dear." I rush around him and lock the door. "You had better follow me to the back, Sir William."

My heart pounds. I'm thrilled to see him but terrified I have caused him harm. He follows, and I search my mind for some bit of knowledge that could explain the glow.

As soon as we're behind the backroom door, he whips off the cloak. His blond hair is shorter than is the style among grand society, and it, too, glows with shimmering blue magic. "What have you done to me?"

His hands glow as well, in the same color that accompanies my magic. Though, perhaps a shade or two darker.

"Nothing like this has ever happened before, Sir William. I have no explanation. Magic is not transferable, at least I have never heard of any such spells." I rush the words, not sure how to help him. Taking his hands, I ease him to the table. "Will you sit? Maybe I can help you release some magic and stop the glowing."

He takes a long breath that expands his already broad chest, making my heart flutter. I'm worse than a child with her first crush.

Finally, his blue eyes meet mine, and he sits. "It came back when I was...excited earlier today. I've tried everything I know to wipe away the thoughts that brought it on, but still, the glowing persists."

Sitting across from him, I take his hands and will the magic back into me. The power creeps close, like a cat sniffing at something new and interesting, but then pulls back, unwilling to come. It doesn't feel quite like my own magic. There is something unrefined and unfamiliar about it.

Rather than toy with things I don't understand, I let go of the desire to pull this power from him and open my eyes. Keeping his hands in mine, I take another path. Maybe I can get to the root of the problem and work it out from there. "What brought on the excitement?"

He stares at me as if he might set me on fire. "It's of a personal nature."

Swallowing down my embarrassment does nothing to keep my cheeks from flaming. He is a man. Men take lovers all the time. There is nothing to be jealous about. "You were aroused? Were you with a woman?"

Head shaking, he pulls his hands from mine and laughs long and hard. "No, Miss O'Dwyer. I did not take a woman to my bed in the middle of the afternoon on a Tuesday. I try to keep my baser instincts in check until at least Friday."

"You are teasing?" It's almost a relief.

"I am. I was, however, thinking of a woman." Again, those stunning eyes lock with mine.

I can't look away. Desire can be a very powerful tool in magic. If somehow, I had transferred some of my magic to him, perhaps the absence, or relief of that need, would deplete the magic. "And the woman is not available, or in a position to relieve this need."

The right side of his mouth pulls up in the most wicked smile. "I don't know the answer to that question, but perhaps you do."

"Me. How can I know what the woman you desire wants? I know I said I'm a witch, but premonitions and mind-reading are not my strongest talents." Perhaps if he brought the woman here. Oh lord, I've lost my mind entirely. Of course, he can't bring a woman who knows nothing of his affections to a witch for divination.

William shakes his head and laughs again. "Are you telling me that lovemaking will cure me of this glowing?"

Hearing lovemaking from his lips sends a thrill down my body, and it transforms into an ache between my legs. I have discussed sex with clients before. It is common for women, and occasionally men, to come to me with their bedroom problems. Surely, I can get through this conversation without melting into a puddle on my kitchen floor. "I don't know for sure. However, desire is very powerful. If you alleviated that desire, it might remove the problem."

Fire flares in his gaze, warming my skin. He adjusts his seat and the glowing increases. "Then, I am to glow like some star in the sky every time I desire a woman for the rest of my life? I'm certain my future wife will be thrilled to know exactly when I'm in need of her." He stands and throws his hands in the air.

I rise as well and touch his shoulder. "Please calm down, Sir William. I'm sure this is temporary. Magic is not transferred from person to person. I have healed hundreds of people with my hands, and this has never happened before. Perhaps you might go to the country for a few days or a week and wait for it to subside."

"It was you," he whispers in a rough voice.

"What was?" I remain close to him but drop my hand as he turns to face me.

"I was aroused by you. The way you touched me, the way you look, how fragile you were, lying on your couch, needing my help. I thought of all of that as I was dressing for the evening. That was when the glowing resumed." Light pours from his face, neck, and under his collar. "Do you still want the lady in question to alleviate my needs?"

"Oh, dear." I don't know what to say. I want him too, but I'm not the kind of woman who beds men I barely know. "I am not a woman of loose morals, sir."

He touches my cheek with the back of his hand in a whisper of a touch. "I suspected not."

"I'm sorry if I gave you the impression I was that type of woman, or that I need a man to keep me." Swallowing down my desire and keeping my voice even is a miracle of an achievement.

He sits and cradles his head in his hands. "You did no such thing. My want of you is only natural. You are very beautiful and kind."

"And beneath you." It pops out of my mouth before I can stop it.

Looking at me, he smiles again. "What do we do, Esme? I cannot go around glowing. I can go to the country, but my mother is there with a house full of servants who will be surprised their employer shines blue like a star in the heavens. It was all I could do to hide it from my valet and butler before I ran out of the house today."

I have no idea how to solve this. "There is a coven here in Windsor. I can inquire with them and see if they have any experience with this. It will have to wait until morning. They gather, at least they used to gather, in the mornings to hear coven business."

"You are not a part of this coven?" No judgment, just curiosity.

"No. I am a lone witch, as my mother was before me." A knot tugs deep in my soul at the thought of my mother.

"Is that common?"

"Most witches belong to a coven for safety and community."

His stomach grumbles. "I was supposed to go to my club for dinner."

"Well, you can't go like this. If I invite you to eat here and stay the night, will you think I'm a loose woman?" I'm sure to regret allowing the object of my affections to spend the night in my home, but I have done this to him, and he can't be out and about in his current state.

"I would think you're a very kind woman and thank you for your hospitality," he says formally.

Turning from him, I close my eyes for a moment and will my good sense to override my burning desire for him. "I have stewed lamb. I'll add some potatoes and carrots and it will be ready in no time."

Even with my back to the table, I feel his presence filling the space. I try to ignore the want of him coursing through me, as bright as his glowing skin, if not so obvious, but it won't leave.

"May I help you in some way?" He's standing directly behind me.

I'd not heard him move, or even sensed him. The stupid infatuation must be dulling my senses. "Do you cook, Sir William?"

He peers over my shoulder as I chop carrots. "I can feed myself in a pinch, but no. I have a cook in my employ."

"How did you learn to feed yourself?"

Moving so that his hip is leaning against my counter, he faces me. "When I was on the continent, I had several occasions where I needed to forage for food. I would harvest a rabbit or some other woodland animal, build a fire and cook it.

My first few attempts ended rather badly, but I got better with practice."

I drop the carrots in the pot and set to work on the potatoes. "I suppose we all do what we must to survive."

Darkness shadows his eyes and the blue glow dims. "Yes." He spots his hands and his gaze shoots to me. "The effects dimmed. Did you see?"

"I did. What were you thinking about?" As he looks at me, the glow increases again.

He studies his hands. "I was thinking about the war. Nothing specific, just the horror of it all."

Heart in my throat, I don't want him to think of terrible times. Yet his gaze is too much. I focus on the potatoes and add them to the pot, then place the heavy iron on the hook in the hearth. "We've been so occupied that I didn't ask you how your leg feels?"

Gaze distant, he rakes his hand through his hair. "I barely have any pain. It's an echo of what was."

It is a very good sign for the healing process. "Sometimes the magic begins the healing, and then the body takes over the work. What you feel is the final stage of your recovery. I'm pleased I could help at least with that."

Having taken a vow to do no harm, it grates at me that I have somehow broken that oath. I wanted so badly to help him. Maybe my personal feelings took over, but my intentions had been good and pure.

If Mother were alive, she'd know what to do. "I'm sure the coven will give us some directions about this phenomenon." I take out two bowls and spoons, and set them with napkins on the table.

William places them carefully in front of each chair. He even folds the napkins neatly. "I believe you had no ill intentions."

The knot in my gut eases slightly.

When the potatoes are tender, I spoon stew into the bowls, then place the pot on a stone near the hearth, where it will stay warm but not cook any further.

We eat in silence while the idea of asking the Windsor witches for help gnaws at me. It isn't that I have anything against the coven, well, not directly. My mother and the witch who previously headed the coven were adversaries.

"What are you thinking that causes you to scowl so?" William takes the last bite of his stew.

"Do you want more?" I change the subject.

"No, thank you. This was very good. It reminds me of a stew the cook of my youth made long ago." As he gets lost in his memory, the lines around his mouth ease.

"I'm pleased you liked it." Despite the glow of blue magic, he has nice hands, strong and callused, as if he does more than sit in his grand house and laze the days away. "The magic wouldn't come to me, but maybe I can teach you how to focus the light so it's not so obvious."

He takes his bowl and spoon to the sink. "What would I have to do?"

There is something out of place and yet perfectly right about his broad shoulders filling the space near my sink. A small pump brings water from the well outside, and he gives it a few tugs until water fills the basin.

"I will clean the dishes." I jump up and rush to the sink. "If you'll wait upstairs, I'll only be a few moments cleaning up."

"Afraid I'll chip something?" His smile is infectious.

"A lady does not like to share her kitchen, is all." I motion for him to head up the stairs and wait.

CHAPTER
THREE

WILLIAM

Her rooms are just as they were the night before. I sit on the couch, but then rise and round the room, inspecting trinkets and books as I go. Touching items that are familiar to her feels intimate, and I don't want to stop. With no business snooping, I can't help wanting to know her better. Something about Esme O'Dwyer calls to me at a level I haven't experienced before.

She is attractive. Beautiful, to be honest, but it's more than that. I can't put my finger on the why or how of it, but she is irresistibly magnetic.

I run a finger over an ornate little box sitting on the plain mantel of unadorned wood. The box has gold filigree and a row of tiny rubies along the edge. It seems quite out of place in the simple apartment.

"It was my mother's. She was a fine lady of society, but lowered herself by marrying my poor Irish father. That box is the only item from her past that she kept." Esme stands in the doorway. She isn't angered by my snooping, nor does she seem surprised.

"This is very fine." I take my hand away and face her. "Do your parents live nearby?"

"My father died many years ago in an accident at the mill. My mother, just last year, from illness." While her voice is steady, sorrow lurks in those extraordinary eyes.

I want to go to her and ease her pain in some way, but it isn't my place. "I'm very sorry. I lost my father several years ago, and I miss him every day. My mother has never been the same. She resides at my country house. It's not far, but distant enough that she is away from the society she no longer enjoys."

She crosses to the chair and sits. "I suppose losing our parents is inevitable. It doesn't make it easier, but we do expect it at some point."

I sit across from her on the sofa. "I suppose so. You were very close with your mother?"

Esme glances at the box and nods. "Yes. We often disagreed, but she was the person I needed most in this world. Now I must fend for myself." She looks at my glowing hands and lets out a long sigh. "I have made a mess of this."

With every reason to be angry and agree with her, all I can do is shake my head. "You will find a way to fix this. We don't even know what caused the phenomenon. If I am willing to be patient and sort it out, you should be kinder to yourself, Esme."

"Must you be so nice?" Her lips pull up in the first smile I've seen from her tonight. It warms my heart.

"Perhaps I can be foul tempered later, or tomorrow, to make you feel better," I tease.

"You would have every right." With a sigh, she takes my hands in hers. "Let's see if we can control this."

Just that simple touch shoots through me as if she is lightning, and I'm the tallest tree in a vast field.

The green of her eyes deepens, and she stares. "Did you feel that?"

"I feel it every time you put your hands on me, and even sometimes when you look at me." I'm being far too honest, but I can't seem to help myself. There is something about us together that is alluring and almost irresistible.

Keeping my hands in hers, she nods. "I thought it might just be me."

The blue glow around my hands deepens, and I clear my throat. "What must I do to control this?"

She draws a long breath and closes her eyes, only opening them after she releases the air. "Do you feel the magic, or is it just the glow?"

It is the strangest thing. Even earlier, I wasn't afraid, only shocked. Then anger filled me. Once it faded, I wondered about the science of such a thing, if there was any. "It feels as if something new, yet familiar, is coursing through my veins."

Squeezing my hands, she smiles. "Good. That's good. Now concentrate on that and put it into a small space outside your body."

"What do you mean?"

"Picture a bubble in the space between our hands and send the magic to the bubble." She pulls her hands from mine. "Like this." Above her right hand floats a pale blue orb. It bounces and pulses with light and energy.

"What is it?" I ask.

Opening her eyes, she bobbles the ball up and down before it erupts and flows over her chest like water and absorbs into her. "It's my magic. Or at least, a manifestation of my magic."

All my life, I have only believed in what I can see and touch. My father frowned upon any fantasies that might take me away from my studies. He'd said not to be mired in imagination. It was the road to Hell. Nothing about Esme is evil. Of that, I'm certain. Goodness flows around her like a warm blanket. "What can you do with it?"

"A great many things, but I'm a healer, and my magic is in kind with that vocation."

With anything good comes bad as well. I learned that in war. Though most of what I saw was bad. I don't want to ask, but I must know. "Then, if it can heal, it can also harm." I close my fists, wishing the blue light away, but only succeed in making it stronger. "I've harmed enough in my life, Esme. I'll not allow whatever this is to hurt a living thing. I'll do away with myself before that."

Intensity flashes in her eyes, and she grabs my hands again, pulling my attention back to her. "This magic doesn't control you. You are its master, William. 'Do no harm' is a way of life. If you fail in that, it would be a great disappointment. However, the first step before we learn how to remove what I left in you, is to control it."

My heart pounds a staccato, but I nod and close my eyes. In my mind, I envision the bubble she made, and push the new sensations rolling through me toward a similar ball in my hands.

Calm settles over me for the first time in years. I open my eyes, and there above our joined hands is a ball of blue light, a darker shade than Esme's was.

"That's quite good. Now command the ball smaller and bring it inside yourself." Her voice trembles with excitement or pride. I can't be sure.

I think about a smaller light and the bubble responds. Then I ask that it go away, and it erupts in a sparkling fountain and fills me again. My skin shines like a sun for a moment, then fades to the blue again.

"What did you do?" Censure rings through her question.

"The sensible thing. I bade it leave me."

She sucks in a slow breath and lets it out. "Of course. Magic is never as simple as we wish, nor as complicated as we hope, my mother used to say. To rid you of the magic, we must understand how you came by it. My healing should not have done this to you, so there is more to the state of things. Try again, but just ask for the magic to remain small and tucked away this time."

My father's voice rings in my head. *Don't trust anything you can't explain. Banish trivial ideas. Stay the course.* He could not have predicted this. I do as Esme instructed and watch as my newly formed ball of light rides a wave into my chest and settles beneath my heart. My hands no longer glow. The new sensation still remains with me but tucked inside. "I don't understand any of this."

She releases my hands and goes to the cupboard, where she removes a bottle of whiskey and two glasses. "You may ask me anything, and if I can, I will answer."

"How did you become a witch?"

She pours two glasses and hands me one. "Witches are born, not made. We have lived longer than humans if the old tales are to be believed."

"You are not human?" Why that should trouble me, I can't say.

She sips her drink. "Not in the strictest sense. Non-magical people may live to seventy or so. I suppose some a decade or two longer. The average life of a witch is almost three times as long."

"You said your mother died last year. Was she very old?"

Shaking her head, she says, "No. Though she had me at

nearly forty-five and could have had more children, perhaps into her sixties or older. I've heard of witches giving birth at one hundred years. But that's not what you asked. Witches are not impervious to disease. Mother became ill, and none of our magic could cure her. She refused the help of the coven, though I don't think they could have helped either."

"How old are you?" I blurt before good manners can be enforced.

A bell-like laugh falls from those full lips, making me long even more to kiss her. "I'll be twenty-five in a few months."

"Forgive me." I drink down the strong spirits in one gulp and put the glass on the table. "I shouldn't have asked such an impertinent question."

"It's all right. How old are you?" A wicked smile turns her from pretty to exotic in a heartbeat.

I lean closer, unable to stop my body from the draw of her. "I've just passed my thirty-first year. I don't know why it should trouble me that you will live hundreds of years beyond my death, but something about you, Esme—" I shake off the rest of the thought. I have already said too much.

"What about me?" She sits forward.

Unable to resist knowing how soft her skin is, I run my knuckles along her jaw. "You mesmerize me."

She closes her hand around mine but doesn't move to stop my touch. She eases closer, her lips parted, and the hint of her pink tongue brushes her bottom lip. "I've done nothing to make it so."

"No." I kiss her cheek. The scent of warm vanilla and lemons fills my head. "Yet I've never wanted anyone with such intensity. Forgive me." My mouth covers hers, and the light inside me relaxes, like coming home after a very long journey and finding my favorite chair just as I left it.

Esme sighs, and when my tongue touches hers, she wraps her hand around my neck and threads my hair.

Her touch is like a torch to dry straw.

I stand, pulling her up with me, and wrap an arm around her waist to pull her close while still cupping her jaw.

Our lips move together as if we've waited all our lives for this kiss. Moving with me, over me, under me, she presses her body to mine, which responds in kind. My shaft yearns hard between us.

Esme presses her hips tight to mine and moans deeply.

Cupping her bottom, I crave more, and am rewarded by her tongue sliding over mine. I kiss her sweet neck, and her pulse thrums for my touch just as mine pounds through me like a marching band. "Esme."

I kiss my way back to those miraculous lips, already parted and panting. Drawing the bottom between mine, and then the top, I revel in how she responds as if made for this moment with me.

This woman has become everything in just one day. *One day.* It crashes over me like a bucket of cold water.

With every ounce of my will, I break the kiss. "Esme, this is not right. I want you, but you are not mine to have, and just yesterday, we were strangers."

She closes her eyes. "No. I know." Pulling back, she brushes her hands from under her breasts to the top of her skirts, wiping me and my touch away. "I share equal blame, William. I should have kept my distance. This could be a product of my magic resting inside you. Once it is gone, the feeling will likely go as well. Then we would be left with nothing but guilt."

I don't bother to explain how ardently I wanted her before she ever laid a hand on me. What would be the point? We are from different worlds, and mine doesn't include witches or shopkeepers. Longing to change my world will not make it so. "Forgive me?"

There is the barest twitch of her lips before she turns serious. "There is no harm and nothing to forgive. I'll get you some bedding for the couch and let you get some rest."

She does as she said, and I lay staring at the dark wood beam on the ceiling for hours. So many feelings and instincts drove me these last two days. There should be many things to regret, yet I can't wish away any of my time with Esme O'Dwyer.

CHAPTER
FOUR

ESME

The bookshop owner next door and I share a water closet just outside my back door. We shared the expense of putting it in. It is a luxury I have never regretted.

On my way back inside, a black-and-white kitten cries out. It sits at the door as if expecting to be let in. I crouch and rub under its chin. A rumbling purr makes me smile.

"Who might you be?" I glance around to see if someone is looking for the little mite, but we're alone, the alley empty due to the early hour.

"Well, if someone comes hunting for you, you'll have to go, but perhaps you need a home. I've never had a familiar. Are you to be my eyes at night, or have you some other power?"

The kitten blinks up at me seriously.

Giving him one more pet, I open the door. I put a bit of last night's stew in a bowl for him and watch as he gobbles it down. "You're in luck. I can cook."

I put on some coffee to brew and, still in my robe, I rush upstairs with a pitcher of water for washing. Kitten at my heels, I nearly trip twice, but make it to my rooms unscathed.

William is a sight to behold with his hair rumpled and eyes full of sleep. Cravat removed, his warm golden skin and smattering of dark blond hair peeks through the vee at his throat.

If the pitcher in my hands wasn't so heavy, I might gawk at him all morning. "Good morning, William. Were you able to sleep at all?"

"Some. Thank you."

I pour half the water in the bowl on the stand where I keep a few kitchen items. "You can wash here, and there's a water closet out the kitchen door." My face heats idiotically. I roll my eyes and am glad my back is to him.

In my bedroom, I pour the rest of the water in my basin and wash up before quickly pulling on a day dress. I hear him talking from the next room. Good lord, he's gone mad already.

I rush the remainder of my toilet and return to the sitting room.

William is sitting on the floor with the kitten, having a very serious and adorable conversation. "If you don't tell me your name, little fellow, I shall make one up for you. What do you think of Darby?"

The kitten, with green eyes, one patched in black fur and the other in white, stares up at him.

"No? Hmm, Dan?"

No response from the beast.

"Jacob is my steward's name. He's a fine fellow. Do you fancy that?"

The kitten cocks its head, and its ears go back.

"I see." Thinking, William scratches a day's growth of beard.

My heart is near bursting. If William hadn't had good sense

the night before, I'd have let him have me. I'd never wanted anyone more. Witches don't always follow the rules of society, and they often take lovers, but I tend to be quite particular, and never would jump into an affair that can't possibly last more than one night. I'm no saint, nor am I a whore.

"I know," William announces. "Simon!"

The kitten gives a loud mew and jumps into William's lap.

Masculine laughter fills my sitting room, and my heart. "Simon it is then."

Holding Simon, William leaps to his feet. "I suppose I should have let you tell me his name. I didn't mean..."

"Don't be uneasy. He appeared at the back door this morning, with no master in sight, and immediately made himself at home. Besides, I enjoyed the naming process more than I should probably admit." My cheeks heat for the second time that morning. I have lost all control of my emotions and it won't do.

He scratches Simon's chin. "He does seem to like the name. Will you keep him?"

I nod. "Animals like Simon are good luck when they find you. I think he's meant to be here. He won't stay if the fit isn't right. At least that's what my mother always said. She had a hawk who stayed with her. She could see through his eyes as he flew over Windsor. After she died, Theo stayed a week with me before flying off. I mourned his loss with my mother's."

Why had I told him all of that? Surely, he doesn't need to know or care about old Theo and my mother. He likely doesn't believe Mother could see through Theo's eyes.

"It was good of him to stay the week with you. I should think he must have cared deeply to have done so, but then it was time to move on." William's eyes fill with sorrow, which he shakes away a moment later.

"Thank you." I search for more to say, but I'm at a loss for words. What he said is in the teaching of Goddess. I doubt he's ever learned such lessons.

He hands Simon to me and brushes the patch of hair from his coat. "As I am no longer glowing like some heavenly star, I thought I might go home and change. Perhaps I can meet you back here in an hour, or would you come with me?"

It shouldn't be such a terrible thing for him to leave and return, but my heart knots at the idea of his departure. Perhaps he will never come back. He might be seduced by darkness with magic not meant for humans coursing through him. It would be my fault if such a fate befell him. "Wouldn't your staff be surprised by me accompanying you?"

Head cocked in thought, much as Simon's had been, William says, "They have been with me since before the war. I think they will adapt to a new friend."

"They will think we are lovers. They will take me for your mistress of the moment." As much as I long to be close to him, I don't want to be the kind of woman who men discard like old clothes.

Touching my chin until I look into his eyes, William presses a chaste kiss to my lips, flooding me with magic and desire. His eyes wide, he says, "I have never had a mistress. And though I have had lovers, never have I brought them to my home. My staff will think you are a friend, and that is what you are, Esme."

"This power between us, William, I'll not lie, I find it as terrifying as I do alluring."

He releases my chin. "As do I. Let me get properly dressed, and we shall see if this coven has any thoughts."

William was right. His staff treats me as if I'm one of the master's greatest friends. They seem unsurprised by my presence, and while I wait, they bring me tea in the parlor. The house is small but very fine, with a curved staircase in the foyer and marble on the floor. The parlor is decorated in forest green, and a cream damask wallpaper that hints at pink.

I sip my tea and sit on an overstuffed chair that costs more than I will make in a year. I pray I don't do or say anything to make a fool of myself. I should be more worried about our upcoming coven visit, but the notion of spilling tea on the crushed velvet nearly has me in a panic.

It's past eleven by the time we take William's carriage to the coven house in the north end of town. It's a respectable house, and from the outside, unremarkable. The lower floor has a meeting room with wooden chairs placed against the walls, should someone need to sit during gatherings. Between the chairs are buckets filled with dirt or water in case of a spell gone wrong. No sofas or tables clutter the room of meeting and conjuring. Through the door on the right is a stillroom with herbs and flowers drying on cords. The coven leader, Sara Beth Ware, lives on the floors above stairs, and if my memory serves, another witch, Minerva, has a room.

I knock, and Minerva opens the door. She is blonde but hides her mass of curls in a matronly cap. I have always liked Minerva, and she is one of the only witches who visits my shop regularly.

Another witch peeks over Minerva's shoulder. Sara Beth keeps her voice soft, but even so, doubt and wariness permeate her question. "Esme O'Dwyer, what an unexpected surprise. Have you finally come to join your sisters in the coven?"

"No, Sara Beth. As my mother before me, coven life is not

for me." I try to keep my mother's disdain from my voice. That was her quarrel, not mine. I only need to honor her wishes, not share her anger.

Minerva stands to Sara Beth's right, her expression sympathetic and calm. Three more witches watch from the far corner. Another witch, wearing an apron, observes from the stillroom. I stay so far away from coven business that I don't know the other four witches. Sara Beth visited once, trying to bring me home, as she called it. Minerva often stops into my shop for a chat, or to exchange thoughts on herbs and spells for healing.

Sara Beth says, "My mother and yours have both gone to Goddess, Esme. Can we not begin again and hope they have resolved their differences in the life after?" She clenches her fists, but her voice remains even.

I feign a long thought. "I was very saddened to hear of your mother's accident. I prayed for your healing as you mourned. However, my mother left this coven because yours would not accept my father into the fold. Have rules regarding male witches changed since your mother moved on?"

Tightness pulls at Sara Beth's lips. "Men turn to the dark far more often than women."

"Have you proof of this? We know that women also turn. It might be an old wives' tale, or perhaps your mother disliked men so much she didn't want to be bothered with them. I have often joined in that assertion. In any case, my mother bade me not be bullied by you, or any other witch, and I will honor her wishes." I draw a long breath and keep it steady despite the shaking I feel within.

All the while, William stands in the shadows near the door, and watches with seemingly little interest, but I can feel his gaze on me. It's ridiculous, but having him here makes me feel safe, despite the reaction I expect once our problem is revealed.

"Male witches have long been a problem. However, when I

see a need to revoke any of my mother's rulings, I shall call a quorum and ask for a vote. This particular mandate goes back much further than my mother. There have not been men in the Windsor coven in over two hundred years," Sara Beth explains.

"I am well aware." I hold my breath, hoping for bravery. "This is not why I have come to you. I am in need of help. While I had good intentions, I have done this man harm."

Minerva gasps and her gaze shoots to William.

Taking a step closer, Sara Beth studies him. "In what way? He looks healthy enough."

"Sir William, please show them." Ready to defend, I pull my magic to me.

William stands up straight, opens his coat and releases the blue magic from his chest.

A gasp rises up from the witches.

Sara Beth lifts her hands, and her palms fill with yellow light.

I jump in front of William. "He is not a witch, and even if he were, he means you no harm."

The witch by the stillroom begins to chant a spell.

The other three rush forward, each ready to cast defensively at William.

I force my own ball of a lighter blue out of me and hold it aloft, while William smartly tucks the magic in him away.

"How dare you bring that creature here?" Sara Beth's eye twitches, and she faces me, gold orbs of magic rising brighter in her outstretched hands.

Not letting my guard down, I rush to say, "Two days ago, Sir William came to me with no magic. He was in need of healing. I drew part of a bullet from his leg and healed him. The effort was almost too much, a mistake on my part. Afterward, this magic grew inside him. I thought it would fade. I've never heard of magic transferring. But it didn't fade, and I was able to teach him some control over it. I have vowed to do no harm, just as you have, Sara Beth. I have harmed him, and I come to you to help me correct this."

Minerva puts her hand on Sara Beth's arm. "She tells the truth. And I don't sense any danger from the man. We would have felt that he was a true witch when he arrived. The fact that none of us knew reinforces Esme's story. Besides, he is a war hero. Someone surely would have noticed if he were a witch."

Sara Beth lowers her hands and nods to the other witches, who cease their spell casting. Striding close, she studies William.

William puts his hands on his hips and pulls his shoulders back as if to allow her a good look.

I don't like it one bit. He looks too fine to be in the company of this many women.

"Lucy," Sara Beth bites out a command, "go and ask the high priestess if she will join us."

The rosy-cheeked witch with thin brown hair runs out the back door.

"You told this witch you had no power?" Sara Beth points to me but keeps her eyes on William.

"I told her nothing on the matter, as I didn't even know such things existed until her touch. Witches and the like were the things of fairy stories. Who is this high priestess and what will she do to me?"

Minerva eases forward and places a hand on my shoulder, sending calm through me with her touch. She says to William, "Prudence Bishop is our high priestess. She will determine if you are a danger, and perhaps can tell us why this has happened."

"Prudence Bishop?" I ask. "My mother spoke of her, but I assumed she was dead by now."

"Not yet, child. Though if Goddess is kind, someday soon I will join her." The scratchy voice comes from the back door. Step by slow step, Prudence Bishop crosses the hall. The members of the coven bow in low curtsies. Even Sara Beth honors the high priestess with contrition.

As she approaches, waves of magic emanate from her. Her dark-blue eyes are full of power. Hunched back and all, she is a force, even at her age. She arrived so quickly, she must live very close, maybe even another apartment within the coven house.

As she touches my cheek, instinct tells me to move into her, but my heart pounds, and I want to run.

"I remember the day you were born, Esme O'Dwyer. Your parents were very proud, and I gifted you a piece of quartz."

My thoughts shift to the shard point of clear quartz sitting on my dresser. "I still have it, Great Mother. I did not know it was from you. I have always had it and cherished it."

She looks into my eyes, and I feel her magic inside me for an instant, then it retreats. "You healed this man?"

"Yes. I went too far and had to use a restorative." I don't want to say too much.

Staring at me until I want to squirm, Prudence smiles. "He tended you while you recovered."

Impossible to lie, so I nod.

Prudence's thin lips twitch with amusement. She moves to William, who gives her a courtly bow like one might give a duchess.

"Sir William Meriwether?"

"Yes, madam."

Pressing her hand to the center of his chest, she closes her eyes. The blue light of his magic surrounds him.

His eyes close.

I push forward to protect him, even if it means going against Prudence and the entire coven.

Minerva grips my arm. "She's only assessing what he has. She'll not harm him. You have my word."

Trusting Minerva is easy when I offer her potions, and she in turn does the same, but I can't risk William. "Great Mother, please stop what you are doing."

A gasp from Sara Beth proves this doesn't happen often. Whatever Prudence wishes is accepted.

The high priestess lowers her hand but looks totally at ease, and not at all put out by my outburst. "I cannot take this gift away as you had hoped, child. You are a witch."

William takes her hand as the glow of his magic slides back inside him. "Madam, I had no knowledge of this power before. How is that possible?"

Moving her hand to the crook of his elbow, she walks with him to a pair of chairs near the wall to the left of the hearth.

I follow but remain standing as they sit.

The other witches gather close to hear what is said.

After several long slow breaths, Prudence says, "Long ago, my kind were hunted and killed for what we were. At that time, many families decided to hide their magic and never use it. For generations, they suppressed their nature, until the power of Goddess could find no way out and went to the shadows."

"And now it has awakened?" William asks.

"Your power is similar in nature to Esme's. When she healed your wound, she unintentionally awakened the magic." Prudence smiles, showing crooked yellow teeth. "I've never seen this in all my years, but I have heard it can happen."

"Great Mother," Sara Beth asks, "why did we not detect him as a witch when he arrived?"

Prudence's shoulders lift in a slight shrug. "He's holding it tightly behind his heart. Interesting that's where you chose to put it, William. If you wish to remain human, you might have put it someplace less powerful, such as your toe." She giggles like a girl at her own joke.

I don't know what to say or even think. "Then he cannot go back to what he was?"

"Not without being bound." Prudence sounds grim.

To spellbind a witch is the worst possible punishment.

"He should be bound." Sara Beth props her fists on her hips. "He knows nothing of magic. He's had no training. He is the perfect object for dark magic to embody."

"Hold your tongue, Sara Beth." I face her, my magic simmering under the surface, ready for the first sign of a binding spell.

Prudence lifts a hand. "Peace, children."

Both Sara Beth and I quiet and face her.

Tears pool in my eyes, blurring my vision. "I don't want him harmed because of my mistake, Great Mother."

Prudence's fearsome gaze burns into mine. "If Sir William chooses binding, he will not be harmed. He will feel the magic in his soul, but not use it. He shall not necessarily miss what he never had. However, Sara Beth has a point. If he chooses to remain a witch, he will need to be trained."

WILLIAM

When I was a soldier, my world got flipped upside down more often than not. The last two days have rocked me more than I'd like to admit, yet somehow it all seems right. I can't explain it.

"Remain a witch. Is that possible?"

"If you wish it," Prudence says. "It is your nature."

I can't even imagine what this would mean to my comfortable life. How would I explain such a thing to Mother?

Esme's eyes shine with unshed tears. "I am sorry, Sir William."

If it's my nature as Prudence says, then I don't know how Esme can blame herself. Regardless, I hate that she's distressed. "I hardly think you could have known that my family had suppressed its nature for generations, or that my magic would match yours to an extent that you could awaken it. It seems this was a strange occurrence of coincidence."

She sighs. "Oh, William, there are no mistakes in magic. This happened because you were meant to return your family to the place nature intended."

Prudence nods. "She tells true, my boy. Goddess makes no errors. You are likely needed, or will be soon. But even so, if you wish to go back to your life as a gentleman, you can do so. Goddess also insists on free will. The choice is yours."

I know nothing of magic or how to use it. Power in novice hands is dangerous, even if my intentions are good. I could harm someone. Yet, if I'm needed...I look from Esme's worried eyes to Prudence. "Who would train me?"

Prudence narrows her gaze. "Esme O'Dwyer would take you to the coven cottage and teach you to use and control magic. She will show you how to conjure and cast. Then the coven will test you against the dark to be sure your heart remains with the light."

"Me? I have my shop to run. I can't go to some cottage" Distraught, she avoids my gaze.

I long to know what is running through that mind of hers.

In a sunny voice, Minerva says, "I would be happy to care for your shop for a few months. I don't imagine you would be gone longer than that. Sir William would be a good student, I think."

I can't stand here and let my fate be decided. There is only one person in the room I can truly trust. I take Esme's elbow. "Will you give us a moment, ladies?"

I guide her across the hall and out the back door. It takes a moment for my eyes to adjust to the brightness of the alley. Being near her sets my body aflame. I should move back, but I pull her into a hug. "I'm sorry, Esme. I have been nothing but trouble to you."

Pulling back to look in my eyes, she studies me as if I'm a madman. "You have no cause to be sorry. Do you want to be a witch and learn magic, William? You might find it difficult to live among society while living among witches. You would have two lives and keep one secret from the other. It's not as if you can stop being Sir William Meriwether. People will recognize you on the street, even if you're a witch. Is this what you want?"

My shoulders ache with tension, and I can't relax. Duty is ingrained in me like the blood that flows through my veins. How can I walk away? I know nothing of their goddess, but two days ago, I knew nothing of magic, and it is real enough. If a deity sought fit to arrange for my power to come forth at this time, how can I run from it? "She said there was a purpose, and you agree with that. For this to happen now, there is some need for me to have magic?"

Esme's lips pull into a straight line before she lets out another long sigh. "Goddess chooses her timing carefully. If your father had been needed, or perhaps it was your mother's side, it would have happened a generation ago. At some point, you will be needed as a witch."

"And if I allow the binding, what happens?"

Despite the warm sun, she shivers. "I don't know. Whatever you were needed for goes some other way than intended. There's no way to know. Still, the choice must be yours. You cannot allow me, or any witch, to persuade you. I will say that most witches would prefer death to binding, but perhaps Prudence is right, and you will not miss what you never had."

I'm no stranger to fear, yet this task seems more daunting than a volley of bullets across a battlefield. "Will you teach me? I don't want to do this with another. I don't trust any others."

"I'll not let you go through this alone. We are friends after all, are we not?" She takes my hand.

Heart in my throat, I kiss her knuckles. "We are friends." Touching Esme feels perfectly right. Only as we cross back into the coven house do I release her and stride to Prudence. "If I agree to go with Esme and be trained, can I change my mind and be bound at a later date?"

Prudence's eyes widen. "Binding is a serious choice."

"If I should turn to the dark magic as Miss Sara Beth fears, I shall want to be bound. I'll not harm anyone." The idea of harming Esme tightens like a knot in my stomach.

Prudence closes her eyes and lets out a long breath. "I think there is little chance of that, child. Your heart is pure and full of light. However, I will bind you should you turn."

I take Prudence's hand. "We have an agreement then."

Prudence's bones creak and pop as she stands. She shakes my hand. "You have my word."

Esme covers our joined hands with hers. "Then we shall go to the cottage tomorrow and begin."

Easing herself back into the chair, Prudence says, "Wait three days, and I will go with you. It will make it seemlier for the few neighbors near the cottage, and perhaps I can be of some help. I am old, and this may be my last chance to do some good in this world."

I nod, and it is agreed.

CHAPTER
FIVE

WILLIAM

I should go home, and at some point, I must. Prudence asked if any of my staff could be trusted to understand what was going to happen and accompany us to the cottage. It wouldn't do to bring any of my household staff into danger. My mind is a jumble of new information and emotions.

Instead of going home, I take Esme and Minerva to the shop, where Esme explains the contents of every shelf. The amount of medicinal knowledge these women keep in their heads is miraculous. At first, it's fascinating. After an hour, it's mind-numbingly boring.

"Miss Honeywell, shall I wait to take you back to your friends?" Abruptly interrupting their debate over the uses of milk thistle was perhaps rude, but if I am to be subjected to a life of herbal remedies, I shall demand to be bound after the first day.

Minerva smiled. "I can walk, Sir William. There is no need to wait on me."

Escaping this dissertation floods me with relief. I bow and pull on my overcoat.

Esme's hand on my arm stops me at the door. "Is something wrong?"

Her looking into my eyes is almost enough to make me reconsider. I switch my gaze to Minerva, who is watching from the counter. When I look back at Esme, I ask, "Is this what my life is to be? I can see that you have a passion for such things, but I'm sure I never shall."

"I don't know what path you will choose for the use of your magic." Her smile is soft like a summer breeze.

"Then there are more choices for someone with our type of magic than salves and ointments?" My brain is numb from the herbal lesson I've overheard this hour.

Joy lights up her entire face. "You can do whatever you want or nothing at all, but you must learn to control your magic, lest it control you."

Flooded with relief, I draw a long breath. "I will be back for you in three days. Send word if you need me sooner."

There is no reason she would have any need for me to return before the appointed day of our departure. Yet, I want her to know I am at her service. I don't even know this woman, but I want more of her. If she is half as affected by me as I am by her, it is a good thing the high priestess is going to the country with us.

"That is kind." She moves back and makes a curtsy. "I will be ready in three days. Goodbye, Sir William."

With a bow, I say, "Until then, Miss O'Dwyer."

I miss her the moment I stride out of her shop. If a man can be bewitched, which I suppose I should find out if one can, I am smitten. As it is totally inappropriate, I shake away the notion and get in my carriage. "Home please, Samuel."

On the ride, I wonder what the future has in store for me. I'm deep in thought when Samuel stops the carriage and opens the door.

Rogers awaits at the door to my house and takes my overcoat.

"Do you know where Dove is, Rogers?" I ask about my valet.

"He is below, sir. Shall I send him to you?"

"That would be helpful. I'll be in my study." I turn and head down the hall to my study, which has a fine library taking up one entire wall. Sun streams in from the large windows behind my desk, and I run my hand along the row of books at eye level. My gaze rises several shelves higher. Some books at the far end were my father's, and his before him. I haven't paid them much attention since I was a boy, but I trace the bindings with their faded titles. After pulling down three tomes, I place them on my desk and pull out a piece of parchment from the drawer. I need to write to my mother. I open the inkwell but close it again.

What do I tell her?

There's a knock, and Dove enters. "You need something, sir?"

Dove and I served together in France. He needed employment when the war ended, and I needed a valet. I can think of no one I trust more. "Dove, may I ask you something in confidence?"

He blinks several times, then straightens. "Of course, sir."

"I'm to take a journey with Miss O'Dwyer and another lady. We're to go to the country, where she will teach me how to use a new skill I've recently acquired. Do you think there are members of the staff besides yourself who would be discreet if they saw things that are impossible?" I am making a complete muck of this.

Tall and lean, Henry Dove wears his brown hair brushed straight back from his forehead, and his dark eyes rarely show emotion. Now they shine with a hint of interest. "I don't know what you mean, sir."

"Perhaps you should sit." I toy with a deep scratch in the top of my large mahogany desk, and indicate the chair in front of the desk.

With an eyebrow raised, he sits.

"It seems there are things in the world that I thought were fairy stories but turn out to be real. My father always told me witches and those tales of mythology were to be ignored and pushed away. I think his father told him the same. I'm certain this was done for several generations, but now those warnings were for naught." In my memories of my father's adamant stance against imagination, I'm mostly talking to myself.

Dove narrows his eyes and leans forward. His voice is barely above a whisper. "Will, what has happened?"

Calling me by my given name shows his concern as a friend. I fold my hands on top of the desk. "I hardly know where to begin. You'll think I'm mad."

"You and I have seen and been through too much for that. And if you are mad, I'll keep your secret, and take you out to spend your days in the country with your mother." It's the first time I've seen him grin since he became my valet.

Taking a deep breath, I tell him everything that has happened in the last two days. At the end of my tale, I let the magic out and show him, lest he really think me insane. "So, you see, I must either have this taken away, or learn to use it. I have no idea if it's a gift or a curse, but that is yet to be discovered."

I tuck the magic away again.

Pale, Henry leans back in the chair. Sitting silently for a long while, he stares at me. Drawing a long breath, he focuses on his hands, then meets my gaze again. "I will go with you, of course. I think Samuel can be trusted, as well as Anne, the downstairs maid. Do you think you'll need more than that?"

Overwhelmed with gratitude, I don't know what to say. For the years we were at war, Henry and I were friends, and then we were not, as our ranks precluded the continuation of our friendship. It seems we are again friends, or perhaps I was mistaken, and we always were. "That will be more than enough. Thank you, Henry."

"How can you be certain these women have no malice in mind by taking you to the country?" Sitting up straight again, he places his hands firmly on his legs as if at the ready to jump up at any moment.

"I'm not certain how I know, but Miss O'Dwyer is of pure heart. I'm sure of it." It's the only thing in the world I feel sure of at this moment. Everything else is a spinning madness.

Standing, he says, "I see."

"You always see too much, old friend," I warn.

His lips twitch the slightest, and then Dove returns to his stoic expression. "It is my job, sir."

"Can you inform Anne and Samuel in some way which I don't sound like a madman?" I hardly see how that is possible, but they have to be told something.

"I will inform them that we are going to the country, and they are needed. If things become...strange, we shall deal with it on a moment-by-moment basis. I believe it will be fine." He bows and leaves the study.

I don't know if Dove is right, but I'm thankful to have someone in my corner during what is sure to be the strangest phase of my life thus far.

Turning my attention to the books, I open the top one. It is a handwritten account of some kind. There is a column on the left with dates and an account of events for each date. It begins on April 1, 1547. The writing is difficult to make out.

I open the center drawer in my desk and remove a magnifying glass.

Margaret Marley was tried and put to death yesterday. Poor Peggy was a good sort and a powerful woman. If she could be removed so easily, we are all in danger.

Heart in my throat, I put the book aside and take up the next.

On the inside cover the inscription reads *Samuel Meriwether*, and beneath it says *with his wife, Sarina Meriwether*.

I turn the page.

For the management of stomach ailments.

A list of herbs precedes instructions to combine them into some kind of salve.

I'm having trouble breathing. Last time I looked at these books, my father caught me and became enraged. He put them up high so I wouldn't reach them. Had my father known about all of this?

The third book is in Latin, and my skills are not up to the task of reading it. Perhaps that is for the best. Reading things I'm not yet equipped to understand might not be wise. I put them aside with the glass, to be packed for the journey. Perhaps Esme or Prudence will find them of value.

Returning to the letter to my mother, I dip my pen in ink and halt as I contemplate what to write.

I spend the next two days getting things in place as if I'm going on an extended holiday. My man of business is informed, will see to the houses, and ensure that my mother is cared for financially. I have told him I will write with my address as soon as I'm able. I have the carriage resprung for the trip. I'm told it's not far, but the carriage will be full with six people in all.

On the morning of our departure, I place the books in a small bag and hand it to Dove. "I suppose this is a new adventure."

"Indeed, sir." Dove hints at a smile, but his eyes show wariness as he waits for me to exit my room.

As I enter the hall, the fact that I'm going to see Esme fills me with excitement. My hands glow. After days of concentrating on mundane things, my magic has escaped from containment at the mere thought of her. Turning, I find Henry gaping. I check the hall and lurch back inside my room before another servant can spot me. "Henry, I'll be down in a few minutes."

"Is there something I can do?" Looking as if he might try to fight the glow out of me, he lifts a hand in my direction.

I sit on my bed and stare at my glowing hands. The cream damask walls close in, and the heavy wood wainscotting looks faraway. The wardrobe grows out of proportion. Everything is distorted.

Even Henry is farther away than logic would dictate.

I shake my head. "I just need to get my emotions under control. I'll be down shortly."

My room grows hazy, and my vision is obscured, as if I'm looking down a tunnel with the walls closing in.

MAGIC TOUCH

Esme is in her kitchen with Simon mewing and rubbing against her legs. "I'll be with you in a moment. Let me get my tools packed, and then into the bag you'll go."

A green, square bag with holes cut on all four sides sits on the table. It appears to be made of burlap and cloth for the purpose of transporting the kitten.

Simon continues his bid for attention until finally Esme picks him up and cuddles him under her chin, and he purrs. "You are going to make us late, little one."

"Esme?" I sound as if I'm talking into a pillow.

She turns, searching the kitchen. "William?"

"You can hear me?" It feels as if I'm floating at the ceiling. I suspect I have died and am now lying on the floor of my bedroom.

"Where are you?" She puts Simon on the floor and continues looking for me.

"I hardly know. I think I've died." Strangely, the idea of being dead doesn't trouble me much. I never expected to survive the war. If my fate is to haunt Esme for all eternity, things could be worse.

She presses two fingers to the side of her head and closes her eyes. "I don't think you are dead, William. Where were you before you came here?"

"In my bedroom about to leave to pick you up. I started

glowing again, everything went out of focus, then I was here." I long to touch her, but I can't find my hands in this daydream or afterlife. Perhaps this is Hell. I'm to always be near here, but never touch her. "How can you be sure I'm not dead?"

"Spirits feel different when they speak to me. Listen to me. Picture your bedroom and ask your magic to go back to the bubble you created when you were in my parlor." Her voice is soft and comforting.

The kitchen fades, and I hear her calling me.

Looking into Henry's concerned face, I'm on the floor in my bedroom.

Henry is white as a sheet. "How do you feel?"

I pick up a hand and see no blue glow. "What happened?"

Helping me to my feet, Henry closes his eyes a moment. "You got a faraway look in your eyes, wobbled, and I eased you to the floor lest you topple off the edge of the bed."

"How long was I on the floor?"

"Not more than a minute." Henry looks ready to faint.

"Sorry to have worried you." I slap his back. "I'm not quite sure what happened. Let's go pick up the ladies. Perhaps the answers lie with them." I could have lost consciousness and dreamed the entire thing. That seems far more likely than I had a chat with Esme in her kitchen across town.

My legs are steady as we head downstairs to the carriage out front.

Samuel waits at the side. "I talked Anne into riding inside for this part of the trip across town, sir. It gets a bit rocky up top whilst in town. She'll sit up with me once the ladies are aboard."

MAGIC TOUCH

I give a nod and climb in.

Anne sits across from me, looking terrified and clutching her hands in her lap. She is perhaps five and twenty, with pale eyes and brown hair that is always tucked under a cap, with just a few curls escaping. A hard worker, she's risen from scullery to first floor maid in just two years.

"It was not mandatory that you make this journey, Anne. Shall I have the driver return you to the house?" I don't like feeling like a bully. My staff has been loyal to me, and I like to think it is because I treat them fairly and pay them well.

Her eyes grow wider still. "Oh, no, sir. I've never left London, is all. It's an adventure, to be sure. I'm just a bit nervous."

"There's nothing to fear. The country has fewer worries than the city." An adventure is a good way to think about this trip. I, too, am heading into the unknown.

"Yes, sir. Dove said the same. I'm fine. I'm sorry to have worried you." She looks out the window.

A few minutes later, we pull up to Esme's store to find her standing by the door with Minerva.

Dove and Samuel jump down and begin loading her two trunks on top.

"Be careful with the small one, if you will?" Esme says as I jump from the carriage, still amazed that I have no pain in my leg.

Watching the trunks being added to mine gives me pause. "Perhaps I should have hired a second carriage or a cart. Do you think Madam Bishop will have much luggage?"

Esme stares me up and down, as if searching for something wrong. "Are you all right? Has anything else happened?"

Anything else. I spot the green bag on her arm and Simon's little pink nose poking through one of the holes. "It was real? I was here talking to you?"

"You talked to me, but you were not here. That's quite an accomplishment for someone who has no training." She hands Simon into the carriage, and Anne takes the bag before Esme sits next to her.

"I can ride backward, Es... Miss O'Dwyer." I offer from the street.

She grins, settling a second bag under her feet. "I don't mind."

We wave goodbye to Minerva, and roll toward the coven house.

Esme says, "I don't think the great mother will have much luggage. I'm told the cottage is not far. Only an hour or so from Windsor. I don't think a cart will be needed."

With her sitting across from me, I'd nearly forgotten I'd asked the question. I shall have to get these emotions under control. Esme can be my friend, but how can she be anything more? Our lives are not synchronous. She runs a shop and I—honestly, I have no idea where my life is headed. I'm a gentleman with lands that pay. I'm expected to marry a lady in my same sphere. As a mistress, Esme would be acceptable, but I would never wish her to debase herself with such a role. That leaves us together as friends, yet apart as anything more. She shall be my teacher, and when this is all over, I'll know my place in the world. If there are battles to wage, I will fight them. Then I shall return to the life I was born to.

It is perfectly reasonable.

CHAPTER SIX

ESME

At the coven house, the great mother waits with one small bag, and the entire coven at her back.

William steps down to assist Prudence, but the coven witches begin weaving a protection spell, murmuring in low tones and circling the carriage.

As he looks from me to the ten women circling the conveyance, William's eyes are wide.

Prudence looks in. "This is a fine carriage. I don't think I've been in one as nice in all my life, and that's a considerable time."

I hold in my amusement. It wouldn't do to laugh. "It is quite fine, Great Mother."

Despite his astonishment at the coven's behavior, William uses great care to help Prudence. "Madam, if you would like to ride forward, I'm happy to ride backward."

"How kind. I would prefer to see what is ahead." Prudence settles into a forward-facing seat. She pats the space next to her. "Come and sit by me, Esme. You will enjoy the ride far better, and Sir William will keep your new friend company."

Giving William an apologetic smile, I do as I'm asked and moved to the bench next to Prudence.

With a soft smile, William tells me it's all right, then returns to watching the witches cast. "How long does this take, Miss Ware," he asks Sara Beth. "Should I continue with my polite attempt at standing amongst women, or shall I abandon my post?"

Sara Beth's lips twitch, and she almost smiles before stopping at the carriage door. "Are you capable of such an abandonment, Sir William?"

He cocks his head and laughs. "To be honest, I have no notion. I have never attempted such a feat."

Sara Beth blushes slightly.

For the first time in my life, jealousy jolts me, but I push it aside as stupidity. William is not mine, and even if he were, such emotions are a waste of energy. A man as good as William would never stray.

Blush gone as if it had never been, Sara Beth says, "We are finishing the protection spell, and you can be on your way in a moment." She rejoins the coven as they make one more turn around the vehicle.

Each witch stops at the door and bids Prudence good travels before Sara Beth leans in. "Your counsel will be missed here, Great Mother. I will send a bird if we are in need. I beg you to take care of yourself and come back to us."

Prudence pats Esme's knee. "Esme will see me cared for, Sara Beth. I will return. We too shall send word should we have need. You are ready to fly on your own. Have no doubt."

The idea that the strong and overt Sara Beth doubts her abilities has never crossed my mind. Seeing worry in her eyes makes me like her more. We still have many years of doubt to overcome, but at least at this moment, I can see her humanity. It makes me worry less about her trying to harm me, or worse, William.

Sara Beth makes a curtsy. "I will do as I believe you would, Great Mother."

"Seek your own counsel and that of your sister witches. You will do well, as your heart is just." Prudence's thin lips pull up in a warm smile.

Sara Beth turns and goes inside the coven house.

Henry rounds the back to ride on the boot.

William climbs up, and Samuel stows the step before helping Anne to the driver's seat. He joins her there and coaxes the horses forward.

Prudence asks, "When did you take on a familiar, Esme?"

A loud meow sounds from the green bag next to William.

"Simon found me a few days ago, and no one has come to claim him. He has a good face and a fine instinct for trouble, I think." The sweet kitten has been good company since staking a claim to my home and shop. It will be interesting to see how he likes a country setting.

William tugs the tie at the top of the bag and pulls it open.

With a mighty meow, Simon pushes his black and white head through the gap. Intelligence shining in his green eyes, he gives us each a look before he settles his gaze on Prudence.

"Oh, I see." Prudence reaches across and lets the kitten sniff her hand. "He's a fine young cat. He'll serve you well for many years."

Simon purrs and rubs his head on Prudence's wizened fingers. He pulls himself completely out of the bag and leaps across to William's lap, where he curls up and purrs so loudly, he can be heard over the rumble of wheels as we make our way out of Windsor.

Once we are out of the city, the ride is pleasant. Sun

streams down, warming the world. With six people, a kitten, and luggage, we are moving at a leisurely pace. A soft breeze brings scents of summer grass and flowers.

"This is quite nice. I've rarely left Windsor," I say, casting my gaze around. "When my father was alive, we would sometimes take rides out to the park to picnic. Mother never wished to go after his death. I once visited a small farm near Eton to help heal a boy. It had this nice earthy scent. My small herb garden cannot compare to the scent of earth in the wild."

"You may like the cottage, my dear." Prudence gazes out the window. "It is full of the elements."

"Maybe I will." The idea of practicing magic in an environment outside my kitchen is thrilling.

William clears his throat. "Esme, I would like to tell Madam Bishop of my experience this morning, if you have no objections."

My heart pounds. When he came to me without his body, I was surprised at first. It takes a special connection or incredible power to travel with one's mind. "If you wish it, you should do as you deem right."

Attention no longer on the scenery outside, Prudence watches William.

Simon yawns then jumps across the carriage to sit in my lap. It's as if he knows I'm uneasy about sharing something that could indicate an intimacy between us. Though it might also mean that William is far more powerful than will be comfortable for the coven's liking.

After a hesitation and another clearing of his throat, William tells of how he left his body and traveled to my home with only the thought of me.

Prudence frowns.

"I shouldn't have told you?" He lowers his gaze to his hands fidgeting in his lap.

"You should, my child. Of course, you should. I only worry that whatever such a gift means may leave us all heartbroken." Prudence brushes a wisp of hair back from her wrinkled forehead. "I have only been able to bring my mind out of my body to seek out one person, and he was not to be mine. It brought both of us misery. I do not wish that for you or Esme. If you can port yourself at will, the skill is considered dark and doesn't bode well."

"Is a skill dark?" William runs his hands through his hair. "In war, skills and deeds were never deemed evil if they were used and done with noble intent. If a man is capable of destroying another, but he chooses to use his abilities to help rather than harm, is the ability still evil?"

At that, Prudence laughs. "I am schooled, and rightfully so. You are right, Sir William. You might use any skill for good. The character of the man or woman makes all the difference."

"Why is this particular skill thought to be evil?" he asks

Her breath rattles a little when she lets it out. "Because the witches who have used those skills have done so with malice. To gather information to destroy witches of the light and take their power." Shaking her head, she brightens. "It could also mean you and Esme O'Dwyer have a strong bond, and the need of each other will always bring you together."

Heat floods up my cheeks. I should have seen such a comment coming, but I was caught up in the darker scenario. "We only met two days before I brought him to you, Great Mother. I assure you there has been nothing between us to shame me."

William's laughter makes me blush even harder. "I think it is safe to say, Madam Bishop, that I am fond of Miss O'Dwyer, and her blush is by far the prettiest thing I have ever seen. However, she tells true."

Prudence shrugs and smiles. "I make no judgment, children. Even at your age, life is short, and good company is hard to come by."

The carriage slows, and the driver yells down, "There's a cart blocking the road, sir. We'll have to stop."

As soon as we stop, William opens the door and jumps out. "Let's see if we can help, Samuel. Henry, please stay here with the ladies."

Both men call out, "Yes, sir," as if they'd never consider disagreeing with William.

Henry is a tall strong man and stands near the door, with his arms crossed over his chest.

"Are you his protector?" I ask.

Gray eyes that have seen too much turn toward me. It's hard to mistake the pain and loyalty along with sorrow inside Henry. "We were soldiers together. Now, I'm his valet, miss."

It's difficult to look at so much pain. "But he trusts you, Anne, Samuel."

He nods. "Anne can cook and is a fine maid. Samuel is a good driver and excellent with all animals. I suppose I have certain skills."

"But loyalty is the skill your employer values most of all?" I can feel the way these two from different worlds have bonded in a friendship, despite the roles they each play.

Focusing down the road toward whatever is taking place to right the cart, Henry says, "Sir William is an employer worthy of a great deal of admiration and loyalty, to be sure."

Prudence shifts. "Young man, will you assist me down so I might stretch my legs?"

Henry offers his arm as a crutch for the elderly witch to climb down.

Unwilling to leave Prudence's side while on an unknown-to-me road, I secure Simon in his bag and follow her out. If anything should happen to the great mother while I am with her, the coven would be inconsolable. While I have no wish to join them, nor do I wish to be on their bad side.

My eyes take a moment to adjust to the bright summer day, and I stand at the side of the carriage for a moment. To the left is a rolling field of grain, and to the right, some deep-green woods. The road ahead is well trod, and already a posting vehicle is stopped behind us. Bags of feed have tumbled onto the road, and at least one has broken open.

A man in his fifties with thinning gray hair and a pot belly shakes his head at the wheel, which has come loose from the cart.

Samuel is dragging the remaining bags from the cart, while William examines the wheel.

With Henry at her side, Prudence strides forward. "What is it, Sir William?"

"His pin's come out. Samuel says we have a spare or two, but we'll need the cart empty before we can lift it to the wheel. I'm just checking to make sure there isn't some other reason the pin came free." He points to where the cotter pin should have been.

"Samuel," Prudence's commands, "go and fetch the replacement pin. I think you've toiled enough with those sacks."

Pushing his brown curls from his eyes, Samuel looks from Prudence to William.

William rises from his knee and nods at Samuel, who rushes to our carriage. He looks at me as soon as Samuel dashes toward our carriage.

The cart driver is shaking his head. "I don't think even your strong back can lift this with ten sacks left in, Sir William. War hero or not, it's too heavy."

"We're going to give it a try, just the same, Mr. Moore. The road is backing up with traffic, and we wouldn't want it to get ugly with the post just behind us." William shrugs.

Samuel darted back, holding up the pin.

"Mr. Moore, is it?" I say, turning the cart driver away from what is bound to be better for him not to see. "I am Esme O'Dwyer. Sir William is conveying my grandmother and me to our home. I'm so glad we met you and had the chance to stretch our legs. I do hate long drives. Where were you heading today before this unfortunate accident?"

He points down the road at nothing. "Have to get this grain to Sorrel's farm. He's going to dock my pay for being late." Mr. Moore's face reddens, and he shakes his head.

I place my hand on his arm and send him a soft infusion of calm. Behind Mr. Moore, Samuel is lifting the cart with no strain at all, William is placing the wheel on the axle, and Prudence is pointing as if she's directing them. What none of them can detect is the shimmer of gold swirling from Prudence's hands as her magic lifts the cart and all its content from the road.

Mr. Moore calms, and his skin returns to a healthier color. "I suppose it will be all right."

"Of course, it will. Look, they've nearly fixed it." I ease Mr. Moore around to see the cart resting on the wheel.

William pushes the pin into place and secures the end. "We'll help you reload, Mr. Moore."

I rush over to Prudence and take her arm so that Henry can help with the sacks. "Are you alright, Great Mother?"

Prudence pats my hand. "Just fine. I'm not so old I can't lift a cart for a few minutes. In fact, while my body has weakened over the years, my magic has only grown. An odd twist of fate. Perhaps we can go back to the carriage, child. They'll be done here in a moment or two, and your little cat will be none too happy to be trapped in that bag."

On the driver's seat, Anne is gaping.

I give her a smile and hope she will grow used to magic. Time will tell.

Inside, Simon is on the floor, with his head and one paw already out of the bag. He looks up when I open the door and gives an unhappy cry. "I don't want you to get lost in the middle of nowhere. Forgive me?"

Once I help Prudence to her seat, I climb up and loosen the top of the bag.

Simon fights his way out before I've completed the task, hisses at me, then curls in a ball in my lap and purrs.

At least he is as forgiving as he is quick to anger.

I pet his head and scratch under his chin until the carriage rocks with Samuel climbing up.

William gets in. "That was rather handy, madam. Thank you."

The carriage rocks again as Henry takes his seat in the boot. A moment later, we're moving again.

Prudence smiles, showing crooked yellowed teeth. At her age, it is a miracle she has teeth at all. "It was nothing. I needed to stretch my muscles a bit. Sara Beth hardly ever lets me cast."

"Whyever not?" I ask.

With a sigh, Prudence closes her eyes. "She fears it will exhaust me."

William leans forward and speaks urgently. "And has it?"

She waves off his worry. "Not at all. I'm nearly one hundred and fifty years old, my boy. Living is far more exhausting than magic."

Eyes wide, he looks at me.

I shrug. I knew she had to be at least that old. She was an old woman when my mother was a girl. Mother told stories about the formidable Prudence Bishop and how she'd outlived all her contemporaries.

"When she was a girl," Prudence says, "I thought her the most beautiful witch I'd ever seen."

"Who, Great Mother?" I ask.

"Was it not your mother you were just thinking about? Your thoughts were so loud, Sir William probably heard them, too." She looks across at him, but when he appears bewildered, she shrugs. "Or perhaps not."

"I was thinking of her and of you," I admit.

"You have her look. Soft hair and green eyes that would turn a bad man good, and a good man bad, the other witches used to say. Of course, your father was a good man and a witch in his own right. He might have changed the coven for the better, but Betty Ware was dead set against men in the coven." Prudence shakes her head, and a sad smile pulls at her mouth. "Betty wasn't wrong about much, but I think she made a mistake where your parents were concerned. Your mother was formidable and loyal to a fault. We needed her. Betty needed her."

"Were they friends?" My mother never mentioned Betty Ware in any way that would indicate a liking for the woman. She snapped with anger whenever the coven was mentioned, and after a while, Father never broached the subject.

She looks at me with passion in those blue eyes. "Oh, yes. The closest of friends during their childhood."

"What happened to separate them? Was it father?" My chest aches with the idea that Mother lost her coven *and* her best friend.

Prudence gives a long sigh. "In a way, it was. Connor O'Dwyer was very handsome and charming. When Louisa Shepherd met him, she fell in love, and so did he. Her family was against the match, as she came from money, while he had none. Even with witches, it's thought best to stay with one's own rank." She frowns. "Determined to have Connor, Louisa went back to Ireland with him, and they married. When she learned she was with child, they returned to England. I think she hoped to be welcomed back. It was a naive hope. By then, Betty had come to lead the coven, and she was angry with her old friend for abandoning England. Many had died in battles during the years your mother was in Ireland. Betty blamed Louisa for those deaths. It was a bit harsh, but Betty was headstrong. She refused to allow a man into the coven, and your mother refused to rejoin her sisters without him."

"Did Betty believe my father would turn to the dark?" I want to cry, but hold it in. My mother had been selfish, but if she had not, I wouldn't be here.

"I don't think she did. It was more that your mother had left, and she was angry and hurt. Your father was known to be a good man. He might have added to the coven. When you were still a small child, perhaps three, the coven was attacked by a dark witch. He killed three witches and dumped their bodies at the door to the coven house."

I gasp. "I never heard this."

Prudence pats my knee, and Simon reaches out a paw to touch her hand. "You are not in the coven and have missed much of its history. Betty was too proud. Rather than ask your parents for help, she devised to burn the dark witch herself. Her heart was true, but her power wasn't up to the task. When she performed the spell, she set herself and part of the coven house ablaze and nearly died. She was never the same after that. She had no power and remained sickly until she died last spring."

Sitting forward to hear every word, William asked, "What happened to the dark witch? Who defeated him?"

"He is not defeated, my boy. He lives." A weary breath pushes from Prudence as she watches out the window. We pass through a village.

"Why didn't he destroy the coven?" I ask, despite my worry that this story is taking its toll on Prudence.

Turning, she locks her sharp blue gaze with mine. "The coven survives because your mother and father came, and cast the dark witch away. They didn't have the power to destroy him, but they hurt him, and for twenty years now, he has not returned."

Confusion and anger wash over me. "And even after that, the coven wouldn't let my father in?"

"I had hoped the tragedy, along with the risk your parents took on behalf of the coven, would have brought the O'Dwyers home. It was my most passionate wish. But too much time and bad feelings had come between them all. I begged your mother to petition for reentry, but she wouldn't. I beseeched the sickly Betty to extend an invitation and bring them home, but she was like steel. So, they never found peace in their friendship or their witchcraft, and both suffered."

The carriage falls silent for a long moment.

William says, "That is a very sad story. Is the daughter as unwavering as the mother?"

I can't tell if he's asking Prudence about Sara Beth, or if he's asking me if I would rather die than bend.

Prudence shrugs, then saves me from having to reply. "Time will tell."

CHAPTER
SEVEN

WILLIAM

The quaint white cottage with brown trim comes into view. "This looks quite nice."

"I think you will find it more than adequate for our needs." Prudence smiles. "I have always loved being here and often wished I could stay in the country."

Samuel slows the carriage and stops at the front door. A girl of perhaps fifteen rushes from the cottage, and stops at the narrow path of white stone that leads from the two steps to the drive.

I jump down and help the ladies out.

When the girl sees Prudence, she runs into her arms. "Great Mother, I have missed you."

"Brianna, my girl. You're so grown I hardly recognize you." Prudence hugs the girl tight and kisses her cheek."

Prudence makes the introduction. "Sir William Meriwether and Miss Esme O'Dwyer. This is my granddaughter Brianna Bishop."

"Granddaughter?" I ask, shocked.

Laughing, Prudence says. "A few generations removed, but too many great-greats makes me feel old."

We all chuckle.

Brianna says, "I've cleaned the cottage for you all. I live just a mile down the lane if you need anything at all. I see you've brought some help, but if you need more, just let me know, and I'll come, or find another to suit your needs."

"Just like your mother." Prudence cups Brianna's cheek. "Efficient and kind."

"Thank you, Great Mother. Shall I stay and see you settled?" She tucks her brown hair under her cap, and looks nervously down the road.

Prudence says, "Run along. I'm sure your mother needs you more than we do."

With a kiss on her grandmother's cheek and a wave, Brianna runs down the road and out of sight.

"Henry?" Prudence calls.

At her side in a moment, Henry offers his arm. "Madam?"

"Will you and Anne get me settled in my room? I need to rest. I'm not as young as I used to be."

I'm speechless as my staff rush to do the witch's bidding without so much as a look back for my approval. "I guess I know where I stand."

Esme's laughter is worth any amount of indignity. "It seems we are both unnecessary, Sir William. Shall we have a look around the property?"

It is by far the most tempting offer I've had in a long time. "I would be delighted."

At my feet, Simon cries.

Esme crouches and scratches his head. "You may stay here or come with us as you wish, little one. We shall be here for a little while, but don't get lost. You are too small yet to find easily."

With a loud purr, he rubs her fingers, then scrambles into the cottage as Samuel hauls one of the bags inside.

"I was surprised to hear that you've not spent much time in the country. I would have thought with all your herbal remedies, you would need some way to gather ingredients." I keep my hands clasped at my back to hold off the desire to touch her.

"Tradespeople sell and barter with me. Minerva has a small garden and trades with me often. I manage, but it would be nice to have a garden and woods closer. I shall make good use of my time here." She runs her hand along the bark of an oak tree.

We wander to the pond that sits like glass, not fifty yards to the right of the house.

Strolling along its bank, she looks right and left. There's a gleam in those green eyes that I can't decide if I love more than life itself, or if I'm wary of the mischief there.

She grins. "Shall I show you a bit of magic then, Sir William?"

"If you'll not use my title when we're alone, Esme, you may show me any manner of thing." The bells of danger ring in my head, but I push them aside.

A gentle blush makes her even more lovely, if such a thing is possible. She turns to the water, reaches out a hand, and mutters a few words under her breath.

A few drops of water scatter as if a pebble had been dropped in the middle of the pond.

Eyes locked on the spot, Esme keeps her hand outstretched. Her gaze is steady, while her face flushes joyfully.

I turn to the water as a fountain begins to gurgle up from the center. It spins and sprays water across the stillness before it shoots up into a geyser. The violence of it fades to a calm wave that crosses toward us.

Esme puts her hand palm up, and the crest of the wave touches her middle finger. Water slides down the finger, into her palm, where she cups it, then sends it back to the pond.

A moment later, there's not a ripple again. It's as if the magic never happened.

Stunned, I sit in the soft grass and look over the still pond. "How did you do that? Is it a spell?"

She sits beside me. "No. Most witches do not need spells to manipulate the elements. We are of the elements, therefore asking is usually enough. Spells are to create magic on a grander scale."

"When you removed the bullet from my leg, was that a spell?" It makes me think of her hand on my leg, which already has my shaft responding.

She sighs. "I thought manipulating the elements would be enough, but the severity of the injury was worse than I anticipated, and I had to use a spell to complete the task."

"I don't think I understand." I pull out a bit of grass and place it between my thumbs before using it to make a loud whistle. I abandon the grass.

A breeze blows out of the south, and the water ripples. Esme points to the effect. "The water responds to the air. When it reaches the earth, it recedes. If there were fire, it would extinguish. The four work together. Because we are of these elements, we can ask that they go against what they are meant to do."

"But water will cut through the earth." I point at the few feet of erosion to the north side of the pond.

"That too, is meant. For what reason, we don't know, but the earth is always evolving for some purpose. When I asked the water to come to me, it did. If I ask the fire to dance on top of the water and the water not to extinguish it, it would. If I want something more specific, like fire to turn to water, I would need a spell."

"Because it's against their nature."

Her grin makes me feel as if I've solved the problems of the world. "Exactly. You learn quickly, William."

Lord, but my name sounds like a prayer falling from her lips. "I don't know what good this does me."

"Let's say you had a splinter," she begins. "I could ask the splinter, which is earth, to lift out of your skin. As a healer, I can ask your skin to close over the space where the splinter was. Your body already knows how to heal, so I would only be asking for a quicker response to what it already does naturally."

"Can I move the water in the pond?" My fingers tingle.

"You won't know until you try."

I continue to stare at the water. "I don't know how to begin."

Esme takes my hand in hers and opens it, palm up.

My pulse ticks harder at her touch. Her hands are soft and strong, with narrow, elegant fingers. It's hard to concentrate, but I focus on what she's telling me.

She traces the deepest crease in my palm. "Inside each of us is water, so water is always a good place to begin. Focus on your magic and release it from the bubble you've put it in."

"I'll glow." I'm at once tempted to pull my hand away, and also hold onto her forever.

She shakes her head. Her voice is even and soft. "I think you glow because of fear. Do not fear what you are, William. Find your magic, and let the bubble go."

Closing my eyes, I let myself acknowledge the bubble of blue power just behind my heart. I poke at it with my mind.

"Let it go, William," Esme whispers.

"I don't know if I can." My heart races, and I gulp for air.

Her hand skims the side of my face in the softest caress. "Of course, you can. You have done much harder things than this, if the newspapers are to be believed."

Opening my eyes, I meet her mossy gaze. "Those acts took only cunning and strength. This is not the same."

She cocks her head. Lord, but she's beautiful. Hand still on my cheek, and the other holding my hand, she asks, "When you were in France, was there never a time when you should have been killed, but for reasons you cannot explain you were spared?"

A half dozen instances clash in my memory.

Her grip on my hand tightens. "Gently, William. Just pick one and tell me."

"When I first arrived in France, I had command of a small band of men meant to spy on French troops. We were to cross enemy lines, and if any of us lived, we would bring the information back to the general. It's dangerous and, often, inexperienced soldiers are used for these missions. It seems less wasteful to risk a man who hasn't amassed the wisdom of war yet." I know this must sound barbaric to her. I never speak of war, because it sounds just as barbaric to me. "I took my men through the killing fields, and as we reached the edge of the woods that separated the French encampment from our position, the world seemed to explode." Trying to banish the sounds of screaming men, I close my eyes.

"It's in the past, William. No need to go back to it, just tell me what happened." Her soft caress on my cheek chases the memories away.

Opening my eyes, I cover her hand with mine. "It was a cannonball. It landed so close, my entire squadron was ripped to pieces. All but me. I lay in a hole almost as big as this pond, covered in mud and..." I break off from describing the rest of the grime that covered me. "I had no explanation for how I survived. Unhurt and alone, I strode into the enemy camp, stole a French soldier's cloak, and gathered the information. I only told my superior that I was the only one to survive an attack."

"Oh, William, what you have suffered." A tear slides down her cheek, and then another.

"I didn't mean to upset you." I wish I could take all my words back. Anything to keep her from sorrow.

"I'm fine." She draws a long breath and meets my gaze. "Can you see that the earth protected you, wrapped you in its embrace and kept you from harm, even as the cannonball maimed it with its power?"

Strangely, that was exactly how it felt. I was an inch under the dirt and mud, and above, my people were barely recognizable. It wasn't possible, but it had happened. Magic. "I've never told anyone that. Even Henry Dove, who was my closest friend in war, and a loyal man to me now, does not know that story."

She drops her hands to her lap. "I'm honored by your trust in me, William. I cannot tell you how much I wish I could take all these pains from you."

"Who would I be if my memory of pain were gone, and who would I be if I didn't remember the men who fell that day?" I swallow down the ache of it and focus on the time before the cannonball, when we were all laughing and joking together.

Esme looks as if she might lean forward and kiss me, but she brushes passion aside an instant later. She sits up straight and looks me in the eye. "Find your magic and set it free, William. Then we will see about water magic."

She's right, of course. I know we can only be friends, and friends are nothing to scoff at. I lost so many in the war, I'm extremely covetous of a good friend. While I have a few, I feel at my core that Esme's friendship will be the most significant of my life.

I take a deep breath, let it out, and close my eyes. Behind my heart, the bubble of blue light shakes and bounces like a puppy that knows it's about to be let out for a run. I give my permission, and lights explode behind my eyelids. Energy blooms in every drop of my blood. I'm frozen and on fire all at once. Pleasure and pain merge as magic fills me until I'm taut with it.

When I open my eyes, I'm on my back, floating, staring into the blue sky. Solid earth bangs against my back, and the grass tickles my skin.

"Easy now, go slow. I thought you'd fly off for a moment there, and I'd have to show all of the neighbors what we're about."

Pressing against my elbows, I sit up. "What happened?"

"You shot blue light for an instant, floated about five feet in the air, then settled down to the ground before your magic slid back inside you." She shakes her head.

"Is that normal?"

Raising both hands, she shrugs. "You are the first I've seen with repressed magic, William. But I'll tell you this, it was a sight to see."

Feeling more myself, I look around, and the world seems crisper. My senses are more acute. I let a blade of grass slide between my thumb and forefinger and can sense the life inside. "I think the world has changed for me."

"How do you mean?" She studies my hand then my face.

A squirrel dashes from the trunk of one tree, across the grass and up another. It's tiny heartbeat echoes in my mind, and I know it's searching for nuts. "I feel life all around me in a way I never have before. Do you hear the trees and animals all the time, Esme?"

"I don't, no." She closes her eyes and breathes in until her breasts stretch the front of her dress.

Forcing my eyes to her face, I hear her heart beating and the blood flowing through her veins.

She smiles, and I hear the pulse of the trees, flowers, a deer close by, and so much more. I hear it all through her mind.

It feels wrong to know more of what she feels and thinks, so I push back from searching her mind.

"It's lovely to open to the world around you." She opens her eyes. "Perhaps I should do so more often. In the city, it's hard to open one's mind without hearing humanity for all it lacks and suffers, as well as the good."

"I can see how that would be uncomfortable." I set aside the fascination with all the life around us. "What would you have me do with my magic now that it's free, and I'm happily not glowing?"

She taps her finger on her bottom lip.

That lip is completely distracting. I long to pull it between mine and kiss her until we're both senseless. I don't know how I'll bury these feelings if we're to be together all the time.

"Perhaps you might try to lift a drop of water from the pond. Water magic is usually a good place to begin, as you won't burn down the county." She grins.

Confused, I stare at the pond. "I don't know how to begin."

"Focus on the water and ask for one drop to rise out of the whole. The water is part of you, as are all the elements. When you ask, the water will respond." Her voice is soft, like a lullaby.

I want to wrap myself in that tone for a lifetime. Lord, but she's a distraction.

Staring at the water, I think about one drop, and in my mind, ask for that drop to rise up.

The pond rises out of the ground as one.

"Too much, William." Esme sounds half panicked. "Ease it back down."

Behind us, the kitten hisses, then growls.

"No, Simon," Esme calls.

Distracted, I let the water free. It splashes to the earth in a vertical wave that soaks the ground around the pond, and us with it.

Simon hisses again and runs back toward the cottage.

Esme sputters and pushes her sopping hair back from her face.

I'm soaked through.

About to apologize, I'm shocked when she laughs. It rolls out of her, musical, gets louder and continues. Holding her stomach, she rolls to her back. "Oh, dear, we shall have to work on your control."

Lying beside her with my head propped on my hand, I look into those green eyes, and I'm lost. I tuck the wet curl on her cheek behind her ear. "I'm so damned attracted to you, Esme. It's hard to think of anything else."

Her laughter fades, and she cups my cheek. "You've been in my heart since long before I met you."

"Have I? In what way?" I thumb the water away from the soft skin under her eye.

She lifts her hand, and with a wave, warm air dries us both. "I read all about you in the paper and saw your portrait. I fantasized about the hero you might be. Then we met, and you are even more than my imagination conjured."

Being called a hero never appealed to me, but having her admiration makes the idea more bearable. "It's distracting from things more important, but I want to kiss you now more than I wish to draw my next breath."

Her chest lifts and falls with quick breaths. Desire courses through her eyes, and I don't need to use magic to feel her want. Maybe it is magic, I don't know. She lifts her head from the warm grass. "You should kiss me, as I can't resist, and honestly, it's all I've wanted since meeting you."

"Will you believe me when I tell you my motives are honorable?" I let my lips ease an inch closer to hers.

She threads her fingers through my hair. "I believe all that is good about you, sweet William."

No man could resist the longing in her eyes, and I have no desire to push her away or keep her at arm's length. Too much thinking at this moment is unpardonable. I lower until my mouth touches hers. Energy pulses around us, and the earth seems to vibrate. I nibble her bottom lip, and then her top. I press my tongue against the seam, and she opens for me.

Her fingers grip my hair while her other hand hugs around my back.

In the damp grass, I shift so my hip presses against hers and make love to her sweet mouth. Passion rises as our tongues slide against each other, over and over again.

I caress down the side of her breast to her waist, and then grip the swell of her hip. My shaft is rock hard, and I have to force some sense into my brain. Breaking the kiss, I spread light kisses on her cheeks. "I swear I have never wanted anyone as I want you, Esme. It's as if my control is lost whenever you are near. I'm a gentleman, you must believe me."

Gazing up at me, she looks like an angel. "I know you, and there is no need for you to defend yourself. I, too, have never felt so compelled to be near someone. I'm no virgin, William, nor do I randomly take lovers. I decided some years ago that lovers were more trouble than the pleasure is worth. Still, desiring you as I do is beyond my control."

Cupping her cheek, I kiss those full, mind-altering lips once more. "I don't know how this can be more than an affair, and I don't want that for you, or from you."

She smiles, but sorrow fills those eyes where I only wish to ever see joy. "Perhaps it's best to not think about the future. We have until you are trained."

Her mention of a time limit on my feelings sits me up. I face the pond, now still after my meddling. "And then we are to be strangers?"

"I hardly think that is possible." She presses her hand to my shoulder. "We are not strangers now."

My temper is rising, but none of this is her fault, so I have only myself to be angry with. I could rail at society, but who would care? "I am not the sort of man to dally with a woman."

"A dalliance is all we can hope for." She sighs. "You must act as your conscience demands, William. I want you and will not turn you from my bed. However, we also have a duty to our magic. You need to learn, and if Prudence is right, there is some purpose to your magic awakening at this time. Danger is coming, and we have limited time to train you as a witch. If making love with me will be a distraction, I think it best to keep our distance."

CHAPTER
EIGHT

ESME

I don't know if I should push him away or pull him in. I want him with such passion it's hard to think, but we are not in the country for an affair of the heart, and he must be trained.

Telling him it can never be more than a distraction played on his conscience, and perhaps that was unfair. It was, however, the right thing to do. We should both concentrate on magic and education, and not on each other.

William turns to me with sharp eyes. "If today is an example of what holding back my desire will be like, it is more likely to be the distraction."

My most private places pulse with agreement.

Running his fingers through his hair, he lets out a long breath. "I don't know the right answer. I only know I want you so deeply it hurts when I'm not touching you. Never in my life have I known such longing."

"Nor I." My throat is too clogged with emotion to say more.

"Could this be some dark magic?" He plucks a blade of grass and rolls it between his fingers.

Anger slides between my adoration and need. "Are you jesting, or do you think there is a spell placed on us? When would such a spell have been cast? I wanted you from before you walked into my shop, but I would never take away your will to choose. I wouldn't want a man who needed to be tricked to desire me."

As I rise, he does too, and takes my hands in his. "Do not be upset. I only raised the question. There is no accusation. I never thought you would bespell me, Esme. Though, I do feel as if wanting you is magic."

I should pull my hands away and take myself back to the cottage. It's insulting to think his desire or mine could only be the product of dark magic. Yet, I can see why he might think so. If his feelings are as strong as mine, it's hard to resist the pull.

"There is a spell." I swallow and pull my hands free. "It's a kind of divination to root out curses placed on people or animals. It will enlighten us to anything forced upon us, and if we are bespelled, it can then be broken."

Still as a statue, he blinks once, twice, then gazes at the ground. "I never meant to offend you. I spoke what was in my heart. I could never believe anything dark about you."

His hesitation makes me feel the "but" after his sentence.

He nods. "But I think you should work the spell that will verify there is no curse." He says the last word so softly it's almost lost in the breeze ruffling the leaves.

"You will do the spell. I will show you how, and as it is common, I have it in my grimoire. You can see for yourself." I shouldn't be offended, but my pride is hurt. He thinks his attraction must be some devilment. What woman wouldn't be offended?

"I know nothing of spells." He takes my hand and rubs his

thumb over my palm. Tension edges out of me with every stroke.

It would be better to snatch my hand away, but he is irresistible, and I thread my fingers through his as we stroll toward the cottage. "Maybe teaching you such a spell and assuring us both that what we feel is in the light isn't such a bad idea."

Simon sits in front of the door and gives me a disgusted glare.

"I think my little man is angry about the splash you gave him." I kneel to scratch his head, and he only holds his anger a second before he closes his eyes and purrs.

"Should we wake Madam Bishop before we attempt the spell?" William asks, taking my hand back into his.

"Let her sleep. This is a simple spell."

He laughs. "You said that about the water, and we nearly drowned."

I squeeze his hand. "I shall be more attentive and give specific instructions."

My trunks are already in my room. Perhaps it would be wiser to take the smaller trunk with herbs, spices, stones and other magical items to another more neutral room, but it's delicious to have him in the room where I'll sleep. I may have lost my mind. Magic or not, whatever this attraction is, I should learn to control it.

Kneeling at the trunk, I open the latch and lid.

William kneels next to me. "What do we need?"

I take a clear quartz crystal and hand it to him. "For purity." I take out several herbs and a vial of blessed water. "You'll need to pull a hair from your head and keep the root intact." I pull one of my own and hand it to him. "Put them in the vial with the water, and then put in a pinch of the cinnamon, and one of the cloves."

He does as I tell him.

I find my spell book and open to the page.

With the vial in one hand and the crystal in the other, I show him where to read. "Out loud and with intention."

He reads, "Fire in darkness be not in mind. Light will show the way. If in these two a curse has been laid, show it now and let them be free. As I say, so mote it be."

I hold my breath as the room sizzles with magic, prickling my skin.

William's eyes are wide. "I feel something rushing along my spine."

"That's the magic." I study him for signs of a dark curse.

When the spark fades and nothing is revealed, I let out my breath.

"What happened?" He's still clutching the crystal and vial.

Easing his hands open, I take both. It takes a lot of energy not to show my relief. I go to the window, open it and pour out the vial before putting both back into my trunk. "There is no curse. One or both of us would have felt pain from the exposure."

I close the chest and latch it.

When I stand, William pulls me into his arms. "I'm sorry. I know you're angry, and you have every right to be. Forgive me. Please, Esme, forgive me." His voice is full of desperation.

The scent of all he is fills me to overflowing. Spices, magic, and William. I could get drunk on him. "There is nothing to forgive. Truth be told, I'm glad we worked the spell and know whatever this is between us is natural."

He releases me and puts distance between us. "I want to show you something. Meet me in the parlor?"

I have never wanted to kiss or be kissed by anyone more. Why must I be a sensible woman? Many witches take a man into their bed just because they want him. I am not one of them. I need more than a quick tumble that leaves me feeling sullied by the act and sorry for the bother.

If it had been a curse, it would have been disappointing, but at least it might have been broken. Then it would be easier to teach him and not yearn for his affection.

My other trunk is in the corner, open and empty. All my clothes have been put away for me. That is a treat. Anne must believe she needs to play maid to me. I will set that straight when I see her.

Clouds roll in from the west, covering the sun and graying the lovely day. With a sigh that sounds hopeless to my ear, I go to the parlor near the front door.

Alone in the parlor, I scan the bookshelves and find many magical tomes that I might like to make use of while we reside in the country. Perhaps I'll grow some herbs to take back to Windsor. The summer won't be a complete loss if I can save myself buying such things from farmers. Perhaps there are some mushrooms to be hunted up in the small woods.

The furniture is old, but of fine polished wood and sturdy fabric. Dark green and gold with touches of red give the parlor elegance. It's clean, as Brianna did a fine job readying the place for her many-times great grandmother. The windows face front, and the first drops of rain dampen the yard.

Simon scurries toward the house, sees the open window, and leaps through. He gives a meow before purring and rubbing his body on my skirt.

I pick him up and give him a cuddle. His fur is damp, but he comforts me with his little head rubbing my chin. "You're a fine fellow, Simon. I'm quite glad we found each other. I feel certain your company will be critical once all this nonsense is over and we're back in the shop."

Alone.

A cool breeze drives the rain to the windowsill. After

putting Simon on the floor, I close out the wet, then rub the chill from my arms.

"Are you cold?" William asks from the threshold.

"It has gotten a bit damp out." I point to the growing storm.

He places three books on the low table in front of the loveseat. "Shall I make a fire?"

Tossing a thought to the hearth, I use magic to light the neatly stacked logs.

William laughs. "That's handy."

I want to run into his arms and never leave. The urge is so strong I have to fight it with considerable will. "I will teach you when you learn some control. Water outside is less dangerous, yet you nearly drowned us. Fire inside could lead to disaster."

Wide-eyed, he nods. "Control would be helpful. It's strange to think of my magic as wild and ill-mannered. I've prided myself on a strict lifestyle since before the army. I never imagined any part of me might be out of control. It's hard to imagine me having magic at all."

I want to comfort him, but all I can do is apologize. "I'm sorry, William. If you hadn't met me, you would still have a life where you were comfortable. Seeking me out has altered the course of your well-planned life."

He rounds the furniture and holds my arms at the elbows. His touch is gentle yet firm. "I have no regrets, Esme."

"How is that possible?" I should pull away, but I long for his hands on me, even in this simple way.

A crack of thunder startles Simon, who jumps onto the loveseat and hides behind a pillow with only his bottom sticking out.

Giving the kitten a brief smile, William leans down and kisses the tip of my nose. "I would never wish you out of my life. Meeting you has changed everything I believed. It has explained parts of my world, and my father, that I never understood. I am not a man to hide myself from the truth, no matter how strange it seems. If that were the case, I would never have come looking for your shop in the first place."

I press my cheek to his chest, and his arms wrap around me. "It would be simpler for you to live in ignorance. It would be wiser for me to ignore these feelings that continue to grow inside me."

His lips press to the top of my head. I've never felt more at home, and it has nothing to do with the cottage.

He sighs. "Maybe I conjured you. You said desire is powerful magic."

Chuckling, I breathe him in. "Why must you smell so damned good?"

Pulling back, he scoffs. "I hardly think that can be after a carriage ride and dousing from the pond. Perhaps the spell didn't work, and you are bewitched."

I know he's joking, yet my yearning for him is so strong, I can almost believe it true. Turning to the books he's brought, I ask, "What have you there?"

"Come and sit." He rounds the loveseat, then waits for me to sit before he settles beside me.

Simon scrambles into my lap and startles with every crack of thunder.

William lifts the first book from the stack. It's old with a worn leather cover. "This is a journal of one of my relatives, Sarina Meriwether. She speaks of the death of a friend during the witch hunts. I didn't read too far into any of these. I thought it best to show them to you and Madam Bishop first."

As if conjured by her name, Prudence shuffles into the parlor with Henry by her side. William's valet seems to have taken it upon himself to protect the great mother.

Prudence pats Henry's arm and releases him. "Have I missed anything?"

With a bow, Henry leaves.

"No," I say. "We had a dowsing when William attempted some water magic. Now, he's showing me some books he brought with him." I don't want to tell her we attempted a curse divining spell. It would give away too much.

Rounding the chaise, Prudence slowly makes her way to the chair adjacent to us. Her dark-blue day dress fits in perfectly with the subdued tones of the parlor. "Where did you find these books?"

"I remembered my father scolding me once as a boy for looking at an old book. At the time, I didn't understand his rage. I also didn't understand the book's content. He moved the books, and I never gave it any more thought until a few days ago. They were on a high shelf tucked at the end." William hands the journal to Prudence.

Once she opens the book, her eyes fill with sorrow. "This is a long time ago. So many good witches lost. Many of the dark betrayed them. You should read this, Sir William. You will learn your family's history."

She hands the book back to him, and he nods. His eyes fill with trepidation, but also agreement. "I will read it. I wonder if my father read it, or if he only hid it as his father did before him."

Wanting to give him comfort, I say, "He may not have acknowledged what he was, but he never burned this book. He kept it, albeit hidden, he kept it for others to find. Don't blame the man for making sure his family was safe. It was his duty, after all."

"Well said," Prudence agrees and smiles proudly.

William frowns, then picks up the second book. "This is a book authored by the same witch, and a man I assume was her husband. Samuel and Sarena Meriwether created this medicinal account."

Prudence opens the book and runs a weathered hand down the pages. After a moment, she says, "It's their grimoire. This is a wonderful find. Most spell books were lost or destroyed during this time. It was often done to hide evidence as so many were dragged away and hanged or burned. We will examine this and see if you can practice with some of the simpler spells."

I take the book from Prudence and read the first page of a spell for headaches. Besides the incantation, it also gives a solid recipe for a tonic, and a poultice to be pressed to the temples. "The tonic here is very similar to the one I use. I've not heard of the damp cloth and herbs for head pain."

"An older way, to be sure, but effective just the same." Prudence points to the third book. The leather cover is dry and torn. "This is something else?"

William hands it to her. "I could not read this, Great Mother. It is in a language that is like Latin, but the words made no sense to me. I thought it best to bring it to you rather than dabble in that which I don't yet understand."

"A wise notion, child." Prudence shivers as she reads. "This is of the old tongue. Latin and Gallic." She closes the book, worry in her eyes. Taking a knitted blanket from the back of the couch, she pulls it around her shoulders.

"What is it?" I ask.

"This book is not of the light. I fear some part of your family was working with black magics, William."

"Should we burn it?" He looks at the fire.

Prudence nods. "It should be done in ritual fire on the new moon if you wish to rid yourself of it."

"I want no part of anything that will do harm." He pulls his shoulders back. "If it is evil, it should be destroyed."

Prudence looks at the first page, and says, "The spells in this book are not all evil, nor is the book itself. The user is where evil may lie." She points a thin finger at the page. "This spell is to make a man do one's will. This spell is forbidden by our laws as it does the man harm. Someone thought it important to keep this book for hundreds of years."

Putting the book aside, Prudence rubs a finger along her temple. "Why would your father and his fathers before him have saved this book? It was not written by Samuel and Sarina. It is far older. Yet, good witches, healers, Samuel and Serena presumably kept this, too."

A shiver runs up my spine. "The new moon is not for ten days, Great Mother. Perhaps we should use that time to learn if this has some value in the light."

Prudence's grim expression eases. "Yes. We should find out what made the Meriwether family hold onto this, despite their resolve to leave behind their magic."

Worry emanates from William in waves that I feel to the bottom of my soul. The idea of something evil in his possession torments him. "If the keeping of this book was deliberate, why didn't my father express it to me at some point? He never said you may never touch these books, but you are ordered to keep them and pass them to the next generation. In fact, he never mentioned them in any way after the day he raged at me for touching them."

"I cannot answer that," Prudence says. "Perhaps whatever we discover will tell you what you need to know."

Anne walks in with a tea tray full of treats.

My stomach growls and my cheeks heat. "I suppose we did miss luncheon."

CHAPTER NINE

WILLIAM

The power coursing through my body is at once familiar and foreign. At first, the bubble of blue light seemed like something apart from me, like a being who lived inside me but separate. The longer I live with my magic, the more I realize it's an extension of me, like an arm or a leg. It was only that I didn't know to miss it until it was awakened.

Behind the cottage is a stillroom, and for the three days we've been in the country, I have met Esme there to work magic spells. It is small, and I like that she must stand close to me. Wild scents of herbs, flowers, spices, and earth fill the room. With walls full of shelves stocked with jar after jar, and a table stretching from end to end, there is barely four feet of space for two people to stand and work. One window lets in light, and we leave the door open, lest we feel trapped.

I have not repeated my confessions of deep desire for Esme,

nor has she indicated any admiration for me beyond friendship.

Being near her is both pleasure and torture.

"You will work a water spell today, William." Esme hands me a bucket of water from the floor.

Holding the handle, I place it on the table. "Last time didn't go very well. Are you certain I'm ready for elemental magic?"

Her pupils dilate, and I wonder if she's recalling the intimacy that followed our drenching on the pond shore. "You have improved and have a better understanding of magic now."

"Still," I say, and scoop a fraction of the water to a bowl and return the bucket to the floor, "perhaps a smaller risk."

Just the hint of a smile appears before she raises her eyebrows. Her shoulder touches mine, and she points. "All right. Now ask just a drop of water to rise from the bowl."

A touch of shoulders while standing in such a place shouldn't arouse me, but I'm distracted by her closeness. Pushing that aside, I want to impress her. A stupid reason to wish to pull a drop of water from the bowl, but desire is important.

I focus on the bowl, then the water inside, and then each drop separates from the whole. The bowl is made up of smaller pieces. Everything around me is a kaleidoscope of infinitesimal dots making up the whole. The water shimmers in every direction, but remains in the bowl, which also shimmers.

Reaching out a hand, I call a drop of water. "From one element to the other, water to air."

A blackbird's heart beats soft and quick from the tree outside. A white rabbit scurries under some brush to hide from a hawk. I hear both of their pulses and their intent.

"Focus, William." Esme's voice brings me back to the water.

As I lift my hand, one drop rises above the rest. It shakes, as if it weighs heavy on the air.

"Now release it slowly." Her voice is soft and calm.

I let my mind be one with the water and tell it to return to the whole.

When it does with the barest of ripples in the bowl, I'm stunned. The individual bits of everything merge and the world comes into normal focus again. "I saw everything."

"You did it." She grabs my arm excitedly.

It's hard to think about the water or my success when I can't forget the way each thing was made up of smaller pieces. Glancing at her, I ask, "Is that the way you see the world when you use magic?"

"What did you see?" She's facing me now, with worry wrinkling her brow.

"The water broken down into smaller bits. The bowl as well. The table, the bottles and jars, and whatever is in each all have smaller elements to them. I could see the essence of everything. I heard the animals outside. I was part of everything, and it was all part of me." I look into the bowl of still water.

Esme cups my cheek, and I face her. She cocks her head. "It is a gift to see this way. To answer your question, no. I don't often see the world as you described. Once, when I was ill, and another time."

Turning in, I kiss her palm. "What was the other time?"

Her breath is quick and rough. "When I healed your leg, I saw inside you in this way."

Glad I hadn't turned to see her broken into the parts that make her, I can't help thinking of her hand on my leg. "Why can I see like this with such a small spell?"

"Maybe we should go ask Prudence." Her eyes are full of

passion and her hand is still on my cheek. The way her breasts are rising and falling is maddening.

I put my hand over hers. "I'd like to come to you tonight, Esme. If you want me in your bed. If you do not, I understand."

"Why did you not come the last three nights?"

I hear no accusation, just honest curiosity. Leaning in, I kiss her forehead.

Her eyes flutter closed, and I kiss her lid. "I don't want to make you feel less than the spectacular woman you are. I can't know how my life will change when things settle down. We hardly know each other. Wanting you is not appropriate or wise for either of us."

She inches back and presses two fingers to my lips. "A lot of reasons against. Perhaps I should have asked why you are asking to come to me now."

"It is distracting to want you so much, to need you so intensely. My heart is overriding my head," I admit.

"Your heart? Are you certain it is your heart doing the thinking?" She leans in until her pelvis grazes the proof of my desire.

I laugh. "Regardless of my natural response, you must believe it is not lust." I grin back at her. "Well, at least not entirely."

"Perhaps if we lay together, it shall relieve the building tension. I feel it as well. Need is a distraction." She takes a step back and draws a long breath. "In the meantime, I'm quite proud of your success, as you should be. You've done well in a very short time."

"Thank you." My power over the water element seems feeble compared to the notion of being admitted to Esme's bed. "If you'll step out and give me a moment to control myself, we can tell Prudence the news and see what she thinks."

Glancing down at my shaft where it presses against the fall of my breeches, she swallows and blushes. "I'll wait outside."

It takes me a few minutes of thinking of benign things, and the evidence of my desire subsides. I'm only human, after all.

Outside, Esme leans against the side of the stillroom. "It's a fine day. Perhaps we should take a turn around the property after tea."

"I'd be happy to walk with you." I'd be happy with any and all time spent with her. She's all I can think about, and I'd be much better off thinking about how my life has turned to complete madness in the span of less than a week.

"What are you worrying about?" she asks on the way to the house.

"My life." I shrug, and open the back door for her to enter.

Inside, we walk down the drafty hall to the parlor where Prudence already waits with a large tray for tea. She looks at peace, sitting on the chair with her eyes closed. When we enter, she opens them and smiles. "You are just on time."

The smell of vanilla and honey from the biscuits makes my mouth water.

After waiting for Esme to sit, I snatch a sweet and sit beside her. "We have news, Madam Bishop."

"Oh?" Her hair is pulled up under a white bonnet, and she pours the tea into three white beveled cups.

Accepting her cup, Esme smiles. "Sir William managed a water spell, and no one got wet. It was quite well done."

"Excellent." Prudence claps. "Why do you look as if there is more to tell?" She focuses those gray eyes on me.

"When I concentrated on the water, I saw everything. Every part of everything. I heard heartbeats and intentions of beasts. The water looked to me as if it were thousands of smaller drops with air in between."

"You have sight. How interesting." She sips her tea.

Esme sits forward. "I have never heard of someone having sight for such a small thing."

Prudence shrugs. "It's a gift. Though I'll not lie, there have been many with such sight that turn dark. It can be a great power to see what makes up the universe. In seeing so much, one's true vision can become blurred."

A rock forms in my gut. "This gift is evil?"

Holding up a hand, Prudence waves it in dismissal. "No. This is powerful and beautiful magic. I merely say that it is a great talent and can be used for evil. Imagine a person of dark heart knowing the nature of water, air, or another person."

"I have no wish to harm anyone. I only wish..." The heaviness inside me spreads to my heart and my head.

Esme's voice is soft. "What do you wish for?"

"It would be better if my magic was simple or ordinary." It's madness. "It would be better if I had no magic at all. Ignorance was bliss."

I plunk the biscuit on the saucer and put my tea on the table before getting up and staring out the window. It's so normal now, but I feel my magic pushing me to see the whole of it. Fighting the urge, I close my eyes.

"You should get some air," Prudence suggests.

Esme stands beside me and takes my hand. "Come, William. We'll go for that walk we talked about. It will help to clear your head."

Down the lane, away from the cottage, Esme keeps my hand in hers. When we pass the pond, we see Simon chasing something up a tree. At the narrow road, we turn left.

Letting go of my hand, Esme folds her arms, so she grips her elbows. "I think you misunderstand magic."

"Do I?" I miss her touch and wish we were the only two people in the country. It's hard to take a deep breath as the worry of darkness and doom fills me to the brim.

"How shall I explain?" She pauses and looks through the canopy of leaves to the blue sky. "Magic is like a coin. Each spell or expression has two sides. On one hand, it can be used for good, and on the other, it can be used for ill. The coin is not right or wrong, it is merely a tool. You are good, and so will use your gift for the light."

"I have done bad things." I want to keep it inside, but I blurt it out before I can stop myself. "In war, I did many things that cost the lives of many men."

"War is just as magic is. There is a job to be done, and it can be done for the good or the evil. You believed what you did for your country was for the side of right." She caresses my arm from shoulder to elbow before pulling away again.

"I'm sure the French soldiers thought they were right as well." Living with the memories of war is harder than anyone ever admits.

"How do I convince you of your own goodness? How do I make you see yourself as I see you?" Her voice is distant, as if she's speaking to herself rather than me.

What she asks is not possible. As the village comes into view, I stop and face her. "What good can the gift discovered today do in the world?"

She beams. "If you were a healer, seeing the essence of a sick person could show you how to treat their ailment. If you were an exorcist, you could see the curse as a blight, and with practice, destroy that which doesn't belong. If you decide to go back to your life as a gentleman, you might avoid pitfalls and wrongdoing by seeing the values of those you deal with. Pushing too hard, without permission, would be against coven law, but allowing others to reveal what they will is not harmful and can be very handy. Your magic is not evil, as you are a good and kind man with a gentle soul."

"Kind words." I wish they were true. The lives I took tell a different tale. "Let's see what the village has to offer."

A man walking toward us touches the brim of his cap. "Good to see you. The old mother hasn't been here in many years. I heard she'd come."

"Hello," Esme says.

A few feet farther, and a woman heavy with child stops us. "How long will the old mother stay? I would like her blessing." She rubs her stomach.

Wide-eyed, Esme holds up both hands and shrugs. "I cannot say for certain. Our plans are not firm. I will tell her of your request. What is your name?"

"Pauline Mercer, my lady. I would appreciate that more than you can know." The woman's grin surely shines all the way back to Windsor.

We meet half a dozen more local people who have requests or good wishes for Prudence.

I suppose, in such a small town, word travels quickly, but I've never seen such adoration for anyone. Prudence is revered, and I can't tell if it's for being so old, or for her good works as a witch.

Esme grins when she sees an apothecary's shop, but then looks at me with worry. "I'd like to go inside, if you don't mind waiting."

I stride to the door and hold it open for her. As she passes, I whisper, "You never need to ask such a thing."

Inside, a man who looks as old as Prudence ambles a few feet to the counter. "Oh, here you are then. I'm Baily Thymes. I heard Madam Bishop had returned. Are you both her students?"

"Only me." I search the shelves as if I know what I'm about, but it's all liquids and powders with labels I don't understand. It's stuffy with damp in the shop.

"I heard you came with servants. Very grand." He smiles, showing off his few teeth.

Esme says, "The old mother needs more help at her age. We came with enough help to keep her comfortable, Mr. Thymes. You have a fine shop."

Even with his stooped shoulders, he stands up a bit straighter. "Thank you, madam. Can I help you with some ailment?"

"I am well, sir. Perhaps another day." Esme turns to leave.

"Wait." Mr. Thymes holds up a hand. "Will you wait a moment? I would like to give you something."

With a slow nod, Esme watches the proprietor grab his cane and make his way to a back room.

"What's this about?" I ask.

She shrugs. "I have no idea."

Voices from the back room indicate that someone else besides the apothecary lives on the premises.

Not sure what to expect from a town full of people who clearly know they are more than caretakers to an old woman, I speak low. "Should we leave, Esme?"

"I sense no malice. If for no other reason, we should stay for curiosity's sake." Her smile could make me stay a thousand years if that's what she wanted.

A few minutes of pacing the small shop, and I'm bored to tears and sick of the damp scent.

Mr. Thymes clomps out with his cane in one hand and a basket in the other. "If you wouldn't mind bringing this to the old mother. Tell her Mrs. Thymes and I would be pleased if she wishes to use our humble shop to see to people."

Esme gives a nod, takes the basket, and says, "This is very kind, and I will deliver your message."

The scent of baked goods and meat fills my head. Whatever is in the basket smells heavenly.

We say our goodbyes and head back toward the cottage. I take the basket from Esme and pull back the linen cloth to find cured ham, sausage, and a loaf of bread. "It's as if she's a queen here."

"I suppose we shall find out why." Esme holds her elbows and lifts her face to the late-day sun. "I think I like the country."

She's so lovely, I want to find a private corner of the world and keep her with me for eternity. It takes several long breaths before I say, "The country suits you."

She cocks her head. "You know, it's strange, but I think so, too."

We walk silently until we reach the lane to the cottage. I've never felt more comfortable with any woman. Men often keep silent in company, especially when at war. However, I was always taught to engage young women in conversation, lest the meeting be awkward. With Esme, there is no uncomfortable moment. Being with her in conversation or silence has a rightness to it.

Perhaps I'm losing my mind with all this witchcraft.

We take the basket to the kitchen and are surprised to find Prudence sitting at the long table shucking peas with Anne.

Anne smiles until she sees me. Then she jumps up. "Sir, I'm sorry. My lady insisted on helping."

I raise my hand for calm. "If madam wishes to assist, who am I to stop her or you from enjoying her company? Be easy, Anne."

Esme takes the basket from me and gives me a warm smile that shoots desire straight to my groin. She puts the basket on the table. "Great Mother, Mr. and Mrs. Thymes have sent a gift and an offer to use their shop. Many people in town have requested blessings and healing. They are quite excited about your arrival."

Putting a pea pod aside, Prudence pulls back the cloth. "How lovely of them. This is most kind. Who else did you see?"

Sitting on the long bench, Esme plucks up a pod and shucks the peas into the bowl. "Pauline Mercer is heavy with child and wondered if you would give your blessing."

Prudence sighs and her eyes fill with tears. "Little Pauline is with child. Last I saw her, she had braids and was chasing a puppy."

I see no reason to be excluded and sit next to Esme. "She's a lovely woman. Grown now. Everyone in town wished to see you. It was quite something. I felt a bit remiss that we didn't go the first day to gather well wishes for you. Will you accept the apothecary's offer to use his shop?"

With a nod, Prudence smiles, then brushes her tears away. "It has been many years since I was here. In the past, when I was younger, I always went to town and helped where I could. Since I've grown older, I don't travel as much, and my return to this place of my birth has suffered. I do send a coven member and gifts each spring."

"I didn't realize you were born here, Great Mother." Esme voices my thoughts as well.

"Oh, yes. This is my home from before I moved to Windsor. It was my grandmother's home before that. She was a powerful witch and saved the town from flood many years ago." Prudence hands the basket across to Anne. "We should make good use of these gifts, my dear."

Anne rushes off with the basket toward the larder.

I try my hand at shucking, but the peas fly in every direction.

Esme and Prudence laugh.

I give up on helping, but I don't wish to leave the good company. "Madam, I can only say that you have been missed here."

CHAPTER TEN

ESME

Did I invite a man to my bed? I can't quite remember how we left it. So many emotions course through me. I want him in my bed, but if he doesn't come, it probably indicates good judgment on his part.

After all, a shopkeeper and a landed gentleman have no business together. Yet, how happy my parents were. They came from different worlds and made a life together.

Witchcraft was their commonality, and love their binding force.

I'm being an imbecile. Love is not what William or I are feeling. Lust, certainly, but love doesn't happen in a few days.

In my nightdress, I comb my hair in the mirror. My curls fight back against my attempts to tame them, but I continue to try.

A soft knock stills my hand and my heart pounds. "Yes?"

The door opens, and William stands on the threshold. His cravat is missing, leaving his shirt open at the collar. Golden

MAGIC TOUCH

hair peeks through the opening. His hair stands out as though he's been running his fingers through it. He wears neither stockings nor boots, and somehow, his bare feet make him seem vulnerable.

"May I come in?"

I swallow my nervous excitement and nod. I put the comb on the dressing table as William closes the door and crosses to me.

He picks up the comb and takes up the chore of taming my curls. "This is like a dream."

"You dream of combing my hair?"

"I do." When he works through a knot, he's much gentler than I am. "I dream of all the little things you must do to be so beautiful."

Simon jumps from the bed, gives a stretch, then jumps into my lap. Absently, I pet him and close my eyes. "I haven't had anyone do this since I was a small child."

His lips touch my ear. "Do you like it?"

"I do." I turn my head and capture his lips with mine. A low sigh escapes me as he pulls me to my feet and drops the comb.

Simon gives an annoyed cry and trots away.

The kiss is gentle at first. William traces the seam of my lips with his tongue, and I open for him. Once our tongues meet the kiss turns desperate.

Low in my belly, I tighten with need, and desire pools between my legs. "William."

He pulls his head back and cups my cheeks with both hands. "Esme, if this is too fast, I will wait for you. Tell me to go and I will."

I wrap my legs around his waist. "I want you. It may be wrong, but by Goddess, I can't deny a desire this strong."

On the bed, he rests me on my back and covers me. His

shaft is hard, perfectly wedged between us, and nestled at my womanhood.

I arch against the teasing hardness and moan.

"Esme. I promise to go slow next time, but I need you so desperately. I long to bury myself deep inside you." His heart beats as one with mine.

I recognize it inside my own thrumming heart. "Yes."

He slides his hand up my leg, pushing my cotton nightgown high. The cool night air touches my thigh and then my bottom. He slips his fingers between my legs and teases my wet center.

"Gods, Esme."

I cry out as he circles my sensitive bead.

When he pulls away, I wrap my arms around his neck and my legs around his hips.

"I only want to take my breeches off, sweetheart." His voice is tight.

With a wave of my hand and a pinch of intention, I remove his clothes and send them to the floor next to the bed.

He startles then laughs. "That's another handy trick you'll have to teach it to me."

"I can't have you disrobing every woman in the county," I tease.

"Only you, Esme. I only want you naked." He pushes his fingers inside me, teasing and coaxing small gasps from me.

I rock my hips up with every plunge. My body tightens. "I need more of you."

A moment later, he presses his shaft at my entrance and slowly enters me. Inch by torturous inch, he fills me.

So tight is my arousal, it snaps, and I find my release. My core clutches at his cock, and he groans into my neck.

"I'm sorry." I had meant to wait for him to find pleasure,

but no amount of imagining could have prepared me for the beauty of having William inside me.

Lifting on his elbows, he meets my gaze. "Never that, sweetheart." He rolls his hips. "I would see your pleasure a million times and die the happiest man in the world."

So slow and deliberate in every stroke, William kisses me just as tenderly. He slides inside me, then pulls back. Each time the base of his shaft rubs my bud until pleasure again tightens inside me.

I claw at his back and lift my hips for more of him. "William." My voice is rough and desperate. It hardly sounds like me.

Each stroke is fuel to the fire roaring within me. Gripping him with my legs, I want more. Need him deeper.

Pulling me tight, he rolls so I straddle him. "Take what you need. I'm yours."

From my position of power, his shaft hits so deep I can't be still. I'm wild with the growing pleasure. I rock back and forth, then rise up on my knees and impale myself over and over.

I have to bite my cheek to keep from screaming with the growing pleasure.

When he presses his thumb to that pearl of delight at the top of my womanhood, I crash over the edge of reason. My body shakes with the fiercest ecstasy I've ever imagined and never believed possible.

William grips my hips and pushes up inside me with three quick thrusts. Groaning, he lifts me from him, then pulls me down, spilling his seed between us.

His kiss is soft, tender, and I never want it to end.

Rolling to his side, he eases me to the mattress. "You're so perfect, Esme. I'll never get enough of you."

That contradicts my idea that lovemaking would relieve

the tension between us, and it should upset me. It should, but I love hearing it.

With a kiss on my nose, he commands, "Don't move."

He's slim-hipped with a muscular bottom. His back is broad, golden, and beautiful. I long to touch every inch of him as he crosses to the basin and pitcher near the wardrobe. He wets a cloth then returns to the bed.

Reverently, he washes his seed from my stomach and thighs. When he presses the damp cloth between my legs, I sigh.

His eyes meet mine, concern wrinkles his brow. "Have I hurt you?"

"No. It feels good to be cared for." Awareness returns, and I squeeze my legs, hoping that after two orgasms, the pressure will relieve my want. But watching him wipe his shaft and abdomen heightens my desire to love and be loved again.

He returns the cloth to the basin then climbs into bed beside me. "I will go if you wish, but I'd like to stay with you awhile. Only if it pleases you."

Rolling, so I'm half covering his chest and my leg is draped over his, I press my cheek to him and listen to the rhythm of his heart. "It pleases me to have you here."

Then he wraps me in his strong arms and kisses the top of my head. "I'm so glad to hear that. I feared you would send me away."

I swallow the emotion building inside me. "I should, but I have neither the energy nor will to deny myself the pleasure of this moment."

"I wish I didn't hear so much worry in your voice. I never want to bring you worry, Esme. Making you happy is what I want most." He skims his fingers along the arch of my spine from my buttocks to between my shoulder blades.

If I could stay like this forever, he would hear only joy in my voice, but life has taught me to be realistic. "I see no end where hearts are not broken."

"Then think not of endings. I want you. You seem to want me in return. My life is a whirlwind of things I never expected right now." He presses his lips to my forehead and is slow to remove them. "Not all I've discovered this last week or so has been pleasant or easy to understand.

"I'm sorry." I want to take the worry from his voice and his heart.

Pushing me to my back, he leans over me and meets my gaze. His eyes are full of emotion that I dare not name. "You shouldn't be sorry for anything. You are the bright light in the storm. I shall never regret a moment spent with you, Esme O'Dwyer, and I pray you shall not regret it either."

Palm to his cheek, I lift my head to kiss his soft, strong lips. "Is it shameless that I want you again so soon?"

"There is no shame in anything we share together, sweetheart." He traces a line with his fingers from my waist to my hip, then cups my bottom to pull me tight against his hard shaft.

I expect and want him to slip back inside me, but instead he kisses my chest, the space between my breasts, then takes my nipple in his mouth. He sucks, licks and nips until I'm wild and writhing on the mattress.

I clutch his head and arch into the delight of his mouth. "William. Good lord, you'll make me into a wanton."

Breaking his connection with my breast, he smiles up at me. "My plan is revealed."

He's so adorable, I'm filled with joy at the sight and feel of him.

Sinking down on the bed, he kisses a path to my navel, my belly, then lightly licks the crease where my thigh meets my body.

I'm mesmerized by him and how every touch drives me higher. Lifting my hips, I'm wild with need for his touch between my thighs.

Kissing lower, he draws a high-pitched gasp from me when his tongue slides between my folds. My mind can't keep up with the rapture of his mouth and tongue teasing and tasting me.

Reaching down, I clutch his hair as he shifts my legs over his shoulders and devours me.

I pump my hips wildly, searching for the culmination of my building rapture.

William slides a finger inside me and then another. Sucking and pumping while his moans vibrate along the sensitive flesh.

My world erupts. Stars explode behind my clenched lids. My body is racked with bolts of pleasure so extreme it's hard to breathe. I shake with the rush of it.

William wraps his arms around me and coos sweet words as he kisses my hair, my cheek, and my forehead. "Esme, you are so beautiful, so sweet, such perfection."

Nothing he's saying is true, of course, but I love hearing the words and dreaming they could be real. I want to give him pleasure, but I'm drifting into the loveliest sleep.

"Esme." His voice is soft and close just as it was in my dream."

I blink. "What? Is it morning?"

He kisses my lips ever so gently. "No, love. It's still dark. I must return to my own bed. I don't want to leave and have you wake not knowing when or why."

Still foggy with sleep, I struggle to work out what he's trying to say. "You must go. I...I understand."

His weight presses along my side. "Look at me, sweetheart."

With much struggle, I open my eyes to find him staring down at me, even more handsome than the portrait I fell in love with months ago. It's hard to imagine not having him in my life. "Hello."

His beautiful lips pull into a grin. "I don't want the house to wake and find us like this. I would hold you day and night if it were proper. I worry about how to make that dream a reality."

Madness. He must have lost his senses. Pushing his shoulders, I sit. Gripping the blanket to cover myself, I still feel exposed. "Don't be silly. Dreams are meant to be that and nothing more. Of course, you must go to your own room and think nothing of it. I'll be ready to resume as your teacher in the morning. Nothing has changed."

I turn away from him. He'll dress and leave, and I'll not watch and wish. I'm stronger than that.

"Esme?"

"What?"

The bed dips, and he sighs long. Clothes rustle, and I imagine him dressing. I close my eyes and wish it wouldn't look childish if I held my ears to block out all sense of him. I swallow emotions trying to clog my throat and push tears into my eyes.

The mattress beside me shifts with his weight. He takes one of my hands from where I clutch the blanket. "I won't believe that last night meant nothing to you no matter how hard you try to prove it to me." He kisses my hand.

"What can one night mean?" I force denial into my voice but keep my eyes closed.

"Please look at me, sweetheart."

It's the plea in his voice that forces my eyes open. "I see you."

His clothes are rumpled from lying on the floor most of the night. His hair sticks out in all directions, fresh from sleep.

He's the most beautiful man I've ever seen.

"If you wish for me to leave the country, I'll do so. I don't want to make you uncomfortable. However, I'm never going to pretend last night had no meaning."

A tear forces its way from my eye and trails down my cheek. "I don't want you to leave. You must learn to use your magic. I am your friend."

"I'm relieved to hear we are still friends." His shoulders relax, and he kisses my hand again.

I pull my hand back, clutch the blanket and sit beside him with my bare legs hanging from the side of the bed. "I will always be your friend, William. I'll not let them bind your magic unless that is what you wish above all else. If you leave here, Sara Beth will find you and you will be bound. Living with that would kill me. I'll not fail you."

"But you are ashamed of our lovemaking." Sorrow burns in his statement.

I pull his hand from his lap and kiss his knuckles. "It shouldn't have happened. You have too much at stake to be distracted by such foolishness. There may be even more at stake if your awakening powers have some purpose in the light. How can we have been so selfish as to take our pleasure and risk ruining our friendship in light of all that?"

"I never believed our friendship was at risk. I only know I wanted you and want you still. I cannot believe a desire this strong can be wrong." With a loud sigh, he rises. Leaning down, he kisses the top of my head.

"You are a good man, William. I knew it from only your portrait," I whisper in my dark room as he walks away.

At the door, he stops. "You are the finest woman I've ever known. I'll not look for another, for I have had perfection."

Before I can chide him for his foolish statement, he opens my door and slips into the hall.

Alone, I curl into the sheets.

With a meow, Simon jumps onto the bed and snuggles up against my chest. He knows I'm sad and wants to take it from me.

"I can't see how happiness is possible now, Simon." I scratch his head.

He stretches long and makes a funny squeaking sound before falling into a soft purr.

"You're right. I shouldn't think so much. We'll just go about our business and let Goddess work out the rest of our lives. Happiness is only ever a dream for a woman like me anyway. I was content before I met Sir William, and I'll be so again when he's gone back to his life." I pet Simon along his back, and close my eyes.

CHAPTER
ELEVEN

WILLIAM

On the afternoon of the new moon, I read the strange grimoire looking for the reason the book was kept in my family for generations. The old language, as Prudence called it, took me a while to understand. It's a strange combination of Latin and Gallic, but with some knowledge of both, I've pushed through.

The spells are about control and power. One to control a man's mind. One to imitate love. A spell to make one person look like another. A spell to manipulate animals, and a death curse. With every page, the spells become more deadly.

Prudence arrives with Anne and sits beside me.

Anne places the tea on the table before leaving.

"Esme has gone for a walk. She said she's tired of being cooped up in the stillroom. I thought you might like some tea and company." Prudence pours me a cup.

I put the book aside, take the tea, and sigh. "I see nothing good in these spells."

"Do you desire to use them?" She pours her own tea.

Shocked, I gape at her. "They are evil. I wouldn't cast to harm another or kill someone. Even to force an animal to do one's bidding strikes me as a terrible undertaking."

Frowning, Prudence nods. "Perhaps that is the point."

"I fail to see your logic, Great Mother." The tea warms me, chamomile to calm the nerves and mint for digestion. This pot of tea was meant to make me feel better, and it has done so. I relax against the sofa cushion.

"Perhaps your family kept it as a test. If you have no desire to use the spells, does that not say something about your character?"

Putting the cup aside, I look from the book to her. "A dangerous test. If I or one of my relatives were dark, they would use these spells. They could kill with them."

"That is so." Prudence hands me my cup and saucer again. "They could have, and you could yet. However, you say you have no desire to use a spell meant for ill. Is that not telling?"

I see her point. "Too large a risk in my opinion."

"Shall we burn it tonight?" She watches me over her cup.

"It would be best. I despair that another Meriwether had not done so generations ago." My heart is lighter with the knowledge that the book will be destroyed.

"It was for you to do. This is meant." Prudence looks at the door just as Esme enters.

"What is meant?" She sits, pours herself a cup of tea, sips, and smiles.

Her smile, though meant for the tea, sears into my heart. "I'm going to destroy the ancient grimoire tonight. Prudence believes my decision is meant to be."

"I see. You have no use for the spells within?" She's watching me so carefully I feel it in my blood.

Shaking my head, I put my empty teacup down. "I would

never use any of those spells. Not in this lifetime nor in the next."

Her lips twitch. "Then we shall make a good fire under the new moon and rid your family of its burden."

As the sun wanes in the west, we light the fire in the yard.

Simon sits watching from the porch with Anna and Samuel.

"Henry, you need not be here. We're only burning a book." I attempt to lighten the grim mood.

"The fact that you feel the need to burn this particular book out of doors with some ritual is reason enough for me to remain close." He cocks a brow. "With your permission, sir."

I laugh. "Of course. Stay if it pleases you."

As soon as the sun leaves none of its light behind, Esme hands me the book. "As we practiced, William."

I stare at the fire, take a long breath, and clutch the old leather. "Guided by not even the moon, I send this evil tome to ash. With salt and Goddess blessing to see, as I will, so mote it be."

I hurl the book into the fire.

Flame as red as blood flashes straight up in a rush that throws me backward and off my feet. The ground knocks the breath from me.

Esme holds on to Prudence, keeping them both on their feet.

Offering his hand, Henry helps me up. "Was that supposed to happen?"

I shrug and caution closer to the column of unnatural fire.

"With my will unscathed. I pray the light. I seek Goddess's will. I abolish the dark's plight. My test is complete."

The fire recedes as if doused. A heaviness lifts from my mind and my heart. It feels as if the old hidden book had shrouded me all my life, and now it is gone, and I am free.

As I look across at Esme, my heart is light and full of something I dare not name.

She offers her smile, and it fills my heart with joy.

Time seems to move more slowly in the country. It's been over a week since we burned that old book, but it feels like months.

As I concentrate on the wick of a white tapered candle, the flame flickers in my mind. It's small and soft, can only light the wick, not set the room aflame.

I have to push aside the memory of nearly burning the stillroom to ash. If Esme wasn't ready with a water spell, we would have perished.

Refocusing, I only see the wick. The stillroom fades from my peripheral vision. Esme's breathing and even her words of instruction shift to nothing. I see the wick. I see the flame. I breathe and flick my fingers lightly toward it.

The wick lights.

As I hold my breath, the room comes back into focus.

I blink. "I did it?"

"You did it." Esme's voice is full of pride.

Turning, I pull her into an embrace and lift her from her feet.

We've hardly touched since the night we made love. I've waited for some sign that she wishes me to return to her bed, but she's been all business ever since. The most wonderful night of my life had little effect on her, it seems.

As I lower her, our noses nearly touch.

Passion lights her eyes but dims a moment later. Her smile fades, and she pushes against my forearms. "I'm proud of you. That was well done."

Releasing her, I move back. "Thank you."

"You learn very quickly. In three weeks, you have managed fire, water, air, and earth spells." She blows out the candle then fans herself. "It's hot. I'm going for a walk by the pond. Perhaps there's a breeze to be had somewhere."

Doubting there is, I fall into step beside her. "Summer in the country is more pleasant than the city, but it's still hot."

"Indeed." She lifts the curls at the back of her neck and turns her back to the slight breeze from the south. "It's better out here."

"The stillroom is quite close. Do you think it's safe to move our work to the parlor, or perhaps we should wake earlier and do magics before the heat of the day?" The pond ripples, and while the breeze is fine, I long to jump into the water.

Simon runs across the grass to the edge of the pond and laps the water.

Kneeling next to him, I don't care that my knees are getting wet and probably muddy. I cup some water and drink. Scooping a handful, I rise and offer it to Esme.

She stares a moment. The fire returns to her eyes like green flames. Dipping her head, but not taking her gaze from mine, she sips from my hand. "Thank you."

My heart is pounding, and blood rushes through my ears. Blood rushes to lower regions as well. I pull back. "I'm thinking a swim might be the only way to cool off."

"A swim?" Her pretty mouth drops open.

"Can't you swim?" I ask.

She grips her elbows and steps back. "Whether or not I can swim is not the issue. We cannot swim together."

Moving so close only a sliver of light separates us, I whisper. "Esme, if I don't cool off, I'm going to ravage you right here on this slope of grass." I draw back. "I'll teach you to swim."

"I have nothing to swim in." She's in a light blue day dress and still wearing an apron.

"Just take off the apron and your shoes and wade in." I pull off my boots, stockings, and coat. "If it were night, we could strip down and just jump in as God intended."

"William!"

Amused, I offer my hand. "You should learn to swim."

"I never said I can't swim." She cocks her head and stares at me.

Hadn't she? "I heard you. I asked if you can swim, and I heard no."

"I never said that." She takes a step away from me.

I'm revisiting the exact conversation. "No. You didn't say it, yet I heard it loudly in my head. I heard you, and I felt the fear you have of the water. No. Not of the water, but of drowning."

Information poured out of her head and flooded into mine. Now her fear shifts to me. She's afraid of me? Afraid of what I might become and that it would be her fault.

"Stop it!" She pushes the center of my chest so hard I stumble back.

Shaking my head, I brush aside the flow of emotions not my own. "I'm sorry. I don't know what happened. All of a sudden, I could hear you, and it was difficult not to listen. It was rude. I realize that. I'm sorry to have made you uncomfortable."

Esme stares at me for a long moment. "You are never to invade another person's thoughts without permission unless it's an emergency."

"It was not something I made an effort at. It was more like a door opened, and I loitered in quite by accident. I apologize." This magic has put a wall up between us, and I want to take every second of the past few minutes back.

Sweat drenches my shirt, running in rivulets down my back, and my desire for her has made me uncomfortably hard. "I'm still going in the pond. Join me?" I hold out my hand.

She shakes her head and sits in the grass where she removes her shoes and stockings.

The sight of her bare calves is too much. Turning, I jump into the pond. It's nice and deep, and within a couple of feet, I can no longer touch the bottom. The cool water is heavenly in the unbearable heat. I swim to the opposite side and let my feet touch the soft bottom.

When I turn, Esme is standing with her feet in the water. She has wrapped her skirt around her arm, so her legs are visible to the knee. She's shapely and beautiful and there is no way for me to stop this burning attraction. Honestly, I don't want to stop.

"Have you changed your mind about a swimming lesson?" I roll to my back and slowly float in her direction.

"No. Anyone might ride up." She checks the road for visitors.

"We've been here over three weeks. Miss Bishop has been our only visitor, and she comes on Friday. As it is Thursday, I find it unlikely you would be seen splashing around in the pond." I stand when I reach her, then walk to the grass, sit, and let the sun dry me.

"Maybe so, but I'll not risk being seen behaving in such a way." She continues to paddle in four inches of water.

Even though I've seen her naked, the glimpse of her legs is charming, and I have to concentrate on not embarrassing myself with a full erection. After all, she's right, someone could see us if they came down the drive. Even as we are, with me wet and her paddling, it's inappropriate and fodder for the gossips. If I'm seen aroused, it would be a scandal.

Thinking of other issues, I pull on my stockings and boots. "I shall go and tell Prudence of this new skill."

Esme strides from the water and picks up her abandoned footwear. "I will go with you. I'm not at all sure how one learns to control such a thing. I've never shared thoughts with another. Even my mother and I couldn't speak without words. Though, she and Father could." She says the last with a dreamy quality.

In the parlor, Prudence sits writing at the small desk in the corner. When we enter, she looks up. "How was your swim?"

"Refreshing," I admit without shame, while Esme's cheeks pinken. "I've exhibited a new magic that has Miss O'Dwyer concerned."

Prudence places the pen in its holder and caps the ink. "Oh? What happened?"

"I heard what she was thinking. I heard it as if she'd spoken out loud. Then it was difficult for me to stop listening." It is best to admit everything. If this is damning, I'll accept the consequences.

Slowly, and with a wince, Prudence stands and shuffles to the chaise. "I assume Esme told you it is considered rude to invade another's mind."

"Unless the circumstances are dire. Yes. She told me." I wait for Esme to sit, and then I lean against the mantel.

Prudence nods. "Read my mind now, William. I give you leave."

I stand up straight. This was not what I expected. "I beg your pardon?"

A warm smile tugs at her lips. "Read my mind. I'm curious

if you can do this on command, or if it was because Esme was broadcasting her thoughts."

In contrast to Prudence's amused expression, Esme looks miserable. Her cheeks are flushed, and she's gripping her elbows so hard her knuckles are white.

Wishing I could ease her concern won't make it so. I focus on Prudence and wonder what she is thinking. "You are thinking that you hope there are cucumber sandwiches with the tea, and something sweet for me to enjoy."

Clapping her ancient hands, Prudence smiles. "Very good. Now. Send me something back."

"How do I do that?"

"Just think it and open the thought to me." Her gray gaze is steady and intense.

I think about the little cakes Anne is so good at making.

"Oh, yes, your Anne is a wonder. You should promote her when we go back to the city." Prudence grins, pleased. "I'm very impressed with your skills, William. How your family has withheld them all these generations is a wonder."

"Does it follow that the previous members of my family had magic? Would they have known and hid it from others?" I recall how angry my father was when he saw me looking at the books. I send the thought to both Esme and Prudence.

Eyes wide with a little panic, Esme pulls her lips into a line.

Prudence shrugs. "He may have known. He may have lit a fire or stirred the wind when he was emotional. I cannot say."

"Is it also forbidden to speak to your minds, or only to invade?" I worry at how uncomfortable Esme is sitting with her back straight and her face grim.

Esme meets my stare. "It is considered intimate."

"So, friends do not communicate in this manner?" I shift my attention to Prudence as she seems less worried.

Opening her arms, Prudence gestures for me to sit in the chair adjacent to the chaise and across from Esme.

With my wet breeches, I hesitate, but then shrug and sit.

She says, "It is something that lovers often share if their bond is strong. It is rare for someone to be able to accomplish this with every witch."

"It is more than rare. It is unheard of." Esme grips her arms tighter and looks as if her shoulders might snap.

"Not unheard of," Prudence corrects. "Rare."

"How rare?" I don't like Esme's obvious concern or the way she's avoiding eye contact.

The women exchange a look.

Prudence sighs. "We only know of one other witch, and he was malevolent in the extreme."

"Was? Then this witch is dead?"

"He is." Prudence's eyes glass over. "I killed him over a hundred years ago. He left me no choice, and still, I suffer from the act."

Esme rises and sits beside the great mother. She wraps her arm around Prudence's thin shoulders. "Tell him the full of it, if you will."

"So long ago, it has become a thing of myth, yet in my mind it might have happened yesterday. His name was Bertram Wells. I was still young, though old enough that I should have seen what he was. He came to Windsor shortly after I left this cottage. Handsome... Oh, even more handsome than you, William. Bertram courted me, and despite warnings from the coven, I fell in love with him. He nearly killed us all in his effort to reach the king. He had great plans to rule England through witchcraft. He might have succeeded if the veil had not been pulled from my eyes in time."

Imagining Prudence as a young woman in love, I lean forward with my elbows on my knees. It seems impossible that the wise witch of today might have been naïve so long ago. "What happened?"

Prudence's laugh is devoid of all joy. "We became lovers and were to marry. He was to be the first male witch in centuries who would be admitted to the coven. Once we were married, he would have had full access to the coven and perhaps could have wheedled his way in to see the king."

"How did you discover his true nature?"

Prudence slumps and Esme rubs her back.

Perhaps I pushed too far. "If this is too painful, madam, it is not necessary to tell me."

Patting Esme's knee, Prudence draws a long shaky breath. "You should know. The power you possess can be used for evil. However, it does not make you dark, William. I still feel nothing wicked in you.

"Bertram was very careful. He and I spoke with our minds, but he could manipulate others without their knowledge. He would plant ideas in witches' heads, and even before our marriage, he climbed the ranks of the coven. Nothing official, of course, but still, I was so proud of his talents and clever mind."

Tea arrives, and we all sit quietly as Anne puts the tray on the table.

Esme pours Prudence a cup and hands it to her before she pours for me and herself.

Prudence puts her cup and saucer down. "It was Sowen. The witches gathered to celebrate, and as the veil between living and dead thinned, we hoped to speak to those who were no longer with us. My mother had passed two summers before, and I longed to see or hear her.

"As the spirits came through, they all looked upon Bertram, but stayed silent. My mother pushed through his spell to keep them away and whispered traitor in my head. Still, I didn't believe her. How could the man I loved so be a traitor? In what way?

"I was a fool." Pale, she picked up her tea. "Willamina Blakely also got a message from her grandmother pointing a finger at Bertram. She accused him, and he struck her down with a forbidden spell. She was dead before she hit the ground."

Esme rubbed Prudence's back. "Tell the rest, Great Mother. I'm sorry, but he must know."

Prudence meets my gaze with a steady gray stare. "The witches went into a frenzy. They threw spell after spell at him, but he was so strong. In his efforts to hold off the onslaught of light magic, his glamor fell. He wasn't the handsome man I fell in love with, but a hideous mangled thing that black magic had twisted and warped. Still, I loved him and begged him to stop and return to the light.

"He laughed at me as if I was a naive child. And I suppose I was. I threw a bolt of power to bind him. I said the ancient binding spell. My sisters gave me all they could to help me bind him for all time. Then it was done."

My heart aches for her pain, so old and yet so fresh in her mind. "How did he die?"

Prudence shakes her head.

After drawing a long breath, Esme says, "It's said he relied on his evil to sustain him for hundreds of years past a natural life, and once he had no magic, he died. He died in the circle of witches on Sowen. His body was salted and burned that very night. The great mother was tried the next day and found innocent of any wrongdoing, as they all had been fooled by him."

"And he was the last witch to have this ability." I touch the side of my head.

"That is known. Yet I sensed no evil or dark when you were

in my head. I only fear what I don't understand. Forgive me." Esme stares at her hands in her lap.

I stand and pace in front of the hearth, then stop and look at the two of them staring at me. "I would give you full access to my mind. I would have you search my heart for anything that might turn to darkness. I do not wish to become a monster."

Prudence struggles to her feet, comes to me, and takes my hands. "You can't become what you are not. Fear not. This magic can be as much a gift as a curse. Bertram was dark because of the choices he made. You will choose better." She pats my cheek. "Esme, take me to my room. I find this talk has exhausted me."

Esme jumps up to do as Prudence asks.

Alone in the parlor, I sit and drink my tea.

Henry clears his throat. "I hardly think you are capable of harming England, Will."

"Eavesdropping is a bad habit." I shift in my seat so I can look at him while he rounds the table and sits in the other chair.

It's rare for Henry to sit in my presence without an invitation. "Still, it's a habit I picked up in the service, and it comes in handy. You would never betray this country or these women."

"No. The man I believe I am wouldn't do those things. I'm just uncertain of what I'm becoming." I swallow down my fears and meet Henry's gaze.

"I see the same man who is my friend. The man who saved my life more than once. I have watched you conjure in that little room, and it is quite amazing, but I have noticed no difference in you, Will."

There is comfort in that. "And you'll tell me, or better yet, tell Miss O'Dwyer, if you notice a change?"

"You have my word." Henry stands, pats my shoulder, and leaves the parlor.

I sit until the tea is cold. I let the sounds of heartbeats both inside the house and out fill me with what is wondrous about magic.

Simon jumps into my lap, and we sit a while longer.

"I'm going up to wash and change, little friend. I suppose you will be the first to know if I'm a bad egg." I scratch the back of his head.

Intelligent eyes stare back at me as if the answer is obvious.

With a bit more hope in my heart, I go get clean from my swim.

CHAPTER
TWELVE

ESME

I've been staring at the spot on the ceiling for hours. I'm never going to find sleep. The fact that I can feel William's arousal and his desire for me from down the hall isn't helping. Though, I can't blame him entirely.

The oppressive heat has eased little from the day, and even with the window open and no blanket, I'm uncomfortably warm.

I push away the connection between us. I've had training against dark witchcraft. Even though there is nothing evil in what William feels or thinks, my training helps to put up a wall between us. Yet, pushing him away hurts more than it should.

It does neither of us any good to give in to the desires. Honestly, it shall be worse for me. He's a gentleman. He can move back to his life without consequence.

Witches take lovers. I remind myself but dismiss the idea of continuing an affair when we return to Windsor. It's better if we are friends. Repeating our encounter will only break my heart, and that organ has no business involved in an affair.

Footsteps in the hall make me hold my breath. I know it's him, as they are too heavy to be Prudence, and the staff wouldn't be so loud. He stops at my door.

Holding still, I let my wall drop and am flooded with desire. It's so strong that when I try to erect my wall again, I'm too distracted to keep his want for me out.

Never has the attention of any man made me so flushed with need.

His footfall moves away, then downstairs and outside. The farther he walks away, the easier it is to push aside our connection. I can't understand why we are like this.

Even at a distance, and with my attempt to break our connection, I feel his relief when he jumps into the pond.

Stay in bed, Esme, I'm screaming inside my head.

In only a shift, I pad from the bed to the door. Holding a moment, I tell myself to get back in the bed. I even order myself to relieve my tension with my own hand. The idea is hollow with William so close.

Does he have me under a spell? I turn the doorknob and go downstairs.

Before I leave the house, I press my head against the wooden door and try to gain some composure. I cast to search for curses or dark magic but find only my own desire drives me across the drive and grass, toward the pond.

The half-moon is enough light to see him naked and swimming away.

I let any remnants of my block fall.

William stops and turns toward me. His head goes under, and he comes up sputtering.

I hold back my laugh. "Don't drown now. It took all my nerve to come out here."

He glides through the water toward me, each stroke easy and strong at the same time. "Do you want that swimming lesson now, Esme?"

"I could hear your thoughts and feelings. It was too hard to push you away," I admit, and ease one bare foot into the water, then the other.

The cool water feels divine, even just on my toes. It can't quell the burn of his nearness. If it were the dead of winter, we would melt this pond in an instant. I close my eyes as he rises from the water and steps toward me.

The first drip of water on my hand lets me know how close he is. "I heard you too, Esme. Is it magic that links us like this? Should we fight some darkness forging this bond?"

Opening my eyes, I look into his. "I don't know why I can't push you aside so we can remain friends."

"Am I evil?" Fear flushes his cheeks, and his shoulders tense.

I cup his cheek. "No, William. There is no evil in you. You have gifts that might tempt a man or woman to use them to gain power. Power can corrupt. Do you wish to manipulate people to rule the world?"

"You mean besides wanting to manipulate you for our mutual pleasure?" He drags me against his wet body.

My breath is shaky. "Yes. Besides that."

He shakes his head. "I have no use for world domination. I'll leave that to gods, goddesses, and kings."

"Will you use your talents to protect and serve the light?" I'm breathless from the warmth of his body and his hard shaft pressed between us.

"I will do what I can for what is right and in service to my king."

I clutch his shoulders to keep my knees from buckling. "Will you teach me to swim?"

His mouth covers mine in a kiss that I feel from my head to my toes. Low in my belly, my womb clenches, and juices slick my most private spot.

"William, I need you, and I don't need anyone." I wrap my arms around his neck and tip my pelvis.

Clutching my bottom, he lifts me, and I grip his hips with my legs as he lowers me to the cool grass.

Hand on the hem of my chemise, he tugs it over my hips to my waist, then breaks contact to drag the thin garment over my head. He sits back on his heels and stares at me. "You are so lovely, Esme. I fear this burning for you is witchery."

"Desire and magic are close companions, but we are under no spell." I tip my hips so his thigh, resting between my legs, rubs me in the most delicious way. My body quivers with sensation.

He covers me, pressing kisses along my collarbone, up my neck, and along my jaw. Breathless, he asks, "How can you be sure this isn't a spell?"

It's hard to make sense of his question, or anything besides his mouth and the caress of his hand on my hip, waist, and breast. "I...I...I divined for magic before I came outside."

He stills. "You also thought this thing between us might be unnatural?"

Leaning on his elbow, he keeps his other hand just below my breast. His thumb circles the skin in a gentle caress.

Rising to my elbows brings my chest against his, trapping his hand between us. "I wanted to be sure. I wanted this to be good and real, not something torrid or forced upon us. Finding no curse or hex, I came to you. You were in my head, thinking the naughtiest desires. How was I supposed to sleep?"

I press my lips to his, and an instant later he devours my mouth. Gripping his hair, I wrap my legs around his hips. "I need you. Please, William."

Wrapping me in his arms, he rolls so that I'm straddling him. "I am yours for the taking, sweetheart."

Rising to my knees, I impale myself on his thick shaft. I bite my lip to keep from crying out. Surely, screams of rapture would bring members of the household out of doors. Folding onto his chest, I kiss my way up to his mouth and rock him in and out of me. My rapture is so close, my pace quickens. "I need..." I rock faster, harder. "I can't..." I fall out of rhythm.

William grips my hips and sets me at a steady pace. His handsome face awash with adoration, he stares up at me. "Tell me what you need."

"I. Need..." Muddled with ecstasy, my brain can't find the words.

Impossibly, William's cock fills me even more. I'm wild with the need to find completion.

His hips rise as mine fall in perfect harmony.

Stabbing up hard and fast, he holds me in place, finds my pearl with his thumb and sends me over the edge. I kiss him hard to muffle my screams as he pumps twice more, pulls out of me, and empties his seed between us.

His kisses gentle after the frenzied release. Nibbling my upper lip then the bottom, he worships me as no one ever has. "You are everything," he whispers.

Naked in the moonlight, I drape my body over him, legs apart and stretched out. I toy with the hair behind his ear and rest my cheek on his chest. "Do you think we need to move from this spot? I would be perfectly happy to die just like this."

His chuckle bumps me up and down, and already he is hard again. "I could make love to you all night and for all the days of my life, Esme."

"Yes, let's do that." I don't recognize my own satisfied and wanton voice.

Trailing his fingers down my spine to the curve of my

bottom, he cups the flesh and pulls me tight against his arousal. "I'm going to teach you to swim first. Then I'm going to taste every lovely part of you until you cry my name a hundred times."

"I like the sound of the second much more than the first," I whine, and grind my hips.

He rolls me to my back in a quick breathtaking move, and hovers above me. His eyes dance with joy and desire in equal measure. "Swim lessons first." With a kiss on my nose, he pops up to his feet. Reaching down to help me up, he's magnificent. Muscled from top to bottom, and his shaft is at full attention.

My mouth is watering. "What on earth do you do with your time that keeps you this fit? I thought landed gentlemen were all soft and squishy."

Wrapping his arms around me, he laughs. "Squishy?"

I'm caught up in the mirth of the moment when I realize he's backed me to the edge of the pond and my feet are submerged.

"I ride, and work in the garden. When I'm able to go to the country, there are a great many chores that need seeing to."

As my knees hit the cold water, I swallow down the rising fear in my chest. "Have you no gardener to tend such things? I've been to your house; it seemed that you had a full staff."

"I like the work and wouldn't wish to get squishy." Taking my hands, he backs into the water until my hips are submerged. Meeting my gaze, he asks, "Okay, love?"

My breathing is choppy. "You'll not let me drown?"

"Never."

Trust doesn't come easily to me. I should run away from this pond and William, but I can't garner the uncertainty I have for most people. Somehow, I know he would never allow any harm to come to me. "What do I do?"

It might be worth drowning to have him grin at me so

beautifully. "Keep walking toward me, and when the water is deep, you're going to lay on your back."

The cold water is heavenly compared to the thick warm air, and I push forward until my shoulders are just above the water.

Not sure how to achieve the next step, I wait, breathing as if I'm already submerged.

Swimming close, William wraps his arm around my waist. "Bend your knees and float. Pick your feet up. I have you."

I lift my toes from the soft bottom. William slides his arm behind my knees and lays me back. "Am I doing it?"

"No. I'm still holding you, but I'm going to let go, Esme. Just wave your arms gently through the water and relax." His arms drop away.

My bottom sinks, but I wave frantically and my hips lift.

"Slow down," he commands.

I do, and I float in one spot. The stars wink down at me, and the moon smiles in approval. "I'm floating."

"You're doing wonderfully." His tone is calm and sure. "Now, lift your head and drop your feet, but keep waving your hands just as you are."

I ease up and let my feet drop. No bottom! My head goes under, and I swallow water. An instant later, William lifts me.

Coughing up the water in my lungs, I feel his legs working under the water.

I kick out and catch his shin.

"Ouch." He grins

"Sorry." I slap at the surface.

"Move your feet back and forth in opposite directions and keep moving your arms through the water." His voice is so calm even as my heart is thrumming loudly in my ears.

It takes me a few minutes before I understand what he

means. Suddenly, I'm afloat, and William releases me. "I'm doing it."

"You are. Quite well, too." He backs away.

The gap between us steadily grows. "How do I follow?"

"Push the water in the opposite direction you wish to move."

Inch by slow inch, I'm swimming. My lungs are screaming, and my arms and legs ache. "Perhaps I had better return to dry land before my energy runs out."

He swims in front of me and closes the distance. "I'll take you back. Put your arms around my neck and relax."

Once I do, he eases to his back with me riding him like a raft. Then, using only his arms, he floats us back to where I can reach the bottom. "I'm very proud of you, Esme. You did brilliantly."

My cheeks heat as I climb the bank to where my night rail lays waiting. I pull it over my head and sit. "Thank you. You are a fine teacher."

William drags on his breeches and sits beside me. "Will you let me take you to bed now?"

I'm trying to catch my breath. My arms and legs feel as if they've been weighted down with sacks of grain. "I shall not tell you no."

Cocking his head, he smiles. "How about if I save the tasting every inch of you for another time and just carry you to your bed and hold you until I must return to my own room?"

"That sounds divine."

Once I'm in his arms, he carries me across the yard. "I like knowing what's in your head, but I do wish I could turn it off. I feel I'm invading your privacy."

Cupping his cheek, I wish I could hold all of him at once and give him comfort. I look at him as he brings us inside and to my room. Once on my feet, I pull off the damp night rail and toss it over the back of the chair. "You will learn to turn it off, and for now, I need no privacy."

He takes his clothes off and places them next to mine on the chair before laying in my bed.

I slip in beside him as a cool breeze flits through the window. "I think the weather is turning. Perhaps we won't need to swim to bear the heat."

Kissing my forehead, he sighs. "What a shame."

Hands on his chest, I rest my chin on them to look at my William. "You really are the most handsome man I've ever seen. How have you avoided the debutantes of your circle for so long?"

His hold around my waist tightens. "I thought you were tired."

"Suddenly coy, William? Have you been married, or are you engaged?" My curiosity is most definitely piqued.

With a twist, he rolls so he's half covering me. His thigh drapes between mine and awakens desire there. Intense blue eyes stare at me, and I brush his hair back from his forehead. He draws a long breath. "I wouldn't be here with you if I were engaged or married. If I had made vows, I would keep them."

Ashamed, I nod. "Of course, you would. I'm sorry. I was only joking."

"I know." His tone lightens. "I was engaged once. I was quite young, as was my fiancée. We were to marry when I got back from the war."

"What happened?" My heart is lodged in my throat.

Pushing up, he sits against the headboard and drags me into his lap. His lips press against my collarbone before he rests his head against me. "I was away a long time." He sighs. "At first, Melody wrote to me every day. Then it was every week. After a year, the letters stopped coming. I wrote to her every week, despite her lack of response. I felt it my duty to correspond. Eighteen months into my deployment in France, I received a note informing me that her affections had shifted to another. While she wished me well, she hoped I would understand that she was nearly twenty now and could not afford to wait forever."

I want to scratch Melody's eyes out on William's behalf. "Good lord, what did you say?"

His shoulders lift in a shrug. "What could I say? I wished her joy and released her from her contract with me."

"You should have called the other man out." My voice is harsh, and I hurt as if the injustice had been done to me rather than him.

William shakes his head. "She didn't love me, and if I'm honest, I didn't love her either. This was a blessing. Even if it was hard to see that at the time. At the moment, I can't imagine I ever wanted to marry Melody."

His lips press to mine, and I open for him. Our tongues touch, and my exhaustion flees as if it never existed.

CHAPTER
THIRTEEN

WILLIAM

Each Wednesday, we bring Prudence to the village, where she heals small ailments and gives advice. Today Pauline Mercer brings her newborn child to see the great mother for a blessing.

I have no true purpose beyond making certain Prudence doesn't overextend herself.

Esme is busy healing many of the more serious ailments.

At the sight of the infant, Prudence brightens, even after the long day has worn her out. "Oh, what a sweet boy you have brought to me, Pauline. I remember when your own good mother brought you in for a blessing."

Pauline blushes. "Mother is too ill to come and see you. She bade me give her regrets."

As if she hasn't heard, Prudence holds the child close and says a few words in blessing before handing the babe back to his mother. "What ails your mother?"

"It is her stomach, Great Mother. She suffers mightily, but

the doctor has done all he can." A tear rolls down Pauline's round cheek.

Frowning, Prudence stands. "If memory serves, your mother lives at the other end of town."

Jumping to her feet despite the burden of holding her baby, Pauline says, "Yes. In the very house where I was raised."

Prudence brushes out her skirts and turns to Esme. "Miss O'Dwyer will continue here in my stead." Once Esme nods, she continues. "Sir William, will you accompany me to Mrs. Kyle's home? Clair is an old friend. If she cannot come to me, then I shall go to her."

"As you wish, Great Mother." I offer my arm, which Prudence takes.

"Will you bring my bag, Sir William?" She points to the satchel with herbs and brews for healing.

I do as I'm told.

Once we are in the street, I ask Pauline, "How far is the walk, madam. Shall I call the carriage?"

Pulling me forward with more force than I would have thought possible, Prudence scoffs. "I'm not so old that a little stroll in the fresh air won't do me good. Don't fuss so."

I share a brief smile with Pauline and walk faster so I can at least continue to offer my arm.

At the end of the village, we stop before a small house, whitewashed and in good condition. The only sign anything is amiss are the dead flowers in the window box. Likely the heat, an unwell Mrs. Kyle, and her daughter recently giving birth are to blame for the poor, sad blooms.

Pauline knocks but enters before anyone calls back. "Mother, I have brought company for you."

The house is dark with drawn curtains and no candles. With the baby in one arm, Pauline pulls back the front curtain to let in some light, revealing a neatly kept front parlor with worn furniture in faded green, and wood that hasn't seen polish in some time. No rug softens the scuffed wood floor.

There are two doors other than the one we entered through. One presumably leads to the kitchen. In the other, stands a gaunt woman who might have once been as pretty as her daughter. Her cheeks are sunken, and dark rings mark the undersides of her red-rimmed blue eyes. She holds tight to the door frame and blinks as if to clear her vision.

Prudence rushes to her. "Clair, my dear, you should have stayed in bed. I'd have come the rest of the way."

"Prudence Bishop?" Clair squints. "I must be seeing things." She stumbles forward and nearly topples them both.

Luckily, it's a small home, and I'm there in an instant to lend each an arm. "Ladies, can I escort you to the sofa?"

Clair's eyes widen as they meet mine. "You've brought a gentleman to call?"

I smile and coax Mrs. Kyle to the sofa. "I'm William Meriwether, madam. It's a pleasure to make your acquaintance."

"Sir William is a student with much potential." Prudence sits beside Clair and takes her hand. "Tell me, what ails you, old friend?"

"The doctor's already written me off, I'm afraid. Stomach is no good. It's dying first just to make my own death more miserable." Clair gives the report without any emotion.

Prudence touches the woman's stomach and then her forehead. She sighs. "I'll not lie to you, Clair. You're sicker than I'd like to begin treatment. Doctors don't know everything, though. Let me ease your pain and start some healing. I've got a fine tea that may help as well. I'll send Esme, a fine healer, to you daily to continue treatment. We'll do what we can for you while we're here. I'll come back to see you next week as well."

Tears run freely down Pauline's face as she rocks the baby in her arms. "Thank you, Great Mother."

"Don't thank me. We may be only slowing the inevitable, but we'll do what we can." Prudence closes her eyes and places her hands on Clair's abdomen.

Some color comes back into Clair's face, and the tightness in her lips eases.

"There now, that's a bit better." Prudence points to her bag. "William, I'll have you make a tea with barley, chamomile, and milk thistle."

I pull out what she listed then move to the door I assume is the kitchen.

"William." Prudence stops my retreat.

"Yes, Great Mother?"

"You must brew the tea with intention." Her gray eyes are alight with meaning.

"I will."

I go into a small room with a cold hearth, a basin, and two pans. Stacks of clean dishes sit on a shelf with several cups and a chipped teapot. Lighting the fire with one of the new spells Esme taught me, I think of the way fire heals and warms. At the well outside the back door, I fill a small pot and hang it over the fire.

While the water warms, I take each herb and place them in the teapot. I want Mrs. Kyle to regain her health and see her grandchild grow to a man. I imagine her with the same round cheeks as her daughter and eating around a table after Michaelmas mass. The family is happy and laughing. A man is holding Mrs. Kyle's chair and grinning.

I take a breath and snap out of the vision. "Herbs to heal and herbs to care. One by one this brew is fair. Each to work the magic free, and find that which I see. As I will, so mote it be."

The water bubbles, and I pour it over the herbs, repeating the spell once more. I wait a few minutes for the tea to darken, then place it on a wooden tray with a teacup next to it and carry it out to the parlor. Placing the tray on a small table, I wait while Prudence opens the lid and gives the tea a sniff.

She smiles at me. "Well done, Sir William."

I pour and hand the simple white cup to Mrs. Kyle. "You must drink the entire pot. It should be pleasant, and at the least, make you feel better."

Mrs. Kyle sips the tea and rests her head back on the sofa cushion. "It's quite good, and it's the first time a man has ever made me tea, let alone a knighted one."

We all laugh, and I say, "Perhaps it shall be a new trend, madam. I quite enjoy the brewing process."

"Imagine that, Mother," Pauline says. "Do you think Bart will be fixing my tea each day?"

Clair grins. "With all you do for that man, it would do him good to make you a bit of tea."

The women continue to speak of married life as if I'm not in the room. After a few minutes, I make my way to the front door. "I'll be just outside when you need me, Great Mother."

I like the sound of women talking, but I'm likely hindering what they might say if I were absent, and if Prudence wishes to say something in private, I don't want to be an obstacle.

The day is very fine with a soft breeze. Esme was right about the weather changing. No more stifling heat that requires dips in the pond. That's not to say we haven't continued swimming lessons, but the cool water was all pleasure and not much necessity.

I walk to an oak tree to the side of the house and lean against the thick trunk. Never in my life did I expect to wind up learning witchcraft in a small village or making healing teas. As Esme strolls down the street toward me, I can think of nothing I want more than what I have here in this place, in this time. I am perfectly content.

"You look pleased with yourself." Esme's smile is everything. She comes to stand next to me.

Running a finger along her silken cheek, I pull away before we are noticed by the townspeople making their way in and out of town. "I am happy. I don't know that I've ever been so before."

"I am glad of it." She opens her mouth as if to say more, but the front door opens, and Prudence shuffles out.

Rushing over, I offer my arm. "How is Mrs. Kyle?"

Prudence stares at me for a long time. "Better than I expected. What did you add to that tea?"

At once delighted and horrified, I say, "Only what you instructed, Great Mother."

Samuel pulls up to the house with the carriage, and I assist both women inside. Once I sit across from them, I continue, "You said to put my intentions into the tea, and I did that as well."

"What has happened?" Esme asks.

"In a moment, Esme." Prudence levels her gaze on me. "William, tell me exactly what you did when you made the tea."

I tell her about the pot, water, fire, and herbs. I repeat the spell I used, then I remember the vision. "I forgot. I actually forgot until this moment. I had a vision of Mrs. Kyle with her family, happy and feasting after church on Michaelmas. It was very vivid and unintentional. I was thinking of my wish to see her healthy and happy, and suddenly I was in the midst of her getting just that. It only lasted a few seconds, then I cast the spell and brought the tea."

Esme sits forward despite the rocking carriage. "What did he do?"

Shaking her head, Prudence smiles. "He healed her of a cancer that I didn't believe could be healed. When I left, she was full of good color and life. Still too thin but asking for some food. Pauline said she'd not been able to force more than a bite or two into her for weeks."

"Will it last?" I want to know.

Prudence shrugs. "I don't know. Your magic may be beyond what I can explain, William. What you did is special."

I think about the vision. "Maybe I only saw what was to be anyway. Perhaps the doctor was wrong, and her stomach was a fugue rather than a cancer."

"I suppose that is possible." Prudence doesn't sound convinced.

"I hope you'll not tell me this is another sign of dark magic." I hold my breath.

"No. Dark magic always takes something away when it gives a blessing. You took nothing, only saw what you wanted and made it so."

Her words strike deeply inside me, and my gaze shoots to Esme. She too, looks shocked. Did I want her and use my magic to draw her in? Was my magic manipulative? I couldn't ask that of Great Mother. We've not been forthcoming about our affair, and I have no idea where asking will lead. To my own shame, I don't even know what Esme wants from me beyond our sojourn in the country.

I'm lost in my thoughts as the carriage rolls down the road back to the cottage. When we arrive, I help the ladies down as if in a fog. How can I know if she truly cares for me, if my magic is of a forceful nature?

"Esme, may I have a word with you?" I whisper as she steps to the ground.

She does not answer as her fingers remain in mine.

"Who is this now?" Prudence says in a sharp tone that makes us both turn to see a young woman strolling determinedly up the lane toward us.

She has long brown hair pulled up in a loose bun, and half of it is hanging around her face and neck. Her light brown eyes assess the situation with keen regard while her lips pull up in a friendly grin. There's something cunning in her gaze, and when she looks me up and down as if I'm a horse to be bought and sold, my skin crawls.

Esme stiffens next to me.

Is she jealous of the way this girl looks at me? I'll save the question for later.

She stops before Prudence, puts down her gray cloth bag, and makes a pretty curtsy. "Hello, Great Mother. I've been sent to assist you."

"Katrina Davidson? Why would the coven send you here?" Prudence stares her down as if to read her mind.

"I only do as I'm told." Katrina says in a light voice. She turns toward Esme and me and makes another curtsy. "I am Trina, if you please."

"Esme, and this is Sir William," Esme says. "What does Sara Beth think you can help with exactly?"

Trina shrugs. "I suppose she thinks I have some talent with magic, and that the great mother might be getting tired after so many weeks away."

Truth be told, Prudence does look tired after a day of blessings and healing. She heaves a sigh. "I shall go and nap then, if I'm so feeble I need a redundancy of help to train one witch." With another loud heave of breath, she allows Anne to assist her into the house.

"What kind of witch are you, Trina?" Esme asks.

Eyes sharp, Trina faces Esme with her hands fisted. "What kind of witch are you?"

Esme's brows rise and she puts down Prudence's medicine bag. "I'm a healer, and my magic is earth in nature."

"And him?" Trina bites out.

"He is standing right here, and it is quite rude to speak of me as if I'm not." I move next to Esme and wonder why so much hostility flows from the girl.

Her expression softens and she dips a shoulder. "Very well then, Sir William. What kind of witch are you?"

"I have no idea," I answer honestly.

"This must be going very badly if you haven't even divined his magics yet. Perhaps that's why I was sent, to help with basics where you are lacking, healer."

Esme takes a menacing step forward, and Trina backs up the same distance. "Do not think to disrespect me, girl. I may not be part of your coven, but I have power enough. You are here, and you may help, but if you think that wicked tongue will win you favor with anyone, you are much mistaken."

The soil under Trina's feet begins to collapse. Inch by inch, it draws her down.

She struggles to free herself and calls to the pond water. A wave surges up.

With a flick of her fingers, Esme pushes the wave back, all the while pulling soil up over Trina. Her hips are buried, and she tries with bare hands to dig herself free. "I'm sorry. I was rude, and I'm sorry. Please, release me."

As the dirt reaches her waist, I begin to grow concerned that Esme won't stop. "Do you plan to bury her over a child's rudeness?"

With a cock of her head, Esme stops mounding the earth. "I just want to make sure my point is well received. I'll not play mother to a girl who doesn't know her place. I'll send you right back to Windsor to explain to the coven why you were not of use."

Another flick of her wrist, and the mound of dirt opens, allowing Trina to jump out.

She brushes the earth and grass from her dress. When she

looks up, her expression is far more contrite. "My apologies to you both. I was rude, and perhaps a bit weary from the road. I have been away from home a long time, and my manners have suffered."

"Very well. There is an extra bed on the lower level with Anne. You will find her good company, and a fine cook and maid. You will treat everyone in this house and village as if they were your esteemed aunt or uncle. Do I make myself clear, Katrina Davidson?" Esme's stern voice is so fierce, it's hard to believe this is the warm, gentle woman I know.

Trina gives a nod and keeps her eyes lowered to her filthy hands. "Is there someplace I can wash, miss?"

"That pond is fed by a stream. You can wash in private if you follow the stream into the woods." Esme points to the east, and Trina trudges off with her bag in hand.

"Why would the coven send another witch?" I ask so that only Esme can hear me.

"Perhaps they don't trust me, and maybe what Trina said about Prudence is true. Though, Great Mother seems quite spry to me. She tires easily, but at her age, so will we." Esme picks up Prudence's satchel and heads into the house.

"Esme?"

She turns back toward me from the doorway.

"Do you think...?" I don't know how to ask what I want to know. If my power is manipulative in nature, is her attraction to me real?

Shaking her head, she smiles. "I don't know the answer to what you're wondering, but I can hear it in your mind, clearly as my own worries."

Walking to the door, I touch her arm and caress up to her elbow. She smells of sunshine, earth, and flowers. I want to bury my face in her soft hair. "Perhaps we should take a step back from whatever this is until we know the truth."

"I want to disagree with you, but I can't." Sorrow spills into her eyes, making me wish I could pull the words back and never even think them.

I press my lips to her forehead. "Friends?"

"Always." She smiles up at me.

CHAPTER
FOURTEEN

ESME

I'll not lie, even to myself. Taking a step back from William's embrace is hard. If it is the nature of his magic to gain what he wants, then he still wants me.

When I look for it, I sense no magic beyond normal desire binding us. I have much time to think on the subject as I trek each day to see Mrs. Kyle. I knock on the Kyle's door, and she calls, "Come in."

Standing by the kitchen door, Clair grins. "I'm feeling almost myself today. What was in that tea the gentleman made me? Never mind, I don't want to know. I'm happy to feel better and see my grandson for a few more days."

"I don't know myself. He has some skills." Despite the fact that we're speaking of tea making and healing, I find my cheeks warm at the thought of William and his talents.

"Indeed, does he?" Clair's smile widens. "Do you have a tender for the man?"

I rush into the kitchen and start boiling some water. "He's not in my sphere, so it's of no consequence."

A little round table has been newly placed in the corner of the kitchen with two chairs. She fondles the table. "Mr. Waller made me this table and brought it to me as a gift. Imagine a woman my age getting a gift from a man. I think if that's possible after being on death's door just ten days ago, then you loving Sir William is nothing to scoff at. Besides, Pauline told me he looks very tenderly at you whenever she's seen you together. Perhaps the fondness is mutual."

I drop herbs in the teapot and clear my mind of all but healing. Once I add the water, I turn toward Clair. "It will not change that he is a gentleman, and I am what I am."

Clair huffs out a breath. "You look fine enough to me, and lovely besides."

I bring the tea to the table with a cup and saucer, and sit. "William is a good man. I'll leave the rest to the fates to decide. I shall continue to be his friend."

While the tea steeps, Clair traces the grain of her little table. "Why do you think a man like Mr. Waller would make me a table?"

"I have only met the man once, when he brought his son to me with a slightly worrisome cut on his hand. It's a fine table, though. Sturdy and good looking, too. Perhaps he heard you were feeling better. I don't know. Did the two of you grow up together?" I pour the tea and slide it closer to her.

She takes a sip. "I married my Patrick when I was just fifteen. He was a fine man, but neither one of us knew anything about life. He kept food on the table and was kind. Died four winters past, and I miss him. Left me enough to live on, which is more than most women around here get. I'm lucky. When I got sick, I thought, well, at least I'll see my Patrick again. Mr. Waller, Ben is his given name, he was a good friend with my husband. His wife's been gone since their youngest was born nearly twenty years ago. Maybe he's lonely. I could do with some company, too. But perhaps we're both too old for all that nonsense."

The vision William had jumps into my mind. Had he done all of this, or had he only seen what was to be? "I think it would be nice for two people to find some company regardless of your ages. Who says having a companion is only for the young?"

While Clair mulls over a man and the table, I reach out with my magic and seek out the area that ailed her only days before. There is no illness that I can see. She's still thin, but that will take time. I've never seen anyone cured of an illness of this nature. Witches can often ease the pain, but to heal a killing cancer and not be harmed in the process is beyond anything I've ever known.

As I saunter back to the cottage, I worry over William. How was power like this suppressed in his family? How did he not know he was special? Was his father as powerful? So many questions and no answers.

I go directly to the stillroom to return the jars of herbs I carried to the village.

The day is warm, and Trina's voice spills out of the open door. "William, you are a wonder. Your hands are more than magic."

I stop. My heart says William wouldn't do anything ungentlemanly with Trina, but my stupid head knows he is a man, and Trina is a very pretty young woman. She's seven years younger than me, and at a prime for marriage, while I am an old maid by such standards.

Within, Simon hisses loudly and bolts from the stillroom.

"That beast got me again," Trina says harshly. She rushes out the door with her hands raised as if to cast, spots me, and freezes. Pointing to Simon meowing at my feet, she complains, "Your cat is a menace."

There's a bloody streak across her hand.

Crouching, I lift Simon into my arms. "He doesn't like you. I can't imagine why."

Once I've given Simon a good scratch under the chin, I put him down so he can run into the house.

Squeezing past Trina, I enter the small room and smile at William, who is deep in concentration over a flowerpot. "What is it you're trying to do, William?"

"He should be healing my hand rather than fussing over that stupid flower," Trina grumbles from the door, as there's barely room for two in here let alone a third.

I put away my supplies and hold my grin.

"I healed your hand from the last time you teased the kitten, and I warned you to leave him alone." He never lets his gaze drift from the pot.

"It's just a scratch. I'm sure you can heal yourself." I fold my cloth bag and put it on the shelf below where William is working. "What's in the pot?"

Trina whines, "But William has such good, healing hands."

My gut twists with an emotion I'm not familiar with. If it's jealousy, I don't like it one bit.

William frowns. "I put a zinnia seed in this pot, and I want to see if I can make it grow. I know this is something you can do."

"Perhaps earth magic isn't your gift." I force myself not to help his seed along, despite the desire to do just that.

"Water magic isn't yours, but you can wield it without issue," he says.

Trina squeezes in behind him, her body touching his. "I told him he's a wonderful student and needn't push himself so hard."

"If I have a purpose, I'll not be unable to fulfill it because I was lax in my studies." He squishes into the corner to get away from Trina's touch.

Grabbing Trina by the arm, I pull her away from him before she can maneuver herself closer and trap him like a rat. I put myself between them, which gains me a warm smile from William. "Perhaps you are going about it the wrong way. I just came from Mrs. Kyle's house. Is it possible you can do with the flower what you did with her health?"

He breaks eye contact with the dirt in the pot and looks me in the eye. "See the flower in a vision?"

"Desire it, William."

Closing his eyes, he links his mind with mine. *Can you hear me, Esme?*

Yes.

I miss you. I miss what we had.

As do I, I admit.

A beautiful white zinnia blooms in my mind.

This is for you, sweetheart.

My cheeks want to heat, but I force them not to in front of Trina.

On a long breath, William opens his eyes and wraps his hands around the pot. A curl of green springs from the soil. It pushes up and unrolls, growing taller by the second. A white bloom erupts from the bud, just as beautiful as the one William sent to my mind.

"Oh, how perfect." I'm breathless with the way his magic works.

Rising to his full height, he lifts the pot and hands it to me. "You are the finest teacher. Thank you."

Trina huffs out a curse, turns, and stomps to the house.

William cocks his head. "One flower managed to get rid of Trina. Show me the nature of my magic, and bless me with your smile. We must keep it alive for a long while, sweetheart." Leaning in, he kisses my forehead.

"You shouldn't say such things out loud or in my head." The mirth in my voice negates my statement almost entirely.

He stands too close and smells of herbs and spices. I'm drunk with his scent. "I know, but I do miss you, Esme. May I come to your room? I'll not ask for your body, but just your time. Time alone with you is so precious to me."

I should say no. We have been ten days with barely a moment alone. My desire for him hasn't waned in the slightest. "How will we know if what we share is truth or magic?"

Taking a step back, his gaze falls to the floor. "Maybe I don't care which it is."

"I don't believe you." I touch his cheek where the hint of a beard rubs my fingers. Dropping my hand, I change the subject. "Why did Simon scratch Trina?"

His lips tug back into a grin. "Because for a smart girl, she can do some very silly things."

In my opinion, Trina is more cunning than smart, but I keep this to myself. I suppose she is bright enough. "What silly thing did she do?"

"She thought to test my skills of levitation on a living thing."

My anger flares. "You didn't levitate Simon."

Gently, he tucks a stray curl behind my ear. "Of course not. I levitated a caterpillar crawling along the sill."

The contact makes me yearn for more. "I still don't know why my cat scratched Trina."

"Because she decided she would show me how it was done properly and tried to lift Simon from the floor. I know this will sound crazy, but Simon looked as if he knew what she was about. Since she's been here, I've seen her levitate many things, but she couldn't lift the cat. After thirty seconds, he hissed and gave his best roar. Then he jumped up on the counter and clawed her outstretched hand." William tries to hide his grin, but he only succeeds in looking even more handsome in the attempt.

"And you healed her?" He should have let her bleed.

He raises his hands as he shrugs. "It was good practice, and I felt a bit responsible."

"Why would you?"

"I kept the cat grounded. I countered her magic. It wasn't right to lift poor Simon. If he were in danger, I could see it, but to manipulate him seemed wrong to me." He shrugged again. "Besides, countering a spell seems like a useful talent."

"How did you know what to do?" My adoration for him grows with every moment. However, I never taught him a counter spell.

"I've been reading my family's remaining grimoire. There was a simple counter spell in it and even a notation about using it without the other witch knowing." His grin is wide.

"You amaze me at every turn, William." The spicy scent of him is like a drug, and I want to wrap myself in him and never let go.

He moves closer until I can feel the heat of him. "It's nice to have even a few minutes alone with you, sweetheart."

I press my cheek to his chest. He's so familiar and perfect. I admit, "I was jealous."

He pulls back and looks me in the eye. "When? Why? Of Whom?"

The rapid questions make me giggle, but I can't meet his stare. I'm ashamed of how I felt when I heard them alone in this little room. "Just before I walked in here, when I heard Trina saying how good you are with your hands. I have no right to jealousy, and I do believe it's the first time in my life I've ever felt such a ridiculous emotion."

Pressing his index finger under my chin, he lifts my gaze to his. "Trina is a very pretty young woman. I'm sure she shall make someone a fine wife, but I'm not interested in her beyond whatever she can teach me of magic. Do you believe me?"

"Of course." I mean it. I know William is not the kind of man who would bed me one week, then chase another skirt the next. He's a man of honor, and he cares for me. Even if our paths are not moving in the same direction, we are friends. He would never knowingly hurt a friend.

His stare drills into me as if he's looking for lies versus the truth. "I don't know what will be between you and me. To be honest, I don't even know what you want from your future. All I can promise is that I'll not ever betray you."

Betray me? He owes me nothing. I'm neither his wife nor his fiancée. There is no commitment or contract between us. I open my mouth to ease his worry, and Trina calls from the house. "Great Mother is asking for the two of you!" she bellows, far louder than necessary.

Sharing a private smile with William, I call back, "We're on our way."

When we enter the parlor, tea is already poured. I place my potted flower on the table.

Prudence raises a brow at the bloom then turns to me. "How is my friend Clair today?"

"She is well, and she has an admirer." I sit and accept a cup of tea.

"Does she?" William asks.

"Indeed. An old friend, and he's made her a table for the kitchen. I found no sign of her infirmity. And other than her need to gain weight, there is no indication that she was ever ill."

"Then William is a healer and likely an earth witch." Trina is pacing behind Prudence's chair.

"Sit!" Prudence points to the chaise. "You're making me dizzy, girl."

With a childish pout, Trina does as she's told. "But I'm right. He's an earth witch."

"Whatever the nature of his magic, he is a very accomplished healer." It's odd how important this is to Trina. I feel that surge of jealousy again, and I don't like it one bit.

"I'm only saying that an earth witch isn't likely to turn to dark. A fire witch is more susceptible to such forces." Trina pops a biscuit into her mouth.

Prudence closes her eyes as if looking for patience. "Trina, will you go and ask Anne if she has any of those nice pastries with the cream inside?"

"Yes, Great Mother."

Once the girl is gone, Prudence takes a long breath. "I can't imagine what Sara Beth was thinking by sending that one to us. She's exhausting and of little use."

"She's powerful." William finishes his tea and puts the cup on the table.

"What makes you think so?" I ask. I haven't seen any great feats of magic from her.

He shrugs and leans back against the sofa. "I can sense it." His gaze is distant and thoughtful. "There's something inside her that's held back, but she has power. Undisciplined and chaotic in her mind, but I have learned a lot from her."

Prudence watches him over her teacup. "I didn't realize you sensed other people's magic, William. This is a skill that I am known for. When did you first notice you had this ability?"

"Perhaps a week ago. I noticed that people both magical and not have a sheen of magic around them. Strong, weak, different colors, I don't know what it all means, but you and Esme have been busy with Mrs. Kyle, so I kept it to myself." He looks from me to Prudence. "Do many witches have this ability?"

"Some, but not many." Prudence puts her tea down. "What do you see in Esme?"

His attention on me makes my cheeks heat, but I don't look away. There's a softness to his gaze when he looks at me. He clears his throat. "Her sheen is green like her eyes or the leaves in spring. It's strong and steady. When she does magic, it burns brighter with flecks of gold."

"It's called an aura, William," Prudence corrects. "And mine?"

"Gold with some orange and red, and very strong. I've noticed when you're tired it dims." He adds the last gently.

"I'm old." Prudence sighs. "And what of our little Trina?"

"Mostly reds, but a lot of gray and muted colors. It's hard to pin hers down. With Esme, it's a green that can't be mistaken. Trina's wavers with her mood." He shakes his head as if he's sorting through it all.

Trina's return to the parlor with a plate of pastries stops the conversation. I wonder over a red aura emanating from a water witch. It would be highly unusual. I wish we were back in Windsor where I have my mother's books to consult.

CHAPTER
FIFTEEN

WILLIAM

The cool nights in late summer give me no excuse for not sleeping. All I can think about is Esme. The way her eyes sparkled when I talked of her aura and the way her soft hair feels sliding through my fingers.

Would she send me away with my shaft half aroused if I went to her room?

She might.

She should.

I throw off my blanket and pull on my breeches, easing from my room and down the hall. Standing in front of her door, I hesitate and am about to return to my room.

The door swings open, and Esme takes my hand and pulls me inside. "You were going to leave."

"I shouldn't have come." I wrap her in my arms. "I can't seem to do without you."

"Nor I you." She presses her cheek to my chest. Her breasts rise and fall against me.

My cock is on full alert, but I only hold her. "Maybe we can talk?"

"It feels as though you have more than conversation on your mind." She laughs.

"That is not my mind, sweetheart, and I may not be able to subdue my desires, but I can behave like a gentleman despite them."

Breaking away from the embrace, she looks up at me. With the moon shining in the window, she's a goddess, pale and bright. "There is something we should talk about."

I kiss her hand and nod.

With a leap, she settles crossed-legged in the middle of the bed. Her white night rail fluffs out around her. She pats the mattress in front of her.

"Are we to sit like two children and gossip?" I climb on to her bed and mirror her cross-legged position.

"It's not gossip." She takes my hand. "It's about the auras you see. Trina said she was a water witch, but usually water magic is silver or blue. I've heard of green, but never red."

"She lifted half the pond on the day she first came to us. Could a witch of another element do such a thing?" I love the feel of her fingers in mine, and use my thumb to rub circles along the back of her hand.

"You nearly drowned us when you first tried." She narrows her gaze but grins at me.

The hushed tones of our voices in the moonlit room are erotic and arousing. Trina is the last thing I want to talk about. "I wonder if we might speak of something else."

Her brows rise. "What would you like to discuss?"

"Anything but another woman, or man." I add the last hurriedly.

"There are no other men. I've not had another lover in

several years. I suspect I will be hard pressed to take another after this sojourn."

The idea of her having a lover when we leave the cottage gnaws on my insides like a poison. "I wouldn't like to know of you with another, but I don't really know what it is you want, Esme."

"What do you mean?"

I turn so that my back is against the headboard and pull her into my lap. It's torture to have her like this and not make love, but I need to touch her. "I've never felt as connected to anyone as I do to you. Will you want me when we return to town?"

With her head on my shoulder, she draws a long breath and lets it out. "How would that work? Will you take me to meet your mother, introduce me to your friends?"

"You say it as if my answer should be no." I don't like where this is going. I'm not a man of great temper, but that doesn't mean I can't be brought to it by passion.

"Of course, you should say no, William." Her voice is soft and full of resignation.

"Why? Why must it be no?"

"How would you introduce me to your mother? I'm sure she is a fine lady. She married a gentleman and produced the same. She raised you to find a woman in your sphere to give her grandchildren who will be admired. I can bring you nothing you need in your life back in Windsor. I have no name or connections to lend to your family. I am beneath you."

It's all I can do to keep my voice low and not wake the entire house. "You are so far above me, you cannot know. I do not deserve your affection, yet I seek it with my very being. I realize society will see it differently. I'm not naive. However, I thought you would see the truth."

Pulling away, she looks me in the eye. Her aura pulses green and gold. "What truth is that?"

I turn so that my legs hang off the side of the bed. Head in my hands, I drag my fingers through my hair. It's grown long since we've been in the country. "You once told me that magic never makes mistakes. You said that things that are meant will come to pass. Why is what we share any different?"

When there is no response, I look over my shoulder.

Esme is again crossed-legged in the middle of the bed. Her eyes are distant and full of tears. "I'm afraid. I fear for you and for myself. It's impossible for what we have to move forward in that world without one or both of us losing everything."

I see the truth in her concerns. If I go to her world, I cannot continue as a gentleman. If she comes to mine, she cannot continue as a witch. "I shall think on what you've said. I do not take your fears lightly." I close my eyes and search the darkness for an answer where my heart isn't shattered. "There must be some middle ground. Is there not, Esme? Is there no existence where you and I find a place together?"

"I know of no such world." Her voice is soft and sad.

Her sorrow makes my chest hurt. "Then we only have this time in this cottage?"

"We had our time, and now we are stealing moments."

As I could find no argument for what she said, I left her room, and now stare at the ceiling of my own. I made her no promises, though she asked for none. Her point is well taken. If she is a bird, I am a fish. How do we make a life between the air and the sea?

Until I have that answer, I will keep our relationship to working on magic and friendship.

Perhaps it is for the best, but my chest aches with the truth.

It's not yet dawn, but the birds begin their song, and I give up any hope of sleep. In breeches and a shirt, I walk to the pond. It's too close to when the others will wake, so I jog through the woods and follow the stream to where it deepens into a small pool.

I drop my clothes on the bank and jump in. The chilly water wakes me up and cools my desire as much as possible. I'm never going to stop wanting Esme. I've accepted that, but bathing helps the physical aches at least.

"Do you want company in there?" Trina leans against a large oak. Her dress isn't properly fastened at the front and hangs off one shoulder. Her feet are bare, and her hair is unbound.

"No. I do not." It's not the entire truth. If Esme were willing, I'd love to have her bathe with me. Trina is a very pretty woman, but she's not the right woman.

Her bottom lip puffs out. "I'm younger and prettier than Esme. Why don't you want me?"

I wade farther into the pool. "It's not about that. I don't recall ever giving you the impression I would be interested in your favors."

She pulls the ties at the front of her dress, and the light blue cloth slides down and pools at her feet. "All men are interested. I learned that by the time I was fifteen."

I turn my back to her. She's clearly unashamed of her body, and she's no reason to be. How did I get myself into this? More importantly, how will I get out? "Trina, why are you doing this?"

"I would think that's obvious." Water sloshes behind me.

It's a small pool. There's not much space to maneuver away. "Spell it out for me, as I'm a bit slow."

"I'm a woman, and I see the way you look at me. I suspect

Esme holds her virtue too tight, and you've been without a woman for some time. You hardly seem like the kind of man to take a servant to your bed, so Anne would be safe. I like a bit of fun." Her fingers touch my shoulder.

Turning, I grab her wrist. "It's a generous offer, but no, thank you." I move to the right to pass her.

She's fast and blocks my path. Her breasts are above the water and her nipples are pointing up in invitation. "Don't run away, William. I'm not going to trap you into a marriage. Witches aren't like those fine ladies you're used to. All I ask is for some satisfaction, and in return, I promise to give you pleasure."

Everything she says is somehow abhorrent. I suppose many men would be flattered and eager, but this is not the woman I want, and despite her obvious attributes, nothing about Trina attracts me. Wrapping my hands around her waist I lift her and toss her into the deepest part of the pool.

I hurry out of the water and pull on my breeches.

Sputtering, she stands up. Her eyes are narrowed on me, and it's obvious she's angry.

"Again, I appreciate the offer, but my answer is no." I pull my shirt over my head.

She climbs out and stands naked in front of me. "Are you under some religious constraints? What kind of man are you?"

I bow. "The kind whose interest lies elsewhere."

Without giving her time to respond, I turn and practically run back to the cottage.

Esme is eating breakfast in the front room. She sees me and raises a brow at my wet hair and shirt.

Trina's voice echoes from outside. She's muttering something about treading on twigs in the woods.

With a shake of my head, I go to my room to dress for the day.

When I return to the front room, I sit across from Esme. "Good morning."

"You went for a swim?" Esme slides the jam across the table as Henry brings me toast.

"I thought to bathe as I couldn't sleep." I spread butter and jam on my toast. Is she jealous? It's possible that Trina made more of a fuss while I was dressing. There's nothing I can do about it, so I meet her gaze and eat my toast.

Prudence arrives and gives each of us a long look before she sits and pours herself some tea. "How are you both this morning?"

"Fine," we say in unison.

Esme pushes her plate away. "I'm going to the stillroom to collect what I need for Mrs. Kyle."

Once she has left, I pray for courage. How am I going to get through the next few weeks with these women?

Outside, Simon chases a butterfly around the grass before running toward the back of the house, where he will likely join Esme.

"Esme's mother was very young when she fell in love." Prudence watches me over her teacup.

"Is that so?" I don't know what else to say, but her pause made me think I needed to comment.

She nods. "She was lucky to find love. It was good and true, the love that Louisa and Connor shared. They were happy."

"It seems they might have been spared such heartbreak. They could have loved for a hundred years. Fate was cruel to take them so young and leave their daughter alone." I don't know why I've said any of this. Only that it's true and poor Esme aches for what she's lost.

Putting down her tea, Prudence folds her hands on the table. "Life is not always fair, as you well know, William. Goddess granted them a great love, and they were happy. The fact that they died before their time doesn't make that love less important."

"Wouldn't they have been more content without all the pain of love and loss? Louisa gave up her family and her coven, and Connor died after such a short marriage." The pain of losing him must have been devastating. It's no wonder Louisa became ill so she could join him.

Prudence's smile is sad. "Perhaps they would have lived uninteresting and contented lives had they never met. They might have even lived a hundred years or more. He died because he wanted to provide more for his family than witchcraft could give them. She died because she wouldn't seek the help that might have saved her."

"Then you agree with me?"

"No." She laughs. "I would give back many years to have a love like those two shared. I would leave my sister witches and howl at the moon if need be. There would be no sacrifice I wouldn't make for a love like that."

"I had no idea you were such a romantic, Great Mother." I finish my toast.

"Love is magic, William. You would do well to remember that. You have studies. Have you not?" She returns her attention to her tea.

Clearly dismissed, I rise and bow before heading to the stillroom.

Esme is rattling jars and shoving them violently into a bag when I enter. Without looking up, she asks, "Did you bed Trina?"

My morning and night have been complete bollocks, and without sleep, my temper is not under control. "Am I compelled to answer that despite how offensive the question is?"

She snaps her head up and glares at me. "You are not required to tell me anything. We are nothing to each other."

With two strides, I close the distance and press her into the corner of the tiny room. "Please don't do this. I have not the patience for this today. I have no interest in that girl, and I'm fairly sure I've told you that before. If you are jealous, for that I am sorry, but I have given you no cause to be."

"Jealous?" Swallowing, she looks at my lips and then at my eyes. "I'm not jealous. It is merely that such a tryst might slow our progress with your training."

"Liar." I pull back. It's not reasonable, but her lie hurts. Until now, we've been refreshingly honest with each other. Now that is changed.

Taking the bag, she squeezes around me and storms out.

Was that our first lover's spat? It's stupid that I'm grinning, but there it is. Instead of waiting for Trina or working in the stillroom myself, I go inside the cottage, go to my room, and pull out my ancestor's journal and grimoire.

After luncheon, I return to my room and the books. Some of the journal passages are hard to read as they speak of things I don't quite understand. Still, there is much about friends being killed, and fears that witch hunters would come for them one night.

I hear Esme in my head before she knocks.

"Come in." Despite our earlier argument, my pulse pounds with anticipation of seeing her.

She opens the door but stays in the threshold. "I came because I owe you an apology."

Standing, I keep my distance. "You owe me nothing. We are

friends, and as such, a small moment of discomfort is forgiven."

Her hair is windblown, and I long to brush it away from her face. She takes one step inside. "Still, I am sorry for my behavior. What you do is not my business, and judging you isn't fair."

I refuse to defend myself when I have done nothing that needs defense. "Thank you for the apology."

She shifts from foot to foot then looks at the journal open on my small desk. "Is there anything helpful in there?"

"I wanted a day away from the women of the house," I admit with a shrug.

Her smile is soft and her lips inviting. I want to lose myself in her mouth and never resurface. "I imagine you have had enough of witches to last a lifetime."

"It isn't easy to be a rooster in the hen house. I shall forever show more admiration for the male fowl in my purview."

"I'll leave you to your solitude then." She turns.

"Wait. I read something I didn't understand. Perhaps you can help?" I point to the book.

At the desk, she looks at the page. "I didn't think this book held any magic."

I hold the chair, and she sits. I look over her shoulder and my senses fill with florals and spices. I flip the page back and point. "Serena wrote that the others were coming for a worship, and then it would be done. She writes about being afraid but knowing it's the right thing."

Esme reads the passage while I read over her shoulder. Maybe I missed something the first time, and it's an excuse to be close to her.

It's the day that will begin my end, and that of my good family. There is no other choice. We must do this, or it will be the end of our line. Somehow, those who would see magics dead can divine it in us.

Millicent thinks it the work of a dark witch. I shudder at the notion of any witch, light or dark, betraying their own kind. It is hypocrisy at its worst.

The amputation will leave me lost, but alive, and that will have to be enough.

Esme rubs her forehead and sits back in the chair, which brings her shoulders against my abdomen. It's hard to think, but even harder to take the step back. With a long breath, I do just that. "After that, the entries are mundane and a bit sad."

She turns the page. "How are they sad?"

"Serena seems to have fallen into a depression after the cryptic event. Even her choice of words becomes less interesting. A few months later, she made her last entry."

Esme flips to the last page with writing.

There's little hope of a life worth living. My boy is safe with his aunt, and she will keep him quiet and away from those who would harm. I know I should be grateful for my life, but I cannot find that hope inside myself.

Should this be read by any caring person, know that I died seventy-two days ago on the night I let them take what was mine by right.

Know that name Forrester and be warned.

Esme shakes her head. "I fear she did herself harm."

"I agree. What do you think she meant when she said that

she died seventy-two days before?" I puzzled over the entry and read both over and over while I hid from the rest of the house.

"I think she had herself bound," Esme says, low as if someone from the past might hear her. "I think she somehow hid her child away, but the only way to save herself was to remove her magic from detection."

My gut twists. "Is that what she meant by amputation?"

She nods. "I think so."

"Know the name Forrester and be warned. What does that mean?" I point to Serena's final words.

Esme shrugs. "Maybe he was a lover or the person who turned her into the witch hunters."

"Would Prudence know more?"

"She is quite old, but Serena Meriwether died nearly three hundred years ago." Esme closes the book. "I suppose it's worth asking, though. Family names in the witching world go back centuries."

"Then you think Forrester is Serena's last effort to claim justice for herself and her family?"

"Perhaps." Esme hands me the book and stands.

We walk downstairs and find Prudence sitting with her eyes closed on the porch.

Her look is faraway when she opens them, and it takes a moment for her attention to return.

"Are you alright, Great Mother?" Esme kneels in front of Prudence and holds her hand.

"Fine. What do you need?" It's a few more moments before Prudence seems her normal, sharp-witted self, but she is clear-eyed and attentive.

Esme and I tell her what we read in the journal.

"Forrester was an old family, but they left this area many years ago. There were rumors the family had been killed by the witch hunters, and others said they turned dark and left to avoid persecution by the Witches of Windsor. No one knows the truth of it."

I sit on the other chair and stare out over the lane and yard. Carrying a sack of vegetables, Trina wanders in from the road.

"Perhaps it was a Forrester who set the hunters against my family. It's possible Serena felt she had nothing to lose by revealing the name in her last entry before she killed herself. To write it in a private journal was little risk to her son. As far as we know, no one has read the entry until now." I hate the idea of the woman in the journal dying alone and desperate, and receiving no justice.

"It was a long time ago, William. It is often best to let such things go, as we haven't the power to change them." Prudence waves at Trina. "It looks like the market was bountiful?"

Smiling wide, Trina pulls out some carrots and greens to show us. "It was good to get out as well. I'll just bring these to Anne in the kitchen."

For the first time since her arrival, Trina doesn't make eye contact with me when she speaks. She avoids looking at me and rushes into the house as soon as Prudence nods approval.

CHAPTER
SIXTEEN

ESME

Mid-September brings a long letter from Minerva. The temperature has cooled, and I'm sitting on a bench in the back garden next to the stillroom. I like the solitude when no one is working. Since William and I broke off our affair, I need time away from him to manage my emotions.

Minerva tells me how much she's enjoying my shop. She gives me a full report on all my customers, who miss me and ask after me all the time.

Simon jumps into my lap, turns twice, and lies down. He's grown to three times the size he was when he came to my back door, and will grow more still. "I think you will miss the country most of all when we return home." I scratch his head.

"Miss Esme?" Trina calls from the other side of the stillroom.

With a sigh, I fold my letter. "I'm here, Trina."

In a white day dress, she rounds some bushes whose

flowers have finished for the year. Only green leaves remain. "Great Mother is looking for you."

Simon hisses at Trina and runs from the garden.

Standing, I brush out my skirts. "I will go directly."

She pokes her head into the stillroom. "Where is Sir William?"

"I think he went to work on water magic in the woods."

With a nod, Trina saunters toward the woods.

Pushing down my jealousy, I head toward the house and find Prudence in the parlor. There's no reason to be uneasy. William is not mine, and even if he were, he's made it clear his interest in Trina is platonic. "Great Mother, did you need something of me?"

"Come and sit." She looks at the letter in my hand. "News from town?"

"Minerva assures me that my shop thrives without me." I tuck the missive into the waist of my skirt.

"I think next week we can head back to Windsor. William is ready to be tested, and all is well here and in the village. I wanted to consult you on something, though."

"Of course." My stomach alights with butterflies. Once we're back in Windsor, I may never see William again. I shall miss our friendship, more than I miss having his affections. He's become such a part of my life.

"As you know, I write to Sara Beth each week and tell her of our progress. The one thing I have kept from my letters is Mrs. Kyle's total recovery from William's healing. Actually, I've not mentioned that we have no source for his magic within the elements either. I may have left out that his magic seems to be desire driven as well." With a steady gaze, Prudence looks me in the eye.

"That seems quite a lot to have left out of your messages, Great Mother. Do you worry that the coven will disapprove of what they cannot understand, or do you have concerns about William's motives?" The gentle butterflies turn to wasps, wrapping me up in an ache I have no choice but to hide.

Prudence shrugs. "I am not beholden to Sara Beth. I didn't mention that you and he are lovers either. That which is not her concern is kept apart."

My face heats. I hadn't realized Prudence knew of our relations. "We have not been lovers in several weeks, though I appreciate you not telling Sara Beth that we were."

Shaking her head, Prudence sighs. "Young people are so foolish and wasteful."

"What do you mean?" I have no notion of what she thinks I have wasted.

She waves off my question. "It makes no difference. I wonder if you think telling the coven about the extent of William's healing abilities will be useful or harm him?"

"I thought that our job is to tell the coven everything and let them decide if William is a danger."

Prudence sits forward with her hands clasped before her and eyes bright with knowledge. "Useful information is what the coven needs and will get. I'll not have that boy bound because of unwarranted fears."

"I'm happy to hear that." Even though William is not for me, and nothing will change that, I will fight to the death to keep him safe.

"Then you do not think the incident with Mrs. Kyle should be disclosed?" Prudence asks.

"Not unless it comes up during the examination." Suddenly feeling nauseated, I stand and look out the window. "Something is wrong."

William and I have closed the link between our minds. It's unseemly to hear his passions for me when acting on them is no longer an option.

"What is it?" Prudence rushes my side and searches the yard.

"I'm not sure, but something is wrong with William."

Prudence grips my face and looks into my eyes. "Open to him, or you'll lose him forever."

With a long breath, I let the wall I've erected in my mind crumble.

William's voice is muffled. His mind is muddy. It's as if he's talking from under a pillow. No. Water. He's under water.

"What do you see?"

There's no time. I break into a run toward the river. "Send help!" I holler.

Holding up my skirts, I jump over a log and scurry through the woods. Leaves fall all around me with the coming autumn. Those at my feet slow me down. My hair catches on a branch, and pain sears my scalp, but I never break stride. At the bathing pool, his shoes lay by the water's edge but nothing else.

I close my eyes and reach into the water with my mind.

There.

I send my magic to pull him out, but something dark fights against me, as if he's lashed to the bottom of the pool.

"William!" Knowing he's dying makes it hard to concentrate. My heart is breaking into pieces. I order myself to calm down and breathe.

"Water and air, find you there. Air and water, hold and share. Part for me the way to see. As I will, so mote it be." Thrusting my hand forward and up, I part the water, pulling it drop by drop away from William.

Somewhere in the distance, I hear someone running toward me, but I push the sound aside. Only the water exists, and it moves to the right and to the left like Moses at the red sea.

At the muddy bottom William and Trina lie unmoving.

Henry and Samuel charge into my chasm and drag the bodies to the bank.

As soon as they are on land, I release the water.

Henry says, "She's breathing, but he's not." He turns William on his side and slaps his back with a resounding crack.

Samuel looks on with wide eyes while he holds Trina on her side.

She vomits up water, and her eyes flutter open.

In my head, I scream for William to come back to me. Kneeling, I place my hands on his chest and sense the water inside his lungs. "Be ready to turn him again."

Henry holds William's shoulders and nods.

I draw the water up.

Water gurgles from William's mouth.

Henry turns him to his side and a fountain of water gushes out of him.

There is no chatter in William's mind. I search for his essence, but he gives me nothing in return. Tears flow freely down my face as I haul him out of Henry's arms and into my own. I press my lips to his and blow my air into his mouth. *"Goddess, do not take him from me,"* I pray over and over again with each breath I give to him. *"Take me too, if you must have him."*

An angelic voice sings in my head. *"I take nothing, child. That was another. However, it is you who brings him back."*

William draws a gasping breath and coughs.

"Tell me you're still in there," I cry holding him to me.

His voice scrapes. "I am here, my sweet."

Still crying, I thank Goddess. Her sweet voice doesn't respond, but I'm just happy William lives.

Samuel carries Trina back to the cottage.

William is too big to be carried, so Henry and I sit with him until he is stronger. His eyes are closed, but he's breathing well. "I heard a voice. It was like the finest music. She told me it wasn't time yet for me to leave my life."

"Goddess. I heard her, too, though her message to me was not the same." I brush the hair from his forehead. He's not had a haircut since we came to the country, and I quite like his unruly waves.

"What does she care if I live or die?" His blue eyes are clear when he looks at me and then at Henry.

"I don't know," I admit.

"Henry?" William asks.

"Yes, Will?"

"I appreciate the save, but would you turn your back for a moment or two?"

A wide grin spreads across Henry's face before he stands and faces the woods.

William cups my cheek, runs his thumb over my bottom lip. "Esme." Threading his fingers through my hair, he pulls my lips down to his.

My body thrums with need and relief. I've never been as tired or as fully awake as at this moment. "I nearly lost you."

"I didn't want to leave you. Trina was drowning, and I jumped in to pull her out. No matter how hard I swam, I couldn't pull away from the bottom of the pool." He relaxes against my lap and arm. "You can turn around again, Henry."

Henry's brows are pinched, and he points to the water. "You're a strong swimmer, and that pool has little current."

"When I arrived, I tried to lift you out, but couldn't move you. That's why I pulled the water away." Had some dark magic gotten hold of them? I had no sense of evil until I sent my magic to the bottom of the pool.

"Quick thinking," William says.

Henry stands with his fists at his waist. "Why would

anyone want to kill you and Miss Trina? What does anyone gain from your deaths?"

"I cannot say." William sits up, closes his eyes, and draws two deep breaths. "I think, if you will both assist, I can make the journey to the cottage."

It is slow, and we are all three exhausted by the time we reach the cottage.

Prudence stands guard at the front door and ambles down to us when we reach the yard. "I've drawn a bath for you, William. It's hot and has what you'll need to recover."

"Is Trina well?" he asks.

"Fine, though shaken. Anne is caring for her, and I've sent for Brianna. She's a fine healer and will stay the night in case we need her."

At William's bedroom door, I stop and let Henry close the door. He will help William.

While I stare at the closed door, my tears begin again.

Prudence wraps an arm around my shoulders. "Come. You need to change out of this wet dress, and you can tell me what happened.

I spare only a few minutes to tell Prudence of the events at the bathing pool. Once I help her settle at the desk in the parlor, I leave her to write a letter to the coven.

Henry, carrying William's muddy clothes and shoes, turns the corner toward the back of the house.

I probably should rest in my own bed, but I knock on William's door.

"Come in, Esme."

There's comfort in him knowing it's me, and in our minds being opened once again.

In the copy tub with steam rising, he sits with his eyes closed. "I missed your clever mind in mine."

With the door closed behind me, I lean on the hard wood. "As did I miss hearing your thoughts."

When he looks at me, I see only love and perhaps worry. "Will you not come closer?"

"I don't want to intrude. I only needed to see you are well." My hand curls around the door handle, but I don't want to go anywhere.

He reaches his hand toward me. His broad shoulders flex with the effort. "Come closer, sweetheart."

There is a chair next to the tub with a towel and William's robe. I lift the items and sit, then clutch them in my lap. "I have never been more terrified than when I sensed you were in danger." It's a hard thing for me to admit, but if I don't let it out, I'll burst with the terror hiding inside me.

His chest lifts and falls with a heavy sigh. "I am alive, thanks to you. There is no need for that tremor in your voice."

Touching his damp neck and tracing a line to his shoulder, I breathe a little easier. Still, my heart aches with fear. "I couldn't move you from the bottom. Something clutched at you and kept you from me." My tears flow freely.

Those bright blue eyes of his are full of worry.

I should be comforting him, but the residual terror clings to me.

He pries my hand free of the towel I'm clutching. "I have strict orders to remain in this healing water for thirty minutes. Take off your clothes and join me?"

"You need rest." My argument is very weak.

"What I need is you in my arms. More importantly, you need to know that I am here and unharmed."

There is no denying it. To touch him, all of him, is exactly what I need. After returning the towel and robe to the chair, I strip out of my clothes. The letter from Minerva falls to the floor. I place it on top of my skirt before bolting the door.

Unashamedly naked, I slink back to the tub and climb in so that my back presses against his chest and my legs slide between his bent knees. Water sloshes to the floor. Closing my eyes, I relax into him, and his arms wrap around me. My voice is more sigh than speech. "Goddess, I needed this."

He presses a kiss where my neck meets my shoulder. "Forgive me for scaring you."

"Never." Then softer. "I don't understand how you could drown, or how you were held. The magic I sensed was dark, and I've never felt anything like it before. It hardly felt like magic."

"What besides magic could do it?" He traces paths up and down my arms before one hand curls around my abdomen and the other under my breast. He holds me as if I might disappear.

"A demon would use magic that would feel so different to me that I might mistake it for something else." Even as the words form in my head, I know there is some truth to them.

"What would anyone, even a demon, gain from my death or Trina's?"

The scents of milk thistle and chamomile fill my senses, and I lean my head back against his shoulder. "I don't know, but we don't know what purpose brought you to me and sparked your magic back to life, or even what you are capable of."

His voice is mixed with a yawn. "I wish I had the energy to make love to you, but I fear if I don't get out of this tub soon, you will have to save me from a second drowning in the same day."

Reluctantly, I get out of the magically warmed water. I use magic to dry myself before handing him the towel. Once he's in his robe, I tuck him into bed and press my lips to his. "I'll come back and check on you."

He pats the mattress beside him. "Why don't you stay?"

"I want to check on Trina. Besides, it's the middle of the day. Don't you think the house will notice if I lay in bed with you all day and night."

Closing his eyes, he smiles. "I have nothing to hide."

"Nor I, William. I will be back." It's harder than it should be to leave him sleeping. Whatever held him to the muddy bottom of the pool might return for him. Perhaps Trina got a sense of the thing.

At the door to the room she shares with Anne, I knock. A chair scrapes the wood floor, and Anne opens the door.

"How is she?"

Anne smiles gently and pulls the door farther open to let me in. "She's fine. Tired and frightened, but unharmed."

The room has two beds, each with a nightstand, a dresser, and a wardrobe. The walls are white, and the floors are dark brown from age. No rug or desk adorn the simple room. In the bed near the wall, Trina is propped up with pillows. Dark rings show under her bloodshot eyes.

"Is Sir William alright?" she asks.

"He is sleeping." I sit on the edge of her bed.

Anne clears her throat. "I'll just get you some hot tea and be right back."

It's the first time since I met Trina that she's seemed unsure of herself. At only eighteen, she's more girl than woman. Staring down at her fingers clasped in her lap, she says, "He would have died to save me."

"Of course."

Snapping her head up, her gaze meets mine. "Why? He doesn't even like me."

"I think he likes you fine, Trina. But the answer to your

question is because it is his nature." My heart swells with love for him. I'm overflowing with it, as well as shame for pushing him away.

She shakes her head and returns her attention to her hands.

"When I tried to lift you from the water, I felt as if something held you down there. Did you feel it?"

Her cheeks grow a patchy red. "I don't know. It all happened so fast, and then the world disappeared for a time."

It's hard to tell if she's lying because she's hiding something, or because she's afraid. Maybe a bit of both, but I need some answers. "I understand you can swim. How did the water overcome you?"

"I...I was trying a water spell. I thought to play a joke and walk on the water. My concentration failed me, I splashed down and breathed in the water. Before I could think, I was at the bottom. Sir William was there, then nothing." She plucks at the worn blanket.

"I'll see that you have a warmer blanket. You might catch a chill after today's events." I get up.

Her gentle sobs turn me around. She wipes her face. "I thought I would be safe. He didn't save me."

It's as if she's talking to herself, so I don't respond. In the hall, Anne is returning with tea. "Anne, I have an extra blanket in my room. Will you bring it to Trina? I worry that she'll be cold and catch a fever."

"Yes, miss. I'll just bring her this tea, and then I'll get the blanket."

"Thank you."

I return to William's room to find Henry sitting in a chair he's brought near the bed.

Head in his hands, Henry is as pale as the coverlet.

William sleeps quietly.

I whisper, "Are you alright, Henry?"

He tips his head up to meet my gaze. "I know I am a servant, but he is the closest friend I've ever had. Once the excitement was over, and I realized he could have been lost... It took a toll on me. But to answer your question, Miss Esme, I'm fine. I am in your debt for saving him."

I shake my head. "There is no debt. I would give my own life to save his. He is far too good to be lost at all, let alone so ignobly."

"He would hate that. If you died to save him, I don't know if he could live with himself. He is in love with you."

Heat rolls up my neck and cheeks. I don't know what to say.

Henry rises and clears his throat. "Forgive me. I am out of line to speak of such things. If you will stay with him, I will take my rest for the night."

"I will stay." I don't know if I can ever leave him. The future is clouded with uncertainty, and that is something I have never liked in my life.

As Henry leaves, Simon slips into the room, jumps on the bed, and curls up next to William. He blinks at me before resting his head on his paws.

CHAPTER SEVENTEEN

WILLIAM

When I wake, every muscle in my body aches. However, the fact that I actually wake at all is a miracle that I'll not take for granted. Another miracle is lying beside me like an angel.

At my feet, Simon purrs and stares at me. I have to move soon, but I'm too happy to have Esme back in my bed and will endure a few more minutes of discomfort while the sun edges over the trees and shines on her cheek.

Simon stretches long and makes a squeak before watching me with those half-lidded golden eyes.

Pulling a leg out from under him, I feel Esme stretch beside me much like the cat. Her mouth opens on a long sigh, and she blinks her eyes open.

"Good morning."

Her smile is warm and inviting. "How do you feel?"

"Lucky to be alive and thankful to you for keeping me in

this world." It's not what she was asking, but I want to make sure she knows how much I appreciate her saving me.

Propping herself against the headboard, she studies me. "You look much better."

"I'm fine." I swing my legs to the floor and receive a grumble from Simon, who jumps down from the bed, onto the windowsill, and with a leap, lands in the tree a few feet away.

Esme's hands touch my shoulders, and her body presses to my back. "If I had known how losing you would feel before, I would never have ended our... I don't even know what to call what we had."

"Romance?" I suggest loving the feel of her, the scent of her. I never want to be apart from her.

"Is that what it was?" She presses a kiss to my back.

I take her hand from my shoulder and turn as I kiss her palm. "It's what this is, Esme. I know you think I will abandon you as soon as we return to town." I hold up a hand to stop whatever she's about to say. "I have no idea how what we have works in the world where we live. If I'm honest, I don't care. What I do know is that I have never felt for anyone what I feel for you, Esme O'Dwyer. I'm learning magic, and that's impossible. How hard can it be for us to stay together?"

Worry crosses her expression before her lips lift in a smile. "I don't have any more answers than you. I know that in the moment you were gone to Goddess, I was in a place far worse than Hell. Perhaps facing the wrath of society and coven is worth the risk for what we have together."

Worry returns to her eyes even as joy rushes into me like a giant wave. "What are you thinking?"

Her moss-green eyes and the most kissable lips in the world make it hard to concentrate. "I was thinking that my mother and father may have said the same thing so many years ago."

My heart expands so that it fills my chest. Just the knowledge that she's thinking about a couple who made a life together is wonderful. "Were they wrong?"

Lifting her shoulders in a shrug, she says, "She suffered daily after he died. She never recovered from the loss."

"My mother suffers in the same way. Would you deny yourself love to avoid a broken heart?"

Her eyes shift to the floor. "I don't know. I thought I would never have to make that choice."

Taking her in my arms, I drag her into my lap and kiss her cheek. "I have not said it because you would not hear it, but I love you, Esme. I have from the moment I first saw you, and even when you made me glow like the moon. I shall never wish for a day when I did not know you. Do you think your mother would have preferred a life without your father, to save her from her despair when she lost him?"

She shakes her head. "I think she would have endured a thousand years of sorrow for the ten full of love and joy that she had with him."

"And you?" Waiting for her reply, I hold my breath.

Taking my head in her hands, she presses her forehead to mine. "I fear for my heart, but it does not change the fact that I love you, William."

Air rushes back into my lungs, and I press my lips to hers.

She opens for me and presses her tongue against mine, and gripping the back of her head, I deepen the kiss. Unable to get enough of her, I lay her back on the mattress and cover her body with mine. I have so many things I want to say, to tell her, but this kiss seems more important at the moment.

Someone knocks on the door.

We freeze.

Esme giggles.

"Who is it?" I am uncomfortably hard, but it is full morning, and Esme probably should have left my room hours before. The house is awake now.

"It is Dove," Henry says as sternly as any schoolmaster.

Wiggling out from under me, Esme stands and pulls her dress from the day before over her head. She's tying the bodice when I give up any hope of ravaging her this morning.

I pull on my robe, tiptoe to the door, and check to make sure she is decent before I slide the bolt. "Good morning, Henry."

Henry scans me from head to toe. "You seem little worse for wear, sir."

There is little point in telling him to call me by my first name, but I still jab. "I am Will when I'm near death, but back to sir in the morning."

"So it would seem." Henry carries a stack of clothes in one hand and a pitcher of wash water in the other. "Good morning, Miss."

Esme pulls on her boots and ties them. "Henry. William, I'm going to get cleaned up and find Prudence. I think we must make arrangements to return to town as soon as possible."

"Because of the near drowning? But I am fine, and you said Trina was also unharmed." I take the clothes from Henry and put them on the end of the bed while he fills the washbasin in the corner.

Shaking her head, she rushes back to me. "You are both fine. It's not that. Something was in that pool with you, and it was not of the light. Some force that I have never felt before held you to the bottom and nearly kept me from getting to you. It means that you are important, as we thought, and whoever gains from your death knows we're here."

My stomach grips. "What if it is the coven who wants me dead?"

Esme cocks her head. "What I felt didn't seem like one of the coven witches, but we shall watch all."

Marching around her, I close the door. I trust Henry completely, and he should know what is said between us now. "I must be very clear with you, Esme. I will do what is right and what protects this country and my king."

"I know." Eyes serious, she pulls her lips up in a soft smile. "I know you, William. No amount of power will sway you against what you believe to be right and just. The Witches of Windsor have protected the English crown for five hundred years. Even as they were hunted and killed, they protected the crown. If that has changed, and I don't believe it has, I stand by you."

Flooded with relief, I kiss her cheek. "I'll meet you downstairs after I've dressed."

With a blush and a look toward Henry, perhaps because of the kiss, Esme nods and rushes from the room.

Brushing out my clothes while I wash up, Henry says, "She saved your life with her own breath, plans to take on whatever evil may come at your side, but upon my seeing a chaste kiss, she blushes like a girl of fifteen. You have a rare woman there, Will. I hope you appreciate that."

"Then you do not worry over the difference in our status or upbringing?" I pat my face dry. Shaving can wait until after we speak to Prudence.

"Is my approval important?" His hand stills.

"To the world, perhaps not, but it is to me." I pull on my shirt and trousers.

Holding my coat so I can slip my arms in, Henry is silent. He tugs it into place and adjusts the shoulder. "If a woman like that looked at me the way Miss O'Dwyer looks at you, I'd save the entire world to be with her, and let social customs be damned. Of course, I am not in your sphere socially. Your mother might disapprove, but I have met few women I like more than Miss O'Dwyer."

"Thank you, Henry. I think my mother will love her despite her lack of elevation. If my father had any of what I have, it's hard for me to believe my mother was ignorant of the fact." At some point, I will inquire about that. Something else worries me. "I feel something big and not at all pleasant is about to happen. Should I be killed, you will tell my mother I suffered an illness. If she was ignorant of the family's talents, she'll only think you mad if you tell her the truth."

Henry's frown is awash with disapproval. "I will do what needs doing on your behalf. Your job is to do what's right and stay alive to confront your mother yourself."

Satisfied, I tie my cravat and go downstairs. In the front room, all three ladies are breaking their fasts with toast and coddled eggs.

"Good morning, ladies. Trina, are you recovered?" I go to the sideboard and fill my plate with sausage and coddled eggs. My stomach grumbles at the scent.

"I am well, Sir William. Thank you for coming in after me." The contriteness of her voice is out of place for the exuberant, selfish girl.

I sit and take a piece of toast from the plate while Anne brings my coffee. "Thank you, Anne. I hardly think drowning with you requires any thanks, Trina."

Trina's face turns red. She focuses on her plate, pushing the eggs around rather than eating them.

I drink a long sip of coffee and bite my toast. I'm ravenous, and eat as if it's been weeks since I've seen food. When my plate is empty, I look up to find the women watching. "I beg your pardons, ladies. It seems I was famished after yesterday's events."

"Indeed," Prudence says. "May I ask you a question, Sir William?"

I nod.

Anne arrives with fresh coffee.

"When you were pulled under the water, did you try to save yourself?" She stares into my eyes as if she's reading something more there.

I think back to yesterday. It all seems so clouded now. "I was going to the pool. Trina was supposed to meet me at the pond, but she wasn't there. I thought perhaps we had gotten our meeting place confused. We were scheduled to work on water magic on a larger scale. I followed the stream, and when I arrived at the pool, Trina was grinning and dancing on top of the water toward me. I laughed. Then she dropped. I called out about that being what she gets for showing off, but then she didn't resurface. I tried the spell for lifting objects, but when nothing happened, I jumped in."

Esme leans forward with her hands folded on the edge of the table. "So, you tried magic first?"

"The memory is foggy, as if it were all a dream." I close my eyes again, trying to remember. "The water was warmer than it's been since the weather cooled. I swam to where Trina fell and dove under. When I saw her, I reached for her, and as hard as I pulled, she wouldn't come off the bottom of the pool. It was as if she were stuck in the mud. Then my foot touched the bottom, and something grabbed it." It's hard to breathe. The memory is like an assault all over again.

"I kicked and pulled, but I couldn't free Trina, and my foot was stuck. I called for Esme with my mind. My lungs filled with water when I could no longer resist the urge to inhale, and everything went black."

"Was there anything else before you awoke on the bank?" Prudence's voice is kind and soft.

"As I told Esme, there was a voice telling me that it was not yet my time, and I should return. My chest screamed with pain, and I expelled the water."

Prudence and Esme both look concerned.

"What don't I know?" I ask.

Esme says, " Goddess does not often speak to anyone. I also heard her yesterday. When I prayed for her not to take you, she told me that it was not she who had tried. In my life, I have prayed to Goddess thousands of times, and it was the first time she answered."

"And you think that means something of note is about to happen." My chest tightens.

"We should return to Windsor by week's end." Prudence stands and places her hands on the table. "Whatever is going to happen, and whoever is behind it, does not want you there."

"I'm not ready to do battle with a witch, good or evil." I don't disagree with Prudence's assessment, but doing no good and getting killed doesn't sound that great to me.

She raises her hands helplessly. "It cannot be helped. Now is when this is happening. You will have to rely on the ability to see and make the outcome you want."

My stomach twists and I wish I hadn't eaten so much. I rise, and with a bow, leave the room.

☽

Tired from caring for me, Esme said goodnight two hours ago and went to bed early. My mind is too full to think about sleep. The entire house is abed as I enter my room. I wish Esme had gone to sleep in my room, but the bed is empty.

As much as I want to hold her and make love with her, I

respect that if she wanted me, I would have found her in my room. Her rest is more important.

Sliding between the sheets, I yawn and close my eyes. Sleep is about to take me when I'm slammed with fear and anger. My heart races, and I sit up.

Even though I feel as if I'm on the battlefield staving off an attack, there's no danger present in my room, and I'm not dreaming.

I get up and push my mind outward, as Esme taught me, looking for the approach of an enemy.

Esme's mind bursts through, screaming, but I can't make out the words.

Before the full image can form in my mind, I'm running from my room. Her door is locked, so I kick in the heavy wood, and it crashes to the floor.

Esme and Trina are in a kind of bubble around Esme's bed. Trina is holding a silver-handled knife in both hands, the tip pointing toward Esme's chest.

Fighting back, Esme holds Trina's wrist.

They both appear to be screaming, but nothing permeates the bubble.

I pound on the bubble, to no avail. "Esme!"

Remembering what Prudence said about seeing the outcome, I think of the bubble only around Trina. "Let her protection from outside become her prison. With no escape to see, as I will, so mote it be."

The bubble flashes red then blue. Trina glows with a red aura inside her prison. Her weapon falls to the mattress.

I push the cage away from the bed and pull Esme into my arms. "Are you hurt?"

Henry, Anne, Samuel, and Prudence stand at the door.

From outside, Simon jumps through the window and hisses at Trina.

Prudence, in a voluminous nightgown, sits on the opposite side of the bed and pulls Esme from my arms. "What happened?" She runs her hands over Esme's body looking for wounds.

Catching her breath, Esme says, "She had an athame and was about to strike when I woke. My magic was dampened by whatever she had around us. I'm sure it was meant to hide what was happening from the house." She turns to me. "How did you know?"

"I felt as if I was back on the battlefield. My heart raced with terror. When I realized it wasn't in my room, I looked for you, and you were there but apart." I don't care about the audience. I pull her back into my embrace.

Prudence's hair is in a long plait, swinging over her shoulder, and she picks up the athame. She stands and studies Trina in the cage. "How did you do this, William?"

"I used her masking spell that surrounded them and turned it into a cage. I saw it and made it happen just as you suggested."

"Remarkable. We leave in the morning," she tells the three at the door. "I'm sorry for the short notice, but we must bring this." She points to Trina, whose face is twisted with hatred. "We must bring this to the coven."

Esme eases back from my arms. "She said that he would forgive her if she brought him my blood. She was mad with her purpose, as if she were possessed."

"She didn't say who he was?" I ask, already knowing the answer.

Shaking her head, Esme breathes raggedly. "Just that she wouldn't fail again. He was angry, and the drowning was a warning. She would bring my blood, and all would be forgiven."

Henry says, "Let's get everything packed. Samuel, get the

carriage and horses ready. I think we'll need to take the cart we use for market, if that's okay, madam."

Prudence nods. "Get the tarp out, too. Trina can ride like potatoes to Windsor. William, do you think you can hold this cage you made?"

"I believe I can." In fact, it took little effort to manage the bubble around Trina.

Henry, Samuel, and Anne rush out, their bounding footsteps ringing on the stairs.

At the door, Prudence turns back. "You can put her in the foyer for now, William. We wouldn't want to forget her here and leave her to starve to death in that thing."

Trina's ferocious glare turns to panic before she screams and clutches at the cage.

Once Prudence leaves, I push Trina into the hallway and lift the door into place with a thought. Clutching Esme's shoulders, I find it hard to catch my breath. "Are you sure you're unharmed?"

She cups my cheek. "I'm shaken. I'll not lie. But I'm not injured."

Pressing my lips to hers gives me the solace I need. "I'm going to put Trina in the foyer and pack my things. I'm sure Henry is busy getting everything else in order. Shall I help you pack?"

Her smile is like a spring day here at the end of September. "I can manage. Thank you for hearing me, William. Thank you for knowing I needed you."

I take her hand and press it to my heart. "You live in here, Esme. When your heart pounds, mine follows."

CHAPTER
EIGHTEEN

ESME

Not one of us found any more rest. William tried to convince me to sleep, but when that failed, we got up and packed our things. I'm tired, but my mind will not quiet after such a night.

In the still room, I gather the bottles and jars, and bundle them into a crate. Leaving the cottage is more difficult than I expected. William and I found something beautiful here. Will it carry over to the city? Can our love survive all we must face to stay together?

Prudence calls from the back door as the sky turns from black to gray. "Come and break your fast, Esme."

With one last look at the stillroom, I lift the crate and return to the cottage.

An hour later, day breaks in full, and Samuel brings the carriage around. Behind him, Henry drives the cart that belongs to the cottage.

"I never suspected a thing," Anne mutters into her handkerchief.

"None of us did." Prudence pats Anne's knee.

Taking one last look at the cottage as we roll down the lane, I try to remember all the good that happened here. Last night's terrors push forward, and I replay the scene for the hundredth time. "Great Mother, what would anyone want with my blood?"

As old as Prudence is, she has generally seemed spry. Today, she looks tired with dark circles under her eyes. "Blood magic is forbidden and powerful. Maybe he hoped to control you."

"Is it possible that whoever controls Trina has her bespelled in such a way?" William asks as he takes my hand in his. His touch soothes me, and despite the others in the carriage, I allow him to rub the back of my hand and ease my tension. His brow furrows. "Will the coven bind her?"

"That is for the coven to determine, William. If she is found guilty, there will be punishment. I don't know if she is under some spell of dark magic, or if she went willingly to the dark." Prudence's sigh reflects exactly how I feel.

We ride in silence a long while before Windsor comes into view. William pulls me close and kisses my cheek before turning to Prudence. "Will I be judged in a similar way as Trina?"

"You will face a tribunal and be tested, and you will pass, William. I have no doubt you will pass. Trina will face a full coven for trying to kill two witches. She has broken our most sacred oath."

"Do no harm," William says before Prudence has the chance.

"Just so," she says.

Worry creases William's brow.

I hate to see it there. "The coven will be fair, and if need be, I will speak for her. If she was not in control of her actions, I'll do what I can to save her."

"Even after she tried to kill you?" Wide-eyed, he stares at me.

"She's just a girl. I'll wait and see what the coven finds, but yes, even though she tried to kill me. It's harder for me to forgive her for trying to drown you." This is the truth. Even if she's under a spell of some kind, it's hard for me to forgive what she nearly did to William. Whatever had him would have killed her, too. Killing me and delivering my blood was some kind of penance.

William squeezes my hand as we round the corner to the coven house. As soon as we stop, he jumps down and hands Prudence and Anne down.

I step down, taking his hand, and watch Henry stop the cart behind us. "Is she still in your cage?"

William nods. "Anne, I can have Samuel take you home."

Anne frowns and gazes at the muddy street for a moment before meeting William's stare. "If you don't mind, sir, I'd like to see this through."

He smiled. "Of course. Samuel, you may stay or go as it pleases you, and as the ladies allow."

"I'll stay if it's all the same, sir."

William nods and rounds the back of the cart. He looks down the lane, where many people are watching our arrival.

Sara Beth, Minerva, and two more witches stroll from the coven house.

Prudence is immediately embraced by Sara Beth. "Great Mother, I am happy to have you home."

Minerva waves her hand, and the onlookers go into their houses. A few return to some other business. "It will only last a few minutes." To my surprise, she hugs me. "When word came this morning that you were coming, I closed the shop. I hope all is well."

I pat her back. It's rare for me to have affection from another witch. I'm surprised, but it's not unpleasant. "We've had a trying few days."

Prudence lowers her voice. "Trina is contained in the cart. She will have to be tried. I'm not sure why you sent her to us."

Eyes wide, Sara Beth strides to the cart and looks under the tarp. "I sent her to help, as her skills are advanced, and her back is strong. How is she held?"

"William holds her in her own magic." Prudence mutters a spell that will shield the area from onlookers. "Bring her inside please, William."

Henry pulls back the tarp.

The bubble holding Trina is intact as William lifts her and moves her through the door and inside. He follows her in.

Trina is pale, and her eyes are wide with fear. She seems thinner even than when we left only an hour before.

Depositing her in the center of the room, William turns to me and raises his brows.

I hear him in my head asking what he should do with her now. Striding to the cage, I meet Trina's gaze. "If you attack, you will be killed. Do you understand?"

Her chest rises and falls fast, but she nods.

"Let her go, William."

Sara Beth holds up a hand. "Sir William, I'm going to want to know more about your magic when this matter is settled."

"Of course," William says. He waves his hand, and the bubble pops, depositing Trina on the wood floor with an unceremonious thud.

She gasps for air as if she'd been suffocated. "He's a villainous dark witch. I might have died in that thing."

I hand Sara Beth the athame Trina tried to kill me with.

"She created the shield to keep any magic, or my screams, from getting out. She intended to kill me and give my blood to whomever she's serving."

"Who is she serving?" Minerva examines the silver-handled blade. "Trina?"

The fire has gone out of Trina's eyes, and she stares up like a lamb. "I serve Goddess and the Windsor coven. Do not believe their lies."

"Great Mother?" Sara Beth asks, her face pale. "This girl was raised in the coven. What say you?"

"She's been away this last year and must have fallen into the hands of evil. I saw her attempt to kill Esme with my own eyes. If not for William, she might have succeeded. Three days ago, she and William nearly drowned, held under water by dark magic. Perhaps whoever she serves was unhappy with her attempts to seduce William."

William's gaze snaps to Prudence.

She sighs. "I may be old, and you may think me ignorant of goings-on, but I see how things are. I know you and Esme have a bond that Goddess favors. I know the girl tried to break that bond and might have succeeded with time."

"One drama at a time, Great Mother." Sara Beth shakes her head. "Why would Trina kill either Sir William or her sister witch?"

I answer, "She said she would be forgiven if she delivered my blood to him."

"Who?" Minerva asks.

Shaking my head, I shrug. "I don't know."

"Who do you serve, Katrina Davidson?" Sara Beth draws close to the girl still huddled on the floor.

"Only you." Trina's voice is barely audible.

Sara Beth crouches. "If you tell me the truth, I may be able to help you. If you lie, and I sense you are full of half-truths and lies, I have no choice but to call a full coven trial. I'll not be able to protect you if you are guilty and show no remorse."

When Sara Beth touches Trina's shoulder, a blue bolt zaps Sara Beth's hand, and she recoils.

When Trina looks up, her eyes are full black. Her hair stands out from her head. "I need no protection from something as weak as you. I was reborn."

Brushing out her skirts as Minerva helps her up, Sara Beth says, "Bring her food. I will call for a full coven." She turns to William. "Can you cage her again once the food is brought?"

"I turned her magic on her to create the bubble. I think I can contain her in a similar magic or perhaps you can jail her in some manner."

Sara Beth says, "I'm curious about your magic. You'll not harm her?"

William narrows his gaze. "No. I will harm none. Will I be allowed to stay for the coven trial?"

Sara Beth nods. "We'll need to hear what you saw and felt during the time you spent with Trina. You and Esme should stay." She looks to Anne, Samuel, and Henry standing just inside the door. "If your people wish to stay, they are welcome."

"When will the trial happen?" William asks.

"I'll send word immediately. We should have ten by dark, and with ten, a trial can be held." Sara Beth's eyes are full of worry and anger.

William bows. "I will send my staff home to rest and care for the horses. They may return if they wish. I will stay. Thank you for your hospitality. I'm sorry that what Trina has done is distressing to you, madam."

Sara Beth's expression softens. "She is a cousin, though distant. I have known her since birth. What evil has seduced her I do not know."

"I wish it were different," he says.

She cocks her head, looks at me then back at William. "That cage you made is special magic. I've not seen the like before. May I feel that which is yours?"

William nods then lifts his chin.

It's all said kindly, but I don't like the idea of Sara Beth touching William. I'm not jealous, but I am uncomfortable. In fact, the jealousy I felt in the country has gone from me completely. I wonder if it was a spell conjured to create a rift between William and me.

I hold my tongue as Sara Beth raises her hand toward William's chest. She stops inches from him and looks at me. "Esme?"

"William is of his own mind. What we share cannot be blemished." I can't stop the truth of that from pulling my lips into a grin.

With only the slightest raise of her brows, Sara Beth presses her hand to William's chest.

Blue light emanates from where she touches him. It folds over her hand and across his chest.

The witches all stare with surprise.

Trina rises like a cat ready to leap out the window.

Simon throws himself at her and scratches her face before hissing and scurrying to the corner by the hearth.

William grabs Sara Beth's wrist and keeps her hand on his chest. With his other hand, he points at Trina. "Stay."

The bubble that appears around Trina flows from William and glows blue before it settles to a clear barrier. This is made from his magic, and is far more beautiful than the magic he borrowed.

Inside, Trina screams, but no sound penetrates the magic.

Releasing Sara Beth, William says, "I wanted to make sure you know the truth of my magic. I will hide nothing, Sara Beth

Ware. What I am, I am. You will either accept or condemn me, but it will be truth, not lies, that sway you."

In my heart, I'm cheering for him, even though I keep silent. What he did was brilliant. There is no evil in him. If there was, Prudence or I would have felt it. It's important that Sara Beth knows this, too.

She draws a long breath and stretches the fingers of her hand that touched his magic. "As I told Great Mother, we shall deal with one drama at a time, Sir William."

Minerva wraps her arm around my shoulder. "That was extremely impressive. I want to know everything about this relationship, Esme."

"I beg your pardon?" I want to tell the world, but never expected anyone to actually ask.

She drops her arm. "Forgive me. I am too familiar. I feel as though you and I are friends, but perhaps I flatter myself."

Taking her hand, I squeeze. "We are friends."

With a grin and a shrug, she says, "What's a little gossip then, between friends."

"I'm not much of a gossip." I can't help my smile. I've never had close friends beyond my mother. The people who frequent my shop often gossip about each other, but I only listen, never add.

"I will teach you. I'm a master of the gift."

We both laugh, and arm in arm, walk to the steps leading to the upper floor. Minerva says, "The others will come up and lay a table. You can help me cook if you aren't too tired."

By the time we reach the top, more clomping follows on the stairs. Above is a sitting room and dining room, along with several doors that I assume lead to bedrooms. Minerva pulls me to a kitchen at the back of the house.

I worry over William, and I'm not comfortable with the

female camaraderie. "I should make sure Sir William is all right, and that Trina is secure."

"They will bring her upstairs, and the rest will settle in the other room while the food is prepared. Sara Beth will summon the full coven and will wish to have privacy for that." Minerva pushes her dark hair back into her bun, and takes two large pots down from hooks over the stove. "You don't have to tell me anything. I'm happy to have your company, and I can tell you all about your shop."

I peek into the dining room as William pushes Trina through a door that looks like a closet.

Sensing me, he turns as he closes the door and gives me a wink.

My cheeks heat, and I rush back to the kitchen. "It seems to me you had everything under control at the shop."

Minerva grins and tells me about Mrs. Cauly and Mrs. Bates. She tells several other stories while we chop vegetables.

A blonde witch enters with a plucked chicken. She places it on the worktable. "I'm Winnie Treacher. I don't think we've ever met, Miss O'Dwyer."

With a nod, I say, "Esme. Nice to meet you."

Several others come in and introduce themselves. Mable Bale is a brunette with large blue eyes and a skill with air magic. Lauren Baxter has sable hair that anyone would envy and can command water. She's also a seer.

They are all very cordial as they bring meat and vegetables to the kitchen, then leave.

"You know they've all gone to flirt with your man." Minerva makes quick work of butchering the chicken into parts.

"He's not mine, but I have no worries even if he were." What I felt in the country must have been a spell. How could

Trina have cast a spell on me, but my divining showed nothing?

"What is that concerned look on your face then?" Minerva's grin is infectious.

"When we were in the country, I was jealous when Trina was close to him. I'm wondering if she manufactured that emotion in me. I had never felt it before, and I don't feel it now. I trust him with my life." It's true. I know William will never betray me.

"What about your heart?" Minerva sears the chicken in a large pot while I peel potatoes.

Every memory with William is full of desire, magic, and trust. "I trust him with my heart as well."

"You are lovers, then." Her smile is sappy, and her gaze drifts far away.

"I don't know what we are or what we will become. William is special, as is his magic. He has a purpose that we have yet to know. We are friends. I will stand by him no matter what the coven says."

Humor drains from Minerva's face. She's serious. "You love him." She holds up a hand to stop my denial. "I can feel it rising from both of you like Goddess from her lair. Do not say it isn't so. Lies are poison. Besides, it should be a blessing to fall in love."

"Your coven may not see it as such. They surely didn't care for the love my parents found." The old bitterness seeps into my gut.

When Minerva is silent, I look up to find her regarding me with regret. "I know you hold Sara Beth responsible for what happened to your parents. Try to remember that was her mother's doing, and the witches that came before. Sara Beth was not born yet. You hold a grudge for what happened, and she holds true to the love of her mother."

"I will try to keep that in mind." It's hard to think of Sara Beth without thoughts of her mother Betty slipping into my emotions. However, Minerva is right. Sara Beth is only a year older than me and was not even a thought when my parents were banished.

"Betty Ware was hard in a great many ways. She thought she knew the right of all things, and it was that which got her killed. I have been Sara Beth's friend since we were in the cradle. She is not as hard, and in my opinion, she is far smarter and more powerful than her mother ever was."

I'm shocked. I don't know if Minerva's revelation is true, but I can sense that she believes it utterly.

Perhaps it's time to reevaluate my feelings about the head of the Witches of Windsor. "I will consider your feelings on the subject as we, too, are friends."

Minerva's smile is bright. "Now tell me all about William?"

As if summoned, William pokes his head in the door. "Do you need help?" He saunters in, filling the kitchen with his broad shoulders and wide smile. "You would be saving me from six very exuberant women if you said you needed me to stay in the kitchen."

I burst into laughter. "Can you peel a potato?"

"It's my favorite chore." He takes the knife from my hand and sits beside me.

Minerva makes a face. "How can we talk about you when you are here, Sir William. It is very inconvenient."

He brightens. "You may ask me directly, as I am far more willing to gossip than I expect Esme would be."

"I am satisfied then." Minerva begins with, "When did you know you were in love with Esme?"

Not even stopping to think, William says, "The moment I first saw her."

My heart is about to explode, but I keep my head down to

hide my blush. I have a stack of carrots to clean and chop, and I focus on them.

"Will you marry her?"

"Minerva." I hold up a hand, stopping both of them.

"Fine." Minerva rolls her eyes. "I read in the paper that your father is no longer with us. Where is your mother?"

"She lives in the country." William handily peels the potatoes and places them in a bowl.

"Will you take Esme to meet her? Do you think they will get along?" Despite Minerva's constant chatter, the chicken smells divine from her cooking. She cuts up some hog that Mable brought and puts it in the other pot.

"I wish you wouldn't answer that, William." My face is on fire. Somehow questioning William has become about me, and I don't like it, even though I'm curious about the answer.

He reaches toward my face but pulls back before actually touching me. His eyes are full of tenderness that makes my heart beat faster.

With a wicked grin, he returns his attention to the potatoes. "I hope Esme will agree to meeting my mother, and I'm certain Mother will adore her."

Meeting his gaze to dispute his notion, I'm met with him shaking his head. "I'm certain she will adore you."

There is nothing to say, so I look at Minerva for assistance.

Her wide grin tells me that I'll get no sensible help from there.

Chapter
Nineteen

WILLIAM

Being the only man at a table of witches is a unique experience. The meal started with seven people, and now, there are nearly twenty.

"Sir William, I have seen your portrait in the royal gallery," Sylvia Pelham says, tearing a bit of bread from the loaf. "It doesn't do you justice."

The ladies laugh and gape at him.

A blonde sitting next to Sylvia fondles a broach pinned to her blue blouse just above her breast. I can't remember all their names, but they are each colorful and interesting.

Esme stiffens beside me. Perhaps she is jealous or disagrees with Sylvia's assessment of the portrait. I can't say as she's again cut herself off from sharing thoughts.

I smile. "I have never cared for that painting, but the king insisted."

Henry arrives and stands behind me. He leans in. "All is

well. Anne and Samuel are waiting below. They could not be convinced to come up."

This gathering might be daunting to anyone. "You were not dissuaded?"

With a grin, Henry stands straight. "It sounds as if you are enjoying yourselves."

A witch with red hair and blue eyes looks at Henry from head to toe. She toys with the lace at the low cut of her green dress. "Life is for enjoyment. There will be plenty of time for serious matters after the meal. Who might you be?"

Henry bows. "Henry Dove. I am Sir William's valet."

"He is also my closest friend," I add.

"Well, Henry Dove, you may come and sit by me, if you like. I am Jennifer Maynard." She pats her shiny hair into place, lowers one shoulder, and bats her lashes at Henry.

Enjoying the attention, Henry obliges and accepts a bowl of chicken stew.

Talk turns to matters I don't understand, and before long, the dishes are being cleared. The women are a swirl of colorful skirts and dresses. None fancy or showing wealth, but neither do they wear rags.

Esme stands to help, but Sara Beth presses her back into the chair. "You cooked. Let us clean up."

Minerva grins from across the table and hands her bowl to Henry, who is clearing with the witches. I rise to help, but Minerva waves me back to my seat. "Let Henry Dove have his time in the sun, Sir William. He'll enjoy it."

Not at all sure what she's talking about, I do as I'm told. "You have been very quiet, Esme. Are you alright?"

"Fine. I'm not used to all the clatter of a crowd." She fidgets with the trim at the waist of her dress, then folds her hands on the table.

Opening my mind, I push gently into hers. *Why have you shut me out?*

She shakes her head. "It's not you. I don't feel comfortable sharing thoughts with so many minds lurking about."

Sara Beth returns to her seat. "Are we lurking?" She picks up her cup of tea.

Despite wine being placed on the table, none of the witches indulge in anything stronger than tea.

"You know what I mean," Esme says. "It's odd enough to allow one person into my head." She gives me a soft smile. "I don't want the entire population of witches in Windsor listening in."

"Fair enough." Sara Beth sighs. "I've never had a talent for hearing the thoughts of others. I can sense evil in a person. If someone is extremely good, that too, leaves an echo."

"You never sensed dark magic had taken over Trina?" Esme keeps her voice soft and kind. She isn't making an accusation, only wondering about Trina.

Sara Beth puts her cup down and heaves a long sigh. Fiddling with a small locket around her neck, she says. "She was sent to Kent for some training with their coven. All reports from the high priestess there were very good. She's been training to see auras and decipher their meanings. She brought back a great deal of knowledge, as well as a beautiful assortment of healing oils. I noticed she was unhappy compared to the carefree girl who left six months before, but I didn't sense any evil in her."

"And now?" I ask.

"Whatever has seduced her hides well. I can tell something is off, but not evil or dark magic. Not in the way I've felt it before, at least."

Minerva's eyes are filled with sorrow. "She was a good girl. Lost her mother two years ago. I never dreamed she would turn to darkness." She heaves a long sigh. "We should give her some food."

With a nod, Sara Beth turns to me, and with a flick of her hand, she opens the cupboard door where I placed Trina before the meal.

I lower the cage and a wave of angry heat pushes from the door.

Trina stalks from the door with empty eyes and her teeth bared. The pale blue dress she wore the day before is wrinkled and skewed oddly. She makes no effort to adjust what must be uncomfortable. "I should have killed you when I had the chance. I waited too long."

Sylvia comes from the kitchen with a plate of food. "Sit and eat. Keep your thoughts to yourself. Your mother is turning in her grave with what you've become."

"My mother was weak and stupid." Trina's gaze falls to the plate. She says nothing more before she sits and eats as if she'd been starving.

It's understandable that she's hungry. She might have eaten earlier if she'd been less violent.

Heart pounding as if something terrible might happen at any moment, I watch her. She's so young, it's a shame to have gone so far astray. "I wonder who seduced you away from the light, Trina."

One by one, witches return to the dining room.

Without looking up, Trina says, "What makes you think seduction was needed?"

"I see auras, too. You were pure honey gold before a dark red covered you. Yet the other still remains. I'm far from an expert, yet I sense another's influence may be the cause. If you were truly evil, your aura would change in full, leaving no trace of the earlier color." Under the table, I brush my fingers along Esme's thigh. I need to know she's there and with me.

I'm afraid for Trina. The witches are perfectly nice, but I suspect there is another side to all of this that I'm not going to like.

Esme takes my hand and squeezes it. She looks at Trina. "What happened to you in Kent?"

"I became." Pushing her empty bowl away, Trina sits back and stares blankly at the wall.

I have a dozen questions about what she means, but I hold back.

Sara Beth stands and her navy skirt swirls around her. She fusses with the locket again. "Minerva, wake the great mother from her nap. Sylvia, take Trina to the hall downstairs. We should see this through."

There is no joy or desire in the high priestess's voice. Sara Beth is resigned to what she must do, but she takes no pleasure in the task.

It gives me some peace that I feel no malice from the witches.

Downstairs, ten chairs form the first circle around one chair, where Trina sits. Sara Beth, Prudence, Minerva, Sylvia, Winnie, Mable, Ellen, Ava, Vivian, and Loralie take the first row of seats like jewels in a row.

The outer circle is filled with other witches who have come in support, along with Esme, Henry, Samuel, Anne, and me.

The long room is lit with dozens of candles, and the doors are bolted. The window blinds are drawn against prying eyes.

In the hearth, a fire burns bright.

Sara Beth remains standing. "Let this circle begin. She turns in each direction as she speaks. "Water, air, earth, and fire form this circle of truth. Be with us and guide our hearts and minds with openness and justice."

The witches all say as one, "Goddess be with us."

"It has been accused that Katrina Davidson tried to kill

another witch, and perhaps two." Sara Beth sits. "What say you to the charges, Katrina?"

With her arms crossed and her eyes narrowed, lips in a thin line, Trina stares at the dark wood floor.

"You will not defend yourself?" Minerva asks.

Frowning, Sylvia searches the circle. "Someone must defend her if she'll not speak for herself."

No one says a word. Only the fire crackling in the hearth breaks the silence.

"I will defend her." I don't know why, but I can't allow her to go without someone to speak on her behalf.

The witches all speak at once, both to me and to each other. There's so much chatter that I can't make out anything.

Prudence rises and holds up a hand. In a light gray dress with a dark sash, she might be someone's grandmother, even my own.

The room silences.

"Sir William Meriwether, you are one whose life may have been taken by the accused. Why should you wish to defend her?"

Standing, I enter the inner circle. "I don't know what power has gripped this girl. I know what she did, but don't believe she had a choice. It goes against my nature to see her harmed if her ability to choose was taken from her."

"As you wish," Sara Beth agrees.

With a sigh, Prudence sits and smooths her skirt.

"What say you to the charges against Katrina Davidson?" Sara Beth asks me.

"I say another influenced her in the room of Esme O'Dwyer, and another's hand held me to the bottom of the pool. I say whatever that force was is malevolent and would have killed Katrina Davidson with me, had we not been saved by Miss O'Dwyer." I know nothing of coven law, but I believe I have the right of it and hope I'm not making matters worse for Trina.

Lorelei is a pretty witch with blonde hair and brown eyes. Her peach dress is too big on her, as if it might have been gifted from a larger woman and not altered. Her angelic voice matches her delicate features to a tee. "If Katrina was forced against her will to commit these acts, she should be cleansed, but not bound."

"How do we prove that she has free will?" a petite witch named Ava asks.

"I want to know what is happening in Kent. Has that coven all gone to the dark? If Trina will tell us, then perhaps we believe she deserves leniency." Sylvia's bright eyes flash with anger.

Arguments boil over between the witches, and Sara Beth lets them go for several minutes before calling for silence. "Esme O'Dwyer, will you tell what you saw and felt at the pool?"

Esme moves beside me in the inner circle and tells them everything she felt, saw, and did when Trina and I nearly drowned.

When Sara Beth calls on me, I step out of my role as defender and tell all that I can remember about the pool, and then all I know and saw in Esme's bedroom when Trina held a ritual knife over her.

Prudence gives her testimony before the witches begin a spirited debate. It reminds me of watching parliament debate a point. Some make grand hand gestures, and others shout. Some are more timid, and wait for a quiet moment to get a word in. Anger, hope, and fear riffle around the room with every point made and fought.

Returning to my seat, I watch and listen as well as I can. I lean toward Esme. "What do you think?"

"Ask for the cleansing. At least then we'll know if she's in possession of free will." She shrugs, and sorrow shines in her eyes.

I stand and march to the center. "May I speak?"

"The defender may address the coven." Sara Beth quiets the witches with a look.

My heart pounds in my throat, and I'm dangerously close to losing my dinner in the middle of a witches' circle. "I am not familiar with your laws or processes. I stand in defense of this woman because no one else would speak for her. What she is accused of is most grievous. If she has not the ability to do good because she is under dark magic's control, or because she is herself dark, seems to be the question. I would ask that a cleanse is attempted. None of us wishes to get this wrong and unjustly condemn a witch to binding. Would not a cleanse give us at least part of the answer we require?"

The witches look at each other, but no one speaks.

Sara Beth says, "A cleansing would tell us if she's bespelled. It won't tell us if she's gone to the dark."

Lifting my hands in the helpless gesture that I feel in my bones, I say, "She is accused of attempting the murder of a sister witch. If she's bespelled, she will be cleared of this charge. If she's not, we are no worse off for trying."

"He's right," Minerva says. "We will have one answer and perhaps it will loosen Trina's lips. Maybe she'd repent and help our cause. If Kent has gone dark, we need to know and take action."

Everyone is talking at once again.

I sit and take Esme's hand for a quick touch before I wait and watch.

Thirty minutes pass before Sara Beth rises. "I call for a vote. Who is in favor of using a cleansing spell to root out part of the truth with regard to Katrina Davidson?"

Everyone in the center circle raises their hand.

Feeling at once relieved and worried, I hold my tongue and watch.

"Very well," Sara Beth turns to each element in turn. "I ask Goddess for her strength. Anyone not in the inner circle who wishes to be spared the sight may do so. I warn those not of or new to magic, this is unpleasant to behold."

No one leaves, though the witches in the far circle mutter to each other, giving the room a ghostly feel.

Esme leans toward me. "You may wish to advise your people to leave. I have not witnessed a cleansing spell, but I understand it can be quite brutal."

With a nod, I go to where Henry, Anne, and Samuel sit at the far end of the circle. "I am advised that this will not be something you wish to see. Perhaps it would be best if you returned home. I shall inform you of the results tomorrow."

Anne's eyes water, and she tears at the handkerchief clutched in her hands. "Will they kill her, sir?"

"I don't think so. They have a rule to do no harm. I think they will try to divine the truth, and her resistance will make that uncomfortable." I wish I knew what to expect, but I'm only guessing based on the coven rules I've seen and learned in the last few months.

Pale and ready to burst into tears, Anne stands. "I'll make my way home, then."

Samuel also rises. "I'll take Anne back to the house."

Henry looks grave but resigned. "I would like to stay, if you wouldn't mind, sir."

"If I'm honest, I'll be grateful to have a friend in the crowd," I admit.

Anne says, "Miss Esme will stand by you, sir. Have no doubt of that."

She's right. Esme will stand with me, even if my stance is

bad for her future. It makes it hard to know what's right. "Of course."

Prudence and Sara Beth move to the hearth and speak in low tones.

I shake Henry's hand, then walk to the center of the circle. I lean in to speak softly to Trina. "You could tell them everything and spare yourself this."

She stares at me with eyes black as pitch. Her body stiffens unnaturally, and she leans in. The rage burning inside her is ugly and forces me to back up. A moment later, her eyes return to normal, and she slumps with her head hanging. For a moment, I think I imagined the grotesque.

"I have nothing to hide, William," Trina whispers, sounding calm and angelic.

"Are you certain?"

The flash of whatever lives inside her returns then fades. "You were kind to speak for me."

When she returns her gaze to the floor, I take my seat next to Esme. I wish I knew more. "Something is inside her. Something evil. I saw it for just a second."

"Then perhaps this cleansing will root it out." Esme's mouth pulls into a tight line.

Prudence returns to her seat. Dark rings mark the underside of her eyes, and her shoulders hunch. "I would ask Esme O'Dwyer to add her strength to the circle, if she is willing, and there are no objections."

Esme closes her eyes for a moment before she takes a deep breath and moves her chair to the inner circle. "I add my power to the cleansing if those here hold no fault."

Most of the witches each give one nod. Sylvia's nod comes after a long pause, but then she too, agrees.

Grim faced, Sara Beth sits. "Gathered here we witches. In

light and in the sight of Goddess. Let none from without see or hear."

An odd pop sounds in my ears, and the noise of the street outside vanishes.

Sara Beth looks around the circle.

My skin tingles with magic.

Sara Beth begins, and her voice rises with each sentence. "This witch to cleanse of spells unkind. This witch to cleanse of evil minds. If forced by spell or possession be, Katrina Davidson. We beseech the light to set her free. Let Goddess fix all that is evil seen. As we will, so mote it be."

Magic pulses in the air.

The witches all lift their arms to the sides with their palms facing away left and right. They don't touch, but light spreads from hand to hand around the circle. When it meets at Sara Beth, a bolt shoots into Trina.

Trina's back arches, her head is thrown back, and her mouth opens on a silent scream. Her brown eyes open and roll back as she convulses and tumbles to the floor.

I stand. Instinct tells me I can't cross the row of witches. Yet it's a struggle not to rush to help.

On the floor, Trina jerks and twists. She gags as if she is choking.

Henry is standing as well. The outer ring of witches looks on in varying states of awe and horror. It is clear that a cleansing spell doesn't happen often.

Trina rises off the floor. Her head moves upright, and when her eyes open, they are black and lifeless. The same presence I saw shows itself while she floats a foot from earth. "This one is mine. Your puny magic cannot root me out of those I own."

Sara Beth's eyes widen, and her skin pales. "Who has stolen this child?"

"You are not worthy to know my name." The voice is part Trina's but deeper and more guttural.

I'm struggling to keep my magic at bay. Everything inside me pushes me to do something to force this demon or witch, or whatever it is out.

Esme turns her head enough to look at me. "William, if you're going to try, do it now. We can only hold a few more moments."

I look from her loving eyes to Sara Beth's hopeless ones, and she nods.

I envision Katrina as a young innocent woman. Her magic pure and good. I don't know what her gifts are meant to be, but I let the image of her purity flow over me.

I reach out with my right hand and slink through the light of the inner circle. My head tingles, as when lightning comes too close.

Lifted from the floor by whatever possesses her, Trina is eye level with me when I grip her head in both my hands. "You were willing to kill her in the pool to get to me, let her go now."

"You are nothing." But the voice is strained.

Meeting the stare of the beast, I push the vision of my magic forth.

The room explodes with white light.

CHAPTER
TWENTY

ESME

Blinding light emanates from William. My skin vibrates with magic. He's at once terrifying and magnificent. Even knowing the purity of his heart, it's staggering to see his magic unleashed.

I'm forced to close my eyes as the light of William's magic envelopes Trina, spreads, and cascades through the room. It takes me a moment to brave a look.

Skin slightly pale, William stands in the center of the circle with Trina limp in his arms.

"Have you killed her?" Sara Beth rises slowly.

Magic pulses in the room as all the witches prepare for whatever may come from the unknown magic that William holds.

His lips twitch, but he gives only half a smile. "She's alive. Unconscious and in need of a healer, but alive."

Minerva, Sylvia, and another witch rush forward and take

Trina from William's arms. They struggle to hold her and lay her on the floor.

"I can carry her wherever you need." Henry strides forward and helps the struggling witches. He follows Minerva up the stairs.

Sara Beth faces William. "What did you do? I have not seen magic of this kind."

"I saw her as she should be." William shrugged.

Standing, I say, "That is the nature of William's magic. While he can wield the elements as well as any witch, his true gift is to see things as they ought to be and alter the circumstances to match."

The circle of witches erupts into chatter over whether or not such magic is light or dark.

Prudence holds up a weathered hand and calls for silence. "I have seen no evil from William." She turns to him. "Did you feel whatever was in Trina? Were you able to remove it?"

"I felt hatred and desire. I saw someone male. I fear whatever it is, knows what I am, and is intrigued rather than afraid." He sighs and sits in the chair Trina vacated.

I stand in front of him and place my left hand over his heart and my right on his forehead. "I just want to be sure whatever that was doesn't lurk inside you."

His smile is tired, but he nods. "I am not afflicted, but you may check." He looks at Sara Beth and Prudence. "You may all check if it will give you ease."

Inside William is all light and love. His heart beats true, and his thoughts are of me, and what he'd like to do once we are alone. I have to work hard to keep a blush from reaching my cheeks. Once I move back, I say. "He is as he always was."

Sara Beth touches his cheek. After several seconds, she drops her hand. "I sense nothing dark or foreign. I'm going to check on Trina."

As Sara Beth climbs the stairs, Henry comes down and stands in front of William. "Are you alright, Will?"

"A bit tired, but otherwise, fine." William struggles to his feet.

I want to go home more than anything. I don't even care if it's my tiny rooms over the shop or William's grand house. However, I know we have to remain with the coven until all are satisfied that William is not a danger to them or the crown.

Unable to stop myself, and with all the witches watching, I throw myself into his arms. "I've never seen anything as magnificent in my life. Magic like yours is a rare gift."

"But is it a gift of Goddess or something else?" Winnie Treacher's blue eyes are wide and fierce.

Kissing the top of my head, William releases me. "Is there no way to ask Goddess and know for certain?"

Lauren Baxter stands. "You would be willing to undergo such scrutiny? Goddess's word is final. If she declares you a danger, we will have no choice but to bind your magic."

"I want no magic that's nature is to harm rather than help. I understand that magic can be used for either, but I have done enough harm in my life, my friends. I never wish to take a life again." He faces the witches that remain as they gather on the hearth side of the circle.

"What if you must defend Esme O'Dwyer or one of your staff?" Winnie's arms cross over her chest.

Henry's eyebrows lift. "You know you're speaking to Sir William Meriwether, a man who defended this nation and nearly lost his life?"

Eyes narrow, Winnie meets his glare. "As he didn't know he was a witch while in France, my question stands."

"I don't see how that makes any difference." Henry moves closer.

William places a hand on his friend's shoulder. "Stand down, Henry."

Winnie's expression softens. "I only mean that before Sir William didn't have power that might afford him the crown should he want it."

"I understood your meaning." William shields Henry by moving in front of him. "I have no desire to be other than I am. The crown is safe from me, and I will defend it with my life. As to the other question, I would die to protect those in my care, as I would to protect Esme. I hope I shall not have to take life, but I am prepared to do what is right." Meeting Winnie's eyes, he adds, "I would do the same for you, Miss Treacher."

Winnie's cheeks turn pink. "I believe you would, Sir William."

Mable Bale turns toward the stairs. "He wishes to be judged by Goddess."

With one arm leaning on the railing, Sara Beth is watching. "You told him that the verdict of Goddess is final?"

"They did," William says.

Ambling to the center of the room, Prudence stands beside William and faces the coven. "I suggest we save another exhausting bout of magic for tomorrow. I, for one, need my rest."

"Agreed." Sara Beth joins us. "Trina is awake and has no recollection of the events these last few days. Her memory before then is spotty. Minerva will try to help her piece things together after she's rested."

"What will happen to her?" William asks.

Sara Beth opens her arms and shrugs. "That will depend on the circumstances of her possession. We shall have to wait and see."

Giving a nod, William takes my hand. "Then if you

approve, High Priestess, we shall go home and return tomorrow afternoon."

For a moment, Sara Beth looks like she might say no. Then she gives him a nod. "If you run, I will find you, Sir William Meriwether."

"I will not run from you or my destiny. I will see you all tomorrow." Hand in hand, we go to the back door of the coven house with Henry at our heels.

Henry says, "I didn't know where you would spend the night, Miss Esme. I have brought Simon to Sir William's townhouse. I hope that was not presumptive."

A carriage waits in the alley. I've no idea how it was arranged, but I'm happy to not have to trudge home after such a night. "Thank you, Henry. That will be fine. I can check on my shop in the morning."

I'm glad to be back in Windsor. As we drive past the castle, I feel relief. "I think I'm better suited to the city."

William lifts our threaded fingers and kisses my knuckles. "What makes you say so?"

"I'm more at ease here. Though I hadn't really noticed my unrest until just now. It's good to be home." I lean my head on his shoulder.

"Is it okay that we're going to my townhouse? If you prefer your shop and rooms, I will follow you there." His cheek rests on the top of my head.

"Perhaps I misspoke. I prefer the city to the country, William, but wherever you are is my home. When I thought you would drown, and I had failed to save you, I knew nothing would ever take me from you again." My chest tightens over what a fool I've been. "Can you forgive me for shutting you out?"

He wraps his hand around my outer thigh and drags me into his lap. "Your concerns were valid. There is nothing to forgive. I will never stop loving you. Even if your goddess banishes me to some hellish solitude, I will love you still."

I meet his gaze and cup his cheek. " Goddess was present when you drew a first new breath on the edge of the pool. If she disapproved, she'd not have given me the ability to breathe life back into you."

"Why did she allow something evil to crawl inside Trina? Is she not one of Goddess's children? Should she not have been protected?" There is no mistaking the anger in William's tone.

"I don't know the answer to that. Choices are made. Perhaps Trina made some bad ones. Hopefully she will tell us what really happened in Kent."

The carriage pulls to a stop, and I slide from William's lap before Henry opens the door and places the step for us.

William jumps down and offers me his hand. I don't need the help, but I take his hand and keep hold of it as we climb the stairs to his townhouse.

Rogers opens the front door. "Welcome home, Sir. I'm happy to inform you that your mother has arrived this afternoon."

I freeze on the top step. "I shall return to the carriage. Please gather Simon for me."

Tightening his grip on my hand, William shakes his head. "Come and meet my mother, please."

My heart has lodged in my throat. "It is late, and your mother will think I'm your mistress or worse. Wouldn't it be better to meet your good mother during normal calling hours?"

His eyes fill with worry. "Please, Esme. Don't run away now."

Is that what I'm doing? Telling myself it's better to be proper is a way of running from a situation that makes me uncomfortable. There is no doubt that this is not how I planned to meet William's mother. In fact, I never gave any thought to actually meeting the lady at all. Foolish on my part. "As you wish, William."

Disheveled from the events at the coven house, William still looks every bit a gentleman as he pulls me through to the parlor. I hope I look more composed than I feel.

Sitting with Simon in her lap, a beautiful blonde strokes the purring kitten's fur. Her black evening dress is formal and dour at the same time. Its high neckline is ringed with a feminine run of white lace that matches at the sleeve. With the same eyes as William, though a bit sadder, she regards us both with a warm smile.

Simon gives a long meow, then resumes his purring.

William crosses and kisses her cheek. "It's good to see you, Mother. What brings you to town?"

Her slim shoulders lift in a slight shrug. "I had a feeling I might be needed."

William watches her with eyes full of love and admiration. "I see you have met Esme's cat, Simon. May I introduce Miss Esme O'Dwyer. Esme, this is my mother, Theodora Meriwether."

I make a curtsy. "A pleasure to meet you, Mrs. Meriwether."

"You are lovers?" she asks, making no pretense at why her esteemed son might be bringing a woman home late at night.

"We are committed to each other." William corrects his mother without denying anything.

Somehow his telling her that warms me, and I feel less nervous. I want her to like me, but it's comforting to know that regardless of his mother's feelings, William and I will not be parted.

Theodora lifts one brow. "I see. Perhaps you have more to tell me about the events since last we wrote to each other?"

"There is more to tell," William admits. He turns to Rogers, the butler who is hovering in the doorway. "Is there anything left from supper, Rogers? I'm famished, and I'm certain Miss O'Dwyer is hungry as well."

"I shall go and check with Cook."

Henry smiles and bows before he, too, leaves us alone in the parlor.

Theodora's eyes narrow. "You had no supper?"

William offers me a seat on an overstuffed sofa across from his mother, and sits beside me. "We had a rather large meal with some friends, but it seems like a long time ago now."

"Friends?"

Simon jumps down and runs over to the curtains, where he bats at the tassels hanging near the floor.

Brushing the black and white hair from her black dress, Theodora examines us both for a long moment. "What is going on? Who are you, Esme O'Dwyer? How did the two of you meet? Who are these friends you dined with?"

On a long breath, William leans back against the cushion. "May I ask you something before I answer, Mother?"

She inclines her head. "Ask."

"Did you know father was a witch who suppressed his gifts?"

Never in my wildest imagination had I expected him to ask her such a thing. I gasp and cover my mouth to prevent further shock from pushing its way out.

In contrast, William's mother is not shocked. She looks perfectly calm, and perhaps even relieved. Her hair is swept into a stylish coif with curls creating a crown. She pats at one side with her palm. "Of course, I knew. He couldn't hide anything from me. He told me when you were three and nearly died in a fall from a horse. He saved you and had no choice but to make a confession."

William stares at the floor. "Why did neither of you ever tell me?"

"If you had not inherited the affliction, there was no point. I'm sure your father intended for you to be told if ever you showed signs of magic. You didn't, so he thought the spell that holds the family benign worked. It worked on him unless he was extremely upset." Sorrow floods her eyes, and she pulls a handkerchief from her sleeve and dabs her eyes. "When you went to war, and said nothing of strange happenings, I kept his secret as well."

"Do you have gifts as well, Mrs. Meriwether?" I keep my voice soft and hope she's not offended by the question.

"I don't know. I sense things. I could tell something was wrong with William. Two days ago, I felt a sense of loss and horror, then relief. I sense now that you are in danger. It is why I returned to Windsor."

"I see."

Rogers returns with a platter of meat and cheeses, along with some fruit and wine.

He places it on the coffee table. "Cook apologizes that she has nothing grander. Anne said you had eaten."

William takes a small plate and napkin, and pops a piece of cheese in his mouth. "Tell Cook this is perfect. We did eat, but it was a difficult night, and this is exactly what we needed."

Rogers bows and leaves.

Once William fills the plate with one of everything on the platter, he hands it to me. "Eat, Esme. I know you're starved."

I don't know why my cheeks fill with heat over him caring

for me in front of his mother, but I know I'm blushing like a girl.

He pours wine and offers a glass to his mother before he fills his own plate.

"You are in love with this woman?" Theodora lifts her wine and sips. Her eyes are the kindest I've ever seen, and when she looks at her son, the love there is vibrant.

Once he's swallowed a bite of ham, he puts his plate aside. "I love her with all my heart, Mother."

"Well, then, I shall not complain." She takes another sip. "You are a witch, Miss O'Dwyer?"

"I am. A healer. I have a shop on the other side of town." After eating a few bites that curb my hunger, I put my plate down and sip from my wine glass.

"And was it you who healed William's leg? I saw when he entered that he no longer limps or grimaces."

"That was the event that awakened his magic. It was not done intentionally. I wanted only to take his pain and help him. Since then, things have become rather—complicated." There's no point in lying about anything. This is the one person who may have answers about William's magic.

"How fascinating. From what my husband told me, his family came from a long line of healers. Is that your gift as well, William?"

"We are not really certain of the full nature of my magic. I can heal, but there is more. What else did Father say?" William sits forward, his eyes sparking with interest.

"He didn't like to talk about his ancestors. He said the sordid past of the Meriwethers was best left buried. I wanted to tell you. I thought it might help if any strange abilities came to light. However, your father said he wanted you to have a normal life with all the society and trappings he and his father had worked so hard to obtain." Tears make her eyes shine bright in the candlelight. She pats them away with her handkerchief. "I understood his wishes, but never thought him right."

"Then why didn't you tell me, Mother? Father has been dead for several years." William's tone is kind.

The love between mother and son is so obvious, I'm struck by how much I miss my parents.

"You were a man grown by the time your father passed. We thought surely you were past an age when any small magic would have appeared. I didn't see the point in telling you something you would never believe. You'd have thought me mad." She finishes her wine.

"Probably so," William admits. "My magic is, I'm discovering, unique. Perhaps that is why it lay dormant for so long."

With a shake of her head, Theodora declines another glass of wine. "Tell me what trouble you are in. Why did I feel I had to come to Windsor?"

"The coven here in Windsor is wary of male witches. They think they may need me for some coming danger, but they will test my magic to see if I follow the path of the light or the dark." Without rancor or fear lacing his words, he says it as if it's to be expected.

Theodora looks at me with wide eyes. "And if your coven finds something they dislike? You will let them harm him?"

Before I can speak, William says, "Esme is not a coven member. She has nothing to do with their decisions."

"My question stands." She narrows her gaze.

"I don't believe they will find any darkness within William. He is the kindest, most thoughtful, and honorable person I have ever known." I raise my hand to stop whatever she opens her mouth to say. "However, if the coven should wish to harm him, I will do all in my power to protect him, as they would be making a grave mistake."

Mollified, Theodora relaxes. "I do not know you, Miss O'Dwyer. Because my son loves you, I must trust you."

She stands and looks at both of us. "You both look ready to drop with exhaustion. I will say goodnight."

Simon cries as he jumps up on the seat she just vacated.

Scratching his head, she smiles. "I like this one."

William rises and kisses his mother on the cheek. "I'm happy to see you, Mother. You look well."

"I will be coming to this judgment." She shakes her head at the argument building in William's eyes. "Don't waste your breath. I will be there, and that is final."

I rise and curtsy. "Goodnight, Mrs. Meriwether. It's a pleasure to meet you."

"And you, Miss O'Dwyer. I'm happy my son found a woman whom he loves with a full heart, rather than some debutante whom he might have tolerated, and been kind to."

I incline my head, but inside I'm brimming with the knowledge that William would have done just what she said. He would have married because he felt he had to continue his family name. His wife would have been lucky to have a man who was kind and warm, but he would never have loved her. Perhaps I flatter myself that I'm the only woman William could ever truly love, but it fills me with joy.

CHAPTER
TWENTY-ONE

WILLIAM

As annoyed as Simon is to get back into the carriage, he is thrilled when we put him inside Esme's kitchen at the back of her shop.

Esme is just as happy to be home. "I didn't know I would miss this place so much. She checks each shelf, running her finger along them. "Not a speck of dust. Minerva kept everything clean and orderly."

The bell above the door chimes. The woman who rushes in is carrying a child of perhaps a year old. He is whining as his mother pats his back. She stops short when she sees Esme. "Oh, Miss O'Dwyer. You've returned. I'm so happy to see you."

"Mrs. Bates, is everything alright?" Esme rounds the counter and reaches for the baby.

His mother relinquishes him without fuss. "Donald is so fussy. I think it might be an upset stomach, but I've tried everything to help him. He just keeps crying and whining."

Mrs. Bates spots me leaning against a shelf and her eyes grow wide. "Sir William. Umm, am I interrupting?"

I give her my most reassuring smile. "Not at all, madam. Your son's comfort outweighs anything I might want."

Esme raises her brow but speaks to Mrs. Bates. "Let's have a look at him." She carries him to the counter. "Donald, what seems to be the problem? Does your tummy hurt."

Worrying her hands, Mrs. Bates follows. "I've not fed him anything out of the ordinary."

Esme wraps her hand around the boy's stomach.

He kicks his feet and flails as if she's killing him. His hand connects with Esme's cheek, causing her to stumble.

In two strides, I cross the shop and lift Donald into my arms. "There, now, big fellow. You can't go around smacking people who are trying to help. Give the lady a hint at what's wrong, and I promise she'll fix you right as rain."

Donald stares into my eyes as if he'd love to tell me exactly what is wrong. A second later, frustration scrunches his face, and he cries more softly as he rubs his stomach.

Esme closes her eyes and feels his stomach. She looks at me with wide, hopeless eyes, then turns to Mrs. Bates. "I think he might have eaten something he shouldn't have. Let's go make him a nice tea. Sir William, will you watch little Donald for just a few minutes while I heat some water for tea?"

"I couldn't ask that of you, sir." Mrs. Bates looks horrified at the idea.

"It would be my pleasure. We'll be fine. Let Miss O'Dwyer show you how to make the tea. Donald and I will stay out here and find something to distract him."

Simon runs through as the ladies enter the kitchen.

Donald points. "CA!"

"We will play with Simon in just a moment. Will you let me

have a look at what's in this stomach and make it all better, my little friend?"

Donald cocks his head and studies me.

My hand spans the boy's belly and halfway around his back. I feel a growth, but it doesn't seem natural. Not a cancer as with Mrs. Kyle. This is similar to the dark I saw in Trina. Not the same, but reminiscent, as if it comes from the same malice. I will attempt to find what it all means later. I can't imagine why anyone would wish to harm this baby, unless they know I will heal him. How does that help the person with malignant intentions?

In my mind and heart, the boy is cleansed of evil and in full health. He grows to a toddler, a boy, and then a man. I release my magic, feel its heat, and let it surround Donald.

As the warmth of magic subsides, I check Donald from head to toe.

He regards me with half-lidded eyes. "CA?"

With a smile, I sit on the floor, and Simon avails himself of the brutal petting from a one-year-old.

As exhaustion takes its toll on Donald, Simon lays across his chubby little legs and purrs.

"Yes, I think he's going to be fine." I scratch Simon's chin and behind his ears.

The ladies return with a cup of tea that's been put in a jar to be heated later.

Mrs. Bates scoops Donald up. "Thank you both for your help and being so kind. I was at my wit's end."

Esme walks her to the door and says goodbye. When she turns back, fear shows in her eyes. "What was that?"

"I cannot be sure, but I think it was a test. One that I had no choice but to pass, and in doing so, gave our enemies information." I tell her what I felt in the boy, and how it came from the same source as whatever was inside Trina.

She wraps her arms around me. "You had no choice. We can't let whatever that is harm that baby even if it did give him something to use against us."

"I know. I think I should go to the coven house and tell Sara Beth what has happened. The timing is suspect as well. Just as we enter your home, poor Mrs. Bates and Donald arrive." I kiss the top of her head.

"I'll close the shop and go with you."

Part of me wants to argue and say she should take care of herself, and let me deal with the coven, but I can't help wanting her with me. I nod. "If you don't mind closing the shop, I won't argue with staying together."

She opens a window in the kitchen for Simon to get in and out as he pleases. "Behave yourself. We'll come back for you if we're going to be too long."

Simon blinks and trots up the steps to the apartment above.

"I'm ready." Esme takes my hand, and we lock up the front of the shop before climbing into the carriage.

When I tell Samuel to take us to the coven house, he asks, "Is something amiss, sir?"

I wish I could give him good news. "I'm afraid so. Once you drop us off, if you'll bring my mother back around three this afternoon, that would be very helpful, Samuel."

"Of course, sir."

Esme sits very close in the carriage and tucks her head against my chest. "I'm afraid, William."

"I know." While I love having her so close, I hate hearing the worry in her voice.

"They would kill that innocent baby to get to us." Her voice trembles, and she tightens against me.

I wrap her more snugly in my arms. "I learned long ago that I can't control the evil of others, be they men or countries.

I can only do what is right. I'm willing to risk everything to be a man you will love, and my mother will be proud of. Let's hope that was the last of these tests."

If I could keep my shiver from reaching her, I would, but I know she feels it.

"Will you close your mind off from me at the coven house, Esme?"

"It's safer to block telepathy, but even closed, I feel you. You know that, don't you?"

"Yes, but I like having you in my head knowing what I know. *Trusting me*." I say the last mind to mind.

As the carriage slows in the narrow streets near the coven house, Esme faces me. "I trust you, William. Never doubt that. I shall always trust that your decisions are in good conscience. When you took Trina's head in your hands, many of the witches feared for her and themselves. I knew you would not and could not do harm."

Interesting. "You could feel the emotions of the other witches?"

She nods. "They were broadcasting their fears at that moment."

"What of Sara Beth, Prudence or Minerva? Did they fear I would do harm as well?" Those three witches know me a little better. Two have gone from mistrust to something cordial.

Esme smiles and tips her chin down as she recalls feelings. "Prudence never doubted you. Minerva was impressed, but not worried for herself or Trina."

"And what about the esteemed coven high priestess?"

"Sara Beth is harder to read. She keeps her emotions tightly bound up. I didn't sense fear, but I saw her eyes widen then a hint of a smile when she realized you had magic beyond what she'd seen before."

"Was it a kind of test?" I dislike the idea of being tested in such a way. "Would they risk Trina if they were unsure of my honor?"

She stares down at the carriage floor. "I am not of the coven, and my mother despised Sara Beth's mother. I may be jaded in my thinking."

"The fact that you know this is a start toward rethinking." My love for her expands with every moment we're together. Even as we close in on the coven, where I may lose her forever, my heart soars with delight in her clever and open mind. "Tell me what you think, even if your views are biased. I will make my own judgments."

Her slim shoulders rise and fall in a long breath. "They believed Trina is a lost cause. They were willing to sacrifice her to find out what you could and would do."

I wish I could disagree with her assessment. Perhaps Prudence believed, but the rest were willing to let Trina die at my hands.

The carriage stops, but neither of us make a move to get out. Samuel shifts the weight as he climbs down.

Esme looks up from the floor. "I will stand by you no matter what the outcome."

My heart aching, I take her hand. "I know, but your life is too precious. Do not risk all for me."

Samuel opens the door and puts the step down.

Like statues, we stare into each other's eyes. My words thrum from within, *I love you.*

A warm smile lights her face and my heart.

A fter we tell her everything that happened at Esme's shop, Sara Beth stares for an uncomfortable moment. "The boy had been magically infected?"

"Yes. I'm sure what I felt in the child had a nature similar to that which was inside Trina," I say.

Minerva pales, shocked to hear that Mrs. Bates' son was ill. "You believe the magic would have killed him?"

With an uncanny ability to remain calm, Esme nods. "What I felt was like a cancer, but different."

"I saw that boy not a week ago, and his only complaint was a slight rash." Minerva's voice is low and grim.

Staring, as if I might run and she would catch me, Sara Beth says, "How can you know? What skill tells you the magic in these two incidents is of the same nature?"

I don't know how to put into words what I felt. "Words fail me. I have no reference to tell you how I know."

Sara Beth throws her hands in the air. "What would be the point of harming an innocent child?"

"To test me, as you will no doubt test me." I stand my ground despite my trepidation over my coming tribunal.

Her eyes flash with anger. "I wouldn't risk an innocent to see if you are of the light."

Softening my tone, I say, "No. Of course, you wouldn't. But you did risk Trina, and you will test me. The magic that infected that boy was malevolent. The user without conscience. His evil seeped from the magic like your sapphire aura seeps from you."

"You see my aura!" Sara Beth jerks back. "I didn't realize you had this ability."

"It would explain how he knows that the magic in Trina and little Donald was similar. Aurors can often match magic. It's a very handy skill." Minerva sits on a wooden chair.

Esme takes it as a cue and also sits.

I wait for Sara Beth to stop pacing and join them, and then I sit beside Esme. "I have learned a great deal about magic, though I know I have much more to learn. I'm willing to submit to your tests, and if you call Goddess, I will allow her to divine my magic as well. I have nothing to hide from you."

One by one and in groups, witches begin arriving at the coven house to witness my tribunal.

My mother arrives with Samuel and Henry. When questioned, they all say they will stand with me throughout the event.

It warms my heart to know that not only my mother, who loves me, would support me, but also a friend and an employee. Worried that the coven witches are not to be trusted, Esme never leaves my side.

However, I sense no ill will, only curiosity and a touch of fear. Minerva was correct. Knowing the nature of each person's magic, along with the ability to sense emotions, is extremely helpful. While I still don't know if I will be allowed to keep my magic, I'm sure these witches mean well. They have a sense of duty to the crown that I respect. Sara Beth feels the weight of a nation and is determined to do what is right.

After they take a few minutes to chat and gossip, Sara Beth, Minerva, and Sylvia move toward the hearth, where three chairs sit in a row facing the center of the room.

The witches each take a chair and move to sit in rows facing the tribunal. They leave a wide gap, and I stand between the onlookers and my judges. My heart beats a little faster. Behind me, Esme sits front and center beside my mother. Henry and Samuel stand like sentinels near the door.

Mother looks as though she might devour anyone who dares harm me, and Esme gives me a smile that doesn't quite touch her eyes. I've shut down the link between our minds. If I'm harmed, I don't want her to feel the effects.

In the center, Sara Beth stands, and the rest of the congregation follow. "The Great Mother honors us with her presence at this tribunal."

Prudence ambles in wearing a blue dress with white lace trim.

Samuel rushes to bring her a chair before returning to the door.

Everyone sits, and chairs scrape the worn floor.

When Prudence has everyone's attention, she says, "I will witness the calling of Goddess and hear her rule. I would ask that whatever our deity decides be the ruling of this coven for ever after. Does the high priestess agree?"

Sara Beth settles into her seat. "I have noticed that Great Mother is fond of this witch." She points at me. "I do not dispute his good work so far, only that men have historically been of the dark, and this coven has long banned them from entry. I will vow to do him no harm unless binding is his wish. If Goddess asks more of me, I will comply. Will this satisfy you, Great Mother?"

Prudence inclines her head. "I am satisfied as ever, that you are a good and fair leader in this coven, Sara Beth Ware."

The hint of a blush fills Sara Beth's cheeks before she faces me. "It is our custom to discuss the situation before calling Goddess. You will then be given time to respond should you wish."

I only nod my understanding.

With her back straight and shoulders pulled back, Sara Beth locks gazes with me. "Sir William Meriwether, you are a witch unbound. Your family suppressed its magic and gave it up for their survival. For fear of darkness entering the coven, men haven't been permitted within for seven generations. We have seen your magic. You have been honest, but still our laws are clear. We must know the danger of a male witch within this city so close to the crown."

Sara Beth's stare falters, and she looks at Esme for a moment before scanning the group. "Open discussion as to whether William should be bound, banished, or accepted within or without the coven walls."

The entire room erupts into chatter. I can't make out what anyone is saying, or even if they favor me or not.

Sylvia holds up a hand and calls for silence. "We have seen his magic is great. He could destroy us."

Minerva says, "He could help us. His magic coming to light when it did, and the knowledge we now have of dark magic possessing Trina is more proof that we will be in need of strong witches."

"It could have been that dark one who awakened his magic," a witch with mousy brown hair calls from the back.

"It was not the dark one. It was Esme O'Dwyer. She may not be one of our coven, but she is fully of the light, as were her mother and father." Minerva seems to be the only witch on my side.

The chatter turns to Esme and her parents and how it was the denial of Connor O'Dwyer to the coven that drove the family away. It seems an age before the conversation returns to my magic and virtues.

Finally, Sara Beth stands and raises her hands. The room falls silent "You are all heard. What say you, William?"

My heart pounds, and I feel fear from so many in the room. I turn to the larger group before returning my attention to the tribunal. "I am new to your ways and those of magic. I feel that which is in me is natural to me, though I knew nothing of it until a few months ago. I have done as I was asked and will accept the ruling of Goddess as my fate."

"May I speak?" Mother stands and looks from me to the witches who would judge me.

If any witch makes a move to harm my mother, I don't think I can restrain myself. She has no defense against their magic.

Sara Beth nods. "Theodora Meriwether speaks for her son."

Mother's face turns pink, and she worries her hands. "William never showed any signs of magic. His father had some, but kept it hidden and restrained. It wasn't always easy for him, but he felt his ancestors were right to subdue their natures. I never agreed, but as it wasn't my gift, I could only lend support. My husband forbade me from telling William unless he showed signs of what they called an affliction. I sense from what has been discussed today, that William's magic is far stronger than that of his father and grandfather. Still, I will say that William is a good and kind man. You will say I am his mother and must say such things." She gives an embarrassed laugh. "Perhaps that is true, but I do not stand alone in my belief of his goodness. Our king takes the same stand. The people of this country also revere him and what he has done for England. William would die to keep this country and all of you safe." She points her finger around the room making eye contact with many of the witches. "You may think what you like, but if danger is near, you will want William Meriwether at your side, even if you're too narrow minded to know it."

Mother sits, and Esme takes her hand.

My heart is so full, it's hard to concentrate.

The room rumbles with comments both for and against what Mother has said. Some agree that I'm a hero, but that magic will corrupt me. Power will poison my mind and heart. Other's rally behind Mother's words.

"Enough!" Sara Beth yells. "We will let Goddess decide."

Sara Beth, Sylvia, and Minerva stand. They walk forward and surround me.

Magic cracks in the air, and the hair on my skin stands up.

This is it. I've given my word and will stand by whatever their goddess says. My heart may beat out of my chest before that happens, but I keep my shoulders back and face Esme.

No matter what happens, I know she will hold true.

CHAPTER
TWENTY-TWO

ESME

Helpless is what I am, watching three powerful witches surround the man I love. I hold Theodora's hand in mine, and we're both trembling. I want to give her comfort, but I'm as terrified as she is.

Gods and goddesses can be fickle.

I push aside my fears and let my heart open to Goddess.

Sara Beth lifts a hand, and a silver cord slips around William, holding him in place. "I bind you for this ceremony as is the tradition. You shall not strike out while our magic opens to greater power."

My heart is pounding so hard I struggle to draw breath.

Sara Beth begins the chant, and Minerva and Sylvia join in. "Goddess mine, your will divine. This man to judge in light or bind. We seek wisdom and beseech thee your advice."

The walls shake. Trina's screams carry from the room above, and light fills the coven house.

I'm tempted to shade my eyes, but I keep them focused on William. I wish he'd not shut me out. I want to reassure him that my love for him is true and constant. But my words are not necessary, because his love for me shines in his eyes and warms me.

The air bubbles with magic.

Then silence deadens the room. Not even the fire in the hearth crackles. No sound comes from the street, and Trina's terror is squashed by the nothingness.

The light fades, and in the circle facing William, stands Goddess. She is both ethereal and solid at once. Her sheer white gown billows in a breeze we don't feel. Her body is curved perfection without a care for modesty. "William Meriwether, you have done well."

Eyes wide, William remains silent.

Goddess smiles at him, and I feel a twinge of jealousy. She turns toward me. "He will never betray you, Esme O'Dwyer. Not even for power such as mine. He would, as his mother said, die to keep any one of you safe."

She turns back to William. "Such loyalty do you command and give in return."

Her gaze turns to the men standing at the door. "Not of magic, yet still so light of heart and open of mind. I shall revisit the minds of men, as they may have grown since last I looked."

Without actually moving, she faces Sara Beth. "Good child, you must follow your own path. Stuck in the ruts made by your mother will only do you harm. This man will be your savior if you let him. Darkness comes sooner than you think. Leave him bound, and you will pay the price in blood."

Sara Beth swallows hard. "Is my goddess telling me that a man should be allowed to join this coven?"

Her shoulders lift and fall like the gentle waves of a pond. "I am not to interfere in the mortal world. I gift you magic and offer counsel with laws to keep you safe. Magic is neither good nor evil. Mortals decide how to use their gifts. Do you think his heart is dark?"

On a shaking breath, Sara Beth says, "His heart is in the light."

I must have been holding my breath, because I gasp in a long, much needed one. It feels as if my entire body has been clenched for hours.

"You will exceed those who came before you." Goddess looks at Prudence, and I swear she winks. "You have done well here."

Unfazed, Prudence inclines her head. "I survive, Goddess. With your grace, I do what I can to teach your ways."

Goddess reaches out and touches William's cheek. "Be wise with your gifts, William. You have much to do and much to learn. Now slip your bindings and hold this house."

Goddess fades away until she is nothing but air.

A chill runs down my spine.

The windows crash inward and a swirl of black rises to the ceiling.

I lift my hands and cast against whatever it is. The dark magic pushes back, flinging me to the floor, and something snaps in my arm.

Bound by Sara Beth's magic, William stands red-faced, struggling to free himself. He closes his eyes, and the silver cord drops away.

Witches are being flung backward as they try to fight the dark cloud of magic.

William's mother wraps her arms around me as if to protect me. "Are you hurt?"

"He needs my help." I'm screaming and fighting to get up. Agony grips me when I try to use my arm. "Help me up!"

Theodora wraps her arms around my waist and hauls me to my feet.

Light pours from Williams outstretched hands and pushes against the evil force pressing down.

Trina runs down the stairs in only a nightgown. Screaming, she throws herself on the ground. "It wasn't my fault. He took you from me."

"What can we do?" Henry and Samuel stand on either side of me.

It's hard to concentrate with my arm likely broken and so many witches throwing magic at the thing growing near the ceiling.

"Hold me up. Keep a hand on me and keep your thoughts on helping William."

Sylvia is crumpled in the corner, unconscious.

Strain and sweat mar Sara Beth's features as she tries to help William hold his magic.

"Minerva! Give what you have left to William. We must stand together." I draw closer and force my energy toward William.

The evil shrinks back.

Dawning widens Minerva's eyes, and she does the same.

Sara Beth commands, "Give him your strength. Let the Windsor Coven be one." She gives William her energy, and the witches still conscious do the same.

A horrible scream rends the air, and the attacking evil crashes out the front door, splintering the wood, and disappearing into the night.

William turns toward me and opens his mind. Immediately, he knows my agony and lifts me in his arms. He sits in one of the few chairs left upright. "I don't know if I have enough left to heal this, my love."

In his lap, with my head against his chest, I'm so relieved

he's alive. "You are alive and saved the lives of these witches. I can suffer a few hours to be healed."

"Whatever it was, it's not dead. It retreated, but it will be back." William speaks loud enough that many witches turn to look at us.

Sara Beth grabs Trina by the arm and hauls her to her feet. "We'll contain Trina tonight and discuss this in the morning." She softens her voice as two other witches haul the crying Trina away. "William, forgive me for doubting you. I would request that you and Esme return tomorrow. We need your help, and I'll not let pride keep me from asking for what is best for this coven and England."

In my head, he asks the question, and I agree. I can't help loving that despite his ability to command, he thinks of me as his partner.

Still cradling me, he says. "We will come. Whatever sent that evil intended to destroy this coven. That implies it intends to gain access to the king. I didn't watch all those men die in France only to have the English throne taken from within."

Minerva rushes over and presses her hands to my arm. "I have to reset the bone."

William's grip on me tightens, and his mind opens to mine completely. *"I have you."*

Keeping his beautiful heart merged with mine, I barely feel the jolt of pain when my bone clicks into place.

Minerva knits the break, and the pain eases to a dull ache. "Better?"

"Yes." I stretch and bend my elbow to test the healing. "Much better. Thank you." Reluctantly, I get out of William's lap and stand.

Sylvia is helped to her feet and up the stairs.

Turning to help with the healing, I'm stopped by Sara Beth. "You should go and rest. I know you gave more than you should have to protect him, and you will heal better if your magic returns naturally."

I want to help, but it's hard to argue with the truth. "We'll return in the morning. If you need us sooner, send word to Sir William's house."

With a nod, she draws me into a hug. "I owe you more than an apology, but please let me start with that, Esme."

Shocked, I accept the embrace then tell her, "You owe me nothing. What was between your mother and mine is past. We have new paths to forge, Sara Beth Ware. It is our destiny to strengthen this coven if we can. Goddess told William to protect this house. We will do just that, if you will let us."

It will probably be the only time I'll ever see Sara Beth cry. Tears stream down her face, and she lights up with a smile at the same time.

We both laugh and hug again.

William and I gather Theodora from where she's helping with the wounded, and head home.

We ride in silence, William holding my hand, and his mother staring out the window at nothing.

When we arrive at his townhouse, Henry hands Theodora down. She turns back to us. "I shall never see anything as magnificent or terrifying as what I witnessed tonight. I was so very proud of both of you. You would have died to protect witches that a moment earlier were judging you." She shakes her head. "Magnificent."

Henry escorts her up the stairs while William and I follow. Too tired to stop and recount the night's events, we climb the stairs to our room.

With a loud cry, Simon rushes into the room and circles our feet before leaping into bed and demanding pets from each of us.

"How in the world did you get here, little one?" I scratch his head and lift him into my arms, letting his attention draw my worries away. Simon is turning out to be a very good familiar.

William pulls me to sit beside him on the edge of the bed. "I couldn't have held that thing much longer if you hadn't given me your energy and convinced the others to do the same."

"It's not your fault." I hate that his voice is filled with regret.

"Why didn't your magic work against that?" He presses his lips to the top of my head.

Simon purrs and rubs his head on William's chest before coming back to me and resting in my lap.

"I'm not certain. Something about the way your magic works, perhaps. My magic is conjured through the elements. Yours comes from desire or so it seems. I don't know." I shake my head, pick Simon up, and put him on the bed before rising. "Perhaps we'll understand more after we rest."

He pulls me between his legs and presses his cheek against my chest. Wrapping his arms around me, he says, "I thought I would lose you. I feared I couldn't save anyone. In one night, that thing could have taken so much from Windsor, and from me personally."

Running my fingers through his hair, I shudder at the vision of him holding back the tide of evil. " Goddess warned us. Did you realize something was coming?"

"Yes. I knew I would have to free myself from Sara Beth's binding."

"And you knew you could?" My heart pounds as it did when the cord first wrapped around him.

He nods against me. "I knew when she cast it, that it couldn't hold me if I wished to be released."

"Yet you stayed bound through the tribunal. Why?" Hands on his shoulders, I pull back so I can see his face.

His eyes are full of fear and worry. "If I am not of the light, I want to be bound. I never want to harm anyone again. I'll protect you with my life. I'll fight whatever evil tries to harm the coven, but for me, there can be no joy in war. I'm not the man I was before I went to France. That man gloried in fighting for his country. He was young and foolish. Death has a way of rooting out the glory of war. We do what we must to protect what and who we love. I love you, my family here in this house, and England. I protect the coven because they protect the king."

"You needn't look like I'll disapprove, William. I know who you are." I cup his cheek and lean in to kiss his lips.

His shoulders relax. "I'm so tired, Esme. Can we make love until my mind is blank and no vision of evil invades my dreams, then fall asleep in a tangle of arms and legs?"

My body tingles with desire at the image he paints. "I would love nothing more."

He slips the bow of my front facing laces before pulling them free and tugging my dress over my hips. Tracing kisses along the curve of my breast, pressed up over the edge of my chemise, his mouth makes an entirely different kind of magic. The stays are also front facing for my ease and he works them free, letting the boned fabric fall to the floor. Two ribbons at my shoulders are all he needs to pull to release my thin chemise, but he sucks one taut nipple through the fabric.

Not even the blaze in the hearth can stop my shiver of delight as he nips the sensitive peak. "William, why am I in such need of you all the time?"

Standing, he pulls the chemise over my head, and I sit on the side of the bed.

Simon jumps away to find someplace less active to sleep.

Once William has removed my boots and stockings, he stares down at my naked body. When his gaze meets mine, he shakes his head. "I know not, my love. Only that you are everything to me. I shall love you all the days of my life and those lives that come after. No other soul can ever speak to me as yours does."

"If that is so, I shall never fear death, only life without you beside me." I reach for him, and he covers me.

His kiss is deep and filled with passion and desperation. His lips devour mine, and his tongue makes love to my mouth, pushing my desire higher.

I know he would pull away and undress, but I use magic to release the fall of his breeches, grab his bottom with both hands, and pull him inside me. I cry his name.

He's still. "Esme." His voice is like a sigh.

Open to his mind, I feel his desire to move, and his hesitance to go too fast. I lift my hips a fraction to take more of him inside. "We can go slow next time."

It's all the encouragement he needs, and he pounds into me. My body burns with need for more as I wrap my legs around his hips. Every thrust slides along my sensitive bud, and I can't contain the cries that roll from my mouth in cadence with our lovemaking.

It's hard to hold back my pleasure. Magic tingles over my skin.

William holds himself on his forearms, yet I feel the touch of his magic between my legs along with his shaft inside me.

"Dear Goddess, William." My body clenches around him as I topple into ecstasy. Pleasure rolls through me, and as he fills me, the sensation heightens again and again.

He's going to pull out. I can hear the hesitance in his mind.

I want all of him, so I clutch him with my legs, my heels digging into his backside to keep him deep inside me as he spends himself on a long keen.

"I couldn't bear to have you spend between us this night.

Are you angry?" I'm still clutching him as if he might escape or disappear.

Collapsed with his head on my chest, he tips his chin up to kiss me. "Coming within your perfect body could never make me angry, love. I only worry that a child of our making will have much to conquer."

"You will marry me?" I don't know why I worry now. I know his heart. Nothing will ever tear him from me. Even Goddess confirms his loyalty. Still, I need to hear him say it.

"Tomorrow, if you wish." His grin is full of joy, and his cock grows hard again inside me.

"Right now is not too soon." I lift my hips, wanting all he has to give.

Pushing up, he slides out, and I groan my displeasure.

With his eyes narrowed and his lips in a straight line, his look is the nearest to scolding he's ever given me. "I'll remove my clothes and not be bullied into bedding you fully dressed a second time."

With a girlish giggle, I hold up my hands in defeat. "As you wish, Sir William."

Eyebrow raised, he stands over me with his fists on his hips. His mouth turns up in a wicked smile. Then his eyes close and his clothes vanish, leaving him completely naked.

There's an annoyed cry from the chair in the corner where the clothes landed on Simon.

"Nicely done." I reach for him.

Lying beside me, he runs his hand down my chest, toys with my nipple, making me arch, before letting his soft caress continue to my stomach. "I'm still a student, but I'm learning. It seems whatever I want from my magic, I just visualize." He circles my navel with one finger. "If I see your pleasure heightened..."

With one of his hands under his head and the other still

tracing circles around my navel, I feel his hand between my legs, the tingle of magic parting my folds and slicking my juices along every sensitive inch. It's hard to get words to form. "This is unfair."

"Shall I stop?" He takes my nipple in his mouth and runs his tongue around and around while his magic does the same between my nether lips.

The orgasm rockets through my body before I can tell him not to stop.

He wraps me in a hug and tells me how beautiful I am. He whispers love words to me over and over again, as if I've done something grand.

Catching my breath, I say, "I think I shall learn some new magic for the bedroom."

"I'm happy to help you practice." He winks and covers me with his warm body.

CHAPTER
TWENTY-THREE

WILLIAM

It's late morning before I wake, and the sun is blinding. Simon is curled at my feet and looks up at me lazily. Esme lies at my side with her head on my upper arm. If my world could stay just like this, it would be perfect. We made love half the night as if we might not see morning, but the sun rose just the same.

Leaning over, I kiss her forehead.

She and Simon both stretch in a similar manner, making me chuckle.

"What time is it?" Her eyes are still closed as she snuggles into my chest.

"Late, my love. We should get up and go to the coven house." My stomach rumbles loudly. "And perhaps eat something, as you have wrung out the last bit of my reserve energy."

A wide smile spreads across her face. "I'm hungry, too."

As I sit up, she does too, and I face her.

MAGIC TOUCH

Completely comfortable, she lets the blanket fall to her waist and cocks her head.

I know she hears some of my thoughts, but I have things to say. "Esme, I think the next few hours or days will be quite busy. We shall not know if we will live or die with whatever is to come. I meant what I said. I will marry you immediately if you would have me."

"English law says banns must be read." Her smile is more warming than the sun streaming through the windows.

"What care I for laws when you are here with me? We could be married by coven law." I want her to be mine for all time, more than I want my next gulp of air.

Those bright green eyes sparkle with joy, and her hair falls wildly around her sweet face. "I'm yours already, but if it will make you happy, I'll marry you for all to see."

It's hard to contain my happiness, but there is more to say. "I have some letters to write. If anything should happen to me, you will be cared for, Esme."

"I can take care of myself."

Pulling her in, I kiss her forehead. "Of course, you can. That's not the point. All I have should be yours. We may have to wait weeks to marry by English law, but my finances can still be managed in such a way that should I be killed, you are deemed worthy to inherit. I'm not a lord whose lands are entailed. I will write to my solicitor and speak with my mother. I will also change my will before we leave the house today."

I hate that the spark fades from her eyes. "Do not die, and all will be well. However, should the worst come to pass, I am able to care for myself as I always have."

Simon jumps on the bed and curls into her lap.

"I would be easier if you let me do this, and if Great Mother marries us today. Then the coven will acknowledge our union." I run my finger down the soft skin along her jaw.

251

She leans into my touch. "I will not deny that marrying you would make me happy, so there is no reason to argue. Do what you wish, but stay alive, and live a long life with me in this world."

"An order from my lady that I am happy to obey."

The coven house is bustling with activity. We go upstairs and are led to a bedroom where Trina lies on the bed clutching the sheets and drooling like a feral animal. When I enter, she screams as if I've stabbed her.

I reach out with magic to calm her, but she bucks violently against my magic. "What is this?"

Sara Beth says, "We don't know. She's been like this since that evil thing came into the house. She wants to leave, but I can't let her. I don't even know if this is her, or some wicked spell."

Turning to Esme, I ask, "Will you help me?"

She steps inside and takes my outstretched hand. "What do you need?"

"I'd like to try to find Trina inside whatever has a hold of her, I feel that your healing magic, along with whatever my magic is, might work." It's the best I can give for an explanation. I still don't know the language of magic well enough, nor do I understand my unique way of conjuring.

Concern etches lines around Sara Beth's mouth. "How will you accomplish this?"

"As gently as possible, High Priestess. I have no desire to harm her more than has already been done. I don't believe her evil. I've seen her aura and think it is shadowed by something unnatural." However I explain, it will not be satisfactory. I know it, yet I must try.

Shoulders back, Sara Beth looks me in the eyes for a long moment. She reaches out and places a hand on my chest.

Esme stiffens.

Sara Beth shifts her gaze and pulls back an inch.

I kiss Esme's hand. "It's alright. She'll not harm me. She only wishes to know my aims are of the light. It is her duty to protect Trina."

Esme doesn't relax, but she nods, and Sara Beth presses her hand against my heart. Her eyes close. Sara Beth's magic tingles as it shifts inside me. After a moment, she opens her eyes. "You may try to reach her but be careful you are not drawn into whatever holds her."

The fact that she cares if I'm harmed is not lost on me. I incline my head and draw closer to the bed with Esme at my side. "We'll go slow. Heal what you can, and I'll search for the light in Trina. Maybe she can tell us something, and we can save her."

"I think you ask a lot, William. Some wounds cannot be healed." Sorrow shines in Esme's eyes.

Prudence comes to the door where Sara Beth and the others have retreated. She says, "I could not reach her. Be careful as you go, children."

Esme places her hand on Trina's sweat slicked forehead.

Trina arches off the bed, and her mouth opens in a silent scream. Wide-eyed, she stares at some horror on the ceiling only she can see.

I round the bed and press my hand over Esme's. Pushing my magic through, I slip like a ghost inside Trina's mind. There are images I don't recognize, like memories, but not mine. It's as if I'm in a dream filled with shadows and smoke.

"Trina?" I call softly in her mind.

A soft cry eddies through the mist of dark and light clouds.

Following the weeping, I move through the image of a

cottage in the woods with flowers growing all around. Then a child playing in a field. A puppy falling in the river and being dragged out to safety.

The crying gets louder.

"Trina, can you hear me? I want to help."

Silence, then a crow dives at me. "Go away."

"I can't do that." I keep moving forward, but the dark is closing in. It's harder to see, and she's stopped crying.

Esme?

I'm here, William. She's put up walls to keep something away. I can't reach her pain.

Keep trying, my love.

"Trina, we only want to bring you back where you belong, and keep you safe."

The crying starts again, and I head in that direction. Despite the darkness, I can make out the form of a girl lying in the mud. I draw closer.

She's curled in a ball in muck that reminds me of the killing fields in France. I swallow the memory. "Trina, take my hand. Let me take you out of there."

Haunted eyes look at me. "He will kill me and send me to a place worse than hell. I cannot come out. I must stay here and hope he forgets about me."

This is not the confident girl who came to the cottage and taught me magic. I have no notion if any of that was Trina. This is a shell of a person, terrified of whatever haunts her.

"Who is it you fear?" I kneel at the edge of the muck.

She shakes her head as though even thinking of telling me will suck her under.

I touch the black mud, slimy and hot. "Come out of there. Let me help you. Let Esme heal you."

A wild smile pulls at her raw lips. Her hair is black with mud, and smudges mar her pale skin. "He's coming for you both, you know. He waited for you to become, and now he sees you are ready to serve. He'll come for you as he came for me, and we will all die or serve."

"No one is coming for me, Trina. I will fight and maybe die, but I'll not go to darkness, nor will Esme. Let us bring you back to the light." I reach out again.

Tentatively, she lifts one arm and reaches her hand to mine.

Her touch burns. Fire licks up my arm.

"It's not real, William!" Esme screams in my head.

Trina must feel the fire too, as she tries to pull away, but I hold fast to her hand and drag her from the filth.

Esme's magic flows over me in a fight against the fire consuming my flesh.

I wrap Trina in my arms. "We're getting out of here, Trina. Hold on."

Cool relief floods my body.

Trina relaxes.

The dark clouds lift from her mind.

Light pours in from the bedroom window. Minerva and Sara Beth are on either side of me holding me up. My body is soaked with sweat, and I can still feel the pain of burned flesh. My hands are bright red, but it's easing away as reality comes back into focus.

Someone behind me pushes a chair against my legs, and I gratefully sit.

The ladies back away and let Esme round the bed and wrap me in a hug. "I thought I'd lose you both." She peppers kisses on my cheeks and forehead.

Sara Beth shakes her head, and her voice trembles. "That was quite a risk for a girl who tried to kill you both."

Eyes light brown and clear, Trina's gaze meets mine. She blinks, and her voice is raw. "Thank you."

I take her hand and squeeze it. "No one should be left in such a place. Tell us who did this to you."

In the barest whisper, she says, "Orin."

Sara Beth kneels by the bed and brushes Trina's hair from her face with a delicate touch. "Orin Sallows is in Kent?"

Tears stream down Trina's face, and she closes her eyes on a nod.

Sara Beth swallows and kisses Trina's forehead. "Rest now, then we'll get you cleaned up. Minerva, give her a sleeping draught, please."

Esme helps me to my feet, and we follow Sara Beth and the others out of the bedroom. I'm too tired to stand on ceremony. I wait for the ladies to sit before taking the first seat at the table, accepting a glass of wine and something I guess is a restorative from Prudence.

She presses her withered hand to my cheek. "You did well, child. A rare marvel you are."

I sip the wine then hand it to Esme.

She only takes one sip then hands it back to me. "You need it more, William. What you did was... I don't know... I've never seen anyone enter another person's consciousness, draw them out of their own hell, then push out the demons. Your magic is far beyond what we have ever imagined."

"I couldn't have done it without you, and I suspect a few others who lent me their energy. I am grateful." The restorative starts to work its magic, and I'm able to sit up straight as the witches gather around the table.

Once everyone is seated, Minerva closes the bedroom door and sits to my left. She pats my arm. "I think she'll be all right with time. She's been through a lot, and it will take a great deal of healing to bring her all the way back."

"Who is Orin Sallows?" I fix my gaze on Sara Beth.

She sighs. "He's a witch who came from Windsor. I heard a

rumor that he recently became high priest of the Kent coven, but I didn't believe it."

"Tell him the rest." Sylvia takes the pitcher of wine from the center of the table and pours a glass.

The other witches take wine and wait with me for more information.

Sara Beth's cheeks pale and her confident eyes are wary. "He was born in Windsor, but my mother sent him away, citing the barring of men from this coven."

I wait, sensing there's more.

"And because he was my suitor. Mother didn't approve of him. I see now, she was right. At the time, I was devastated. Orin begged me to go with him when he left, but I couldn't leave my mother. I was young, barely sixteen. What did I know of love?" she asks, as if the past means little, but there's pain in her eyes that tells another story.

"Do you think he wants vengeance on this coven?" I clutch my wine a little too tightly.

Esme presses her hand to mine, and I ease my grip. I can't help my protective instincts. It's who I am.

Sara Beth shrugs. "I can't imagine he's waited all this time to seek revenge for a broken heart. If he's dark, and it seems he is, he'll want more than revenge on me. He'll want access to the crown."

"He'll not have that." I slam the cup on the table. The wine splashes over my hand, and I take a long breath. "Forgive me. I let my emotions overrule my good sense."

Standing, Sara Beth takes her wine and sighs. "William, you have in less than twenty-four hours saved this coven and that child." She points to the closed bedroom door. "You may rant all you want."

With a chuckle, I lift my cup to her before we both drink. "What will you do? Will you attack Kent?"

Thoughtful, Sara Beth paces the room. "No. We cannot leave the castle unprotected. That is likely what Orin wishes. He knows we don't have the numbers to mount an attack *and* protect the king. He must have grown very powerful to have sent that thing last night, but he cannot have sent it from Kent. No. He must be close."

I stand and face her. "How can I help?"

Stopping her pacing, she faces me across the table. "Sir William Meriwether and Esme O'Dwyer."

Esme pushes her chair back and stands beside me.

Sara Beth takes a long breath and holds it before letting her shoulders down. "It is my fervent wish to invite you both to join Windsor Coven. My heart is heavy with so much regret for things that were done in the past. Let me make amends and welcome you into this family of witches."

Inside Esme I feel trepidation turn to joy. It's surprising, but there's no mistaking her desire to be a part of a family of witches.

"I would ask for a condition," I say, and Esme smiles up at me.

With a loud laugh, Sara Beth says, "There should always be conditions when an invitation is issued."

In a calm, soft voice, Prudence says, "Perhaps there should. We have too long been of a single mind, and it nearly got us all killed and left the crown vulnerable to dark magic."

Sara Beth sits. "What is your condition?"

"That the Great Mother marry Esme and me in your tradition and immediately." I remain standing and take Esme's hand.

With a look at Minerva, and then at Sylvia, Sara Beth says, "My mother would say your children will be too powerful and tip the balance. I begin to question a great deal of what my mother believed. She ruled by fear. Her own, and that of others. It is too heavy a burden to continue in this way. I want to be a priestess who listens and rules with love. Is that not possible?" She turns to Prudence, sitting at the foot of the table.

"My child, you are not your mother. Betty was a good woman and a fine leader for her time. She didn't see any way to do this but on her own, and not asking for help cost her life. You are far smarter and more powerful. You see the value in love and in the witches who would be loyal to you. The decision is yours." Prudence opens her arms then lets them settle on the table.

Sara Beth turns to Esme and me. A wide smile breaks across her face, turning her from pretty to beautiful in an instant. "You are granted your condition. Gather your mother, who I know will not wish to be excluded, and your people, and we shall celebrate this night."

I'm about to ask questions, but Esme tightens her grip on my hand.

Sara Beth gives orders to have the lower level prepared for a wedding. She also sends Minerva, Vivian, and two other witches to the castle to fortify the magical defenses.

"We should go and get ready. But I have no gown suitable for a marriage." She looks down at her day dress. "This will have to do."

Once we're in the carriage, I pull her into my arms. "I would marry you in rags, my love. But I think we can find you a gown. Let's see what Mother can do."

Her face pinkens to the most charming shade. "I wouldn't want to be a bother to anyone."

"You will offend her if you don't let her help."

Samuel drives quickly through Windsor and jerks the horse to a halt in front of my townhouse.

In the foyer, I call for Mother and the staff. Once everyone has gathered with shocked expressions at being summoned, perhaps for the first time ever in such a way, I announce, "Miss Esme O'Dwyer has agreed to become my wife. We shall save the traditional English ceremony for banns to be read. However, tonight, at the stroke of midnight, a wedding in the bride's tradition will be held across town. I would be pleased if any of you wish to attend, and not offended if some of you prefer to remain here."

Mother is agape for several unladylike seconds before she snaps her mouth closed. "We need a gown. Anne! Take two footmen and find my trunk in the attic. Those dresses will need some alterations, but they should do nicely."

Esme leans toward me. "Is she happy or put out? I can't tell."

"I think happy." I kiss her hand.

Staff run in every direction. Cook calls for Mirna, the scullery maid. "We'll not show up without a full pot with all the fixings. Come on, girl, seven hours, and we'll be at the wedding of Sir William and his lady."

Dove marches forward. "May I offer my congratulations, sir, miss? I'm very happy for you both."

I offer my hand. "Thank you, Henry. Will you stand as my best man?"

For just an instant, emotion overwhelms Henry's eyes. It's gone just as fast. "It would be my honor, Will." He shakes my hand then rushes up to my rooms, probably to brush out my best suit.

Mother grabs Esme by the hand and drags her away, saying how thrilled she is.

Esme looks back at me with terrified eyes.

I shrug and head upstairs with more joy than I have in my entire life.

CHAPTER
TWENTY-FOUR

ESME

I never in my life expected to marry anyone. It's just not that common for a witch to marry. A lone witch might. My mother became a lone witch so that she could marry my father.

I have been ordered to wait in the carriage outside the coven house. It's the first moment I've had to catch my breath and think about agreeing to join the coven. My mother might be rolling in her grave.

The door swings open, William jumps in, and takes my hands. "What's wrong?"

"Nothing."

"If you're going to lie, you'll have to close your mind off, my love. I know something is troubling you. If you don't wish to marry so quickly, I'll call all of this off. I'll wait for you no matter how long you need. I thought this was what you wanted." The abject despair in his handsome face is near comical.

"I was thinking about my mother's reaction to joining the

coven. I want to marry you more than anything." Leaning forward, I kiss him soundly on the lips.

He relaxes. "Did she forbid it?"

I let loose the sigh that's been building. "Mother never forbid anything. She told me not to be bullied or do another's bidding for their sake. She disliked the coven because they wronged her."

His gaze softens. "Do you think that perhaps she would see my acceptance as a sign that the coven has changed and made amends? Perhaps she would be appeased. Or perhaps you believe your mother would not approve of me as your husband?"

"I think she would love you. I can't imagine anyone not loving you. You are all that is good in the world." I ease off my bench and into his lap, wrapping my arms around him. "I hope Mother is happy with my decision, as it was mine."

He squeezes me and kisses my cheek. "It was. If you'd been opposed, I would have declined."

"I know." It's perfect to know without trepidation that this man would never go against my wishes and needs. When our minds first connected, I thought it would be an invasion of my privacy to have another in my thoughts and feelings. I couldn't have been more wrong. Knowing him as I do is the greatest blessing.

"William?"

"Hmm?" he hums against my neck.

"Will you marry me now?"

As he pulls back, the brightest smile lights his already too handsome face. He slips out from under me, and backs out of the carriage, still holding my hand as I join him on the street.

Alight with candles and magic, the coven house is open for all to see. They've not closed the blinds as they did when the tribunal and trial were going on. People outside are welcome to see the marriage take place, even if they don't understand the ceremony.

Magically placed lights dance above like tiny fairies skittering across the walls and ceiling. The hearth crackles with a good fire to keep out the chill of fall. Candles light the tables as well as form an aisle on the floor to guide William and me to where we'll be joined.

As soon as we enter, Theodora rushes over with wide eyes. "Oh, Esme, you're quite beautiful."

Looking down at my pale-green gown, I thank her. "This is the finest dress I've ever worn. You are too kind to let me wear it."

"It is yours, dear. I'm sure your husband will buy you all the fine dresses you will need for a life I can only imagine will be very interesting." She gives William a stern look.

"I shall lavish her with everything I have. You needn't worry, Mother." He squeezes my hand where it rests on his arm.

"Isn't the hall lovely?" Theodora asks. "William, did you know, you and Esme will be joined for all your lifetimes? Minerva told me that witches believe we live many lives."

The look he gives me sends flutters to my stomach. His warm eyes and joyful smile are full of love for me. "I think Esme and I have been joined many times in past lives. No one shall ever convince me otherwise. It's not possible to love someone so utterly with only one life to guide the heart. We are meant through time and time again."

My sigh mixes with Theodora's, and then we both giggle like young girls.

"I suppose we should get started, if you're ready," Sara Beth says from the far side of the lighted aisle.

William looks at me. "Esme?"

"I'm ready."

The witches, along with most of William's staff, gather outside the rows of candles.

We start at the near end and walk together toward Prudence.

Henry stands at the front as the best man, while Minerva has honored me by standing as my maid of honor. The butterflies in my belly have turned to bats. I can't imagine why I'm nervous. This is everything I want but never knew I did. Joy flushes my cheeks with heat, and I know I'm grinning like some town idiot.

Prudence smiles and lifts a silk ribbon.

William and I face each other, and he takes my left hand in his.

Speaking a spell, Prudence magically lifts the ribbon. "Bound through time, these two souls renew their vows to have unto each other only and forever. Neither man nor god may separate them through time, magic, or battle. For each time they are from the earth, they will seek their togetherness with Goddess and again in every lifetime."

The ribbon slips around our hands and wrists, joining us as one.

Sara Beth hands a silver goblet to Prudence, who waves a hand over the cup. "Wine to bring you joy and abundance." She hands it to me.

I take a sip of the rich wine before handing it to William.

His eyes have not left mine. It feels as if he sees my soul and loves what he sees. He sips the wine then passes it to Henry, who drinks and passes the goblet on for all to drink of our happiness.

Minerva places a broom on the floor in front of us. We're both wearing the silliest grins as William takes my other hand and we jump over the broom.

The wedding guests cheer, and we're surrounded by well-wishers who hug and kiss us.

With the end of the magic that tied it, the ribbon slips away, but William snatches it before it can tumble underfoot. Gaze still fixed on mine, he presses his lips to the satin and tucks it into his coat pocket.

It's such a small gesture, but tears prick my eyes.

Wilma takes my hand and pulls me into a hug before a pianoforte is rolled in and Sylvia begins playing a lively tune.

Townsfolk wander in, and everyone dances.

Laughing and twirling around the room, I catch a movement at the edge of my vision. At the back of the room, Trina is curled up on the stairs peering through the spindles like a lost child.

It takes some maneuvering, but I extricate myself from the dancing and go to the steps. "You're welcome to join the party, Trina."

She's clean and fresh-faced in a simple cream dress. Her hair is tucked under a sweet bonnet, but she won't meet my gaze. "You cannot wish me at your celebration, Miss Esme. After all I did, you must hate me."

I hate the catch in her voice. "Neither I, nor Sir William hate you. We'd not have helped you if that were so. He risked quite a lot to pull you from that dark place. Do you think he would have done so for someone he didn't care about?"

Lifting her chin, she cocks her head and finally looks me in the eye. "I think your husband is too good and would risk his life for most people. That's why he was a war hero and that's why he saved this coven from Orin. Where others fear, he jumps in and stands firm. You are very lucky to have won his heart."

I love the sound of "your husband," and I can't disagree

with anything she said. William is the bravest person I've ever known. I reach out toward her. "Come and join the dancing."

She shakes her head. "After how I behaved in the country, and the evil you saw inside me, I cannot." She buries her face in her hands.

Sitting a step below her, I take her hands from her face. "That was not you. You were harmed by someone as surely as William's drowning. You were taken and used in a terrible way, but that was not you, Trina. This coven will stand by you and see you well again. It will take time to heal your heart and mind, but you will be whole again." I cup her cheek and brush a tear away with my thumb.

"Do you think so?" Doubt laces her question.

"I know it. I felt the healing begin this morning. William and I will help you if you let us." I have no need to ask him, I know his heart.

"How shall I ever face him?" Her cheeks burn bright red. "I acted like a trollop then became a monster."

William must have sought me out and heard the nature of our conversation. He reaches out both hands. "Two beauties like you shouldn't be sitting like wallflowers. Come and dance with me."

Love overflowing, I take his hand and stand beside him.

Staring at her feet, Trina shakes her head violently.

William kneels so that he can see her downcast face. "Trina, will you not dance with your friend and the groom?"

"I don't know how you can call me friend." Her tears drip on the stairs.

He places a finger under her chin and lifts her gaze to his. "I have been in your heart, Trina, and you have been in mine. I know you are good and kind. We are friends in a way that most people can never understand."

Wide-eyed, she looks ready to jump into his arms like a

child. Instead, she nods and takes his hand. "I will dance with you and your bride."

The other witches are happy to see Trina join the party. A young man from town looks particularly happy to see her. His sandy blond hair is overly long and shadows one brown eye, but the other is focused on Trina.

In William's arms as the music slows, I feel at home. "There will be a battle to come."

"Yes." He kisses the top of my head.

"Trina will need a great deal of healing." So many worries tumble through my mind.

"She will and should come and stay with us to be cared for by you, and so she has a family who loves her." He's so good it's almost too much.

"You don't think the coven will give her what she needs?" I press my cheek to his chest, as most of the townspeople have left in these early morning hours.

His chest expands with a deep breath. "They will care for her, but it was this coven who sent her away when she was not ready. They put her at risk because they thought a girl without family should learn to be useful, even though she was vulnerable. If her mother were still alive, would they have sent her to Kent?"

"I don't know, but I would think her mother would have known she'd not be strong enough to fight dark magic," I admit.

"If you don't wish to bring her into our family, I understand. She has wronged us both, but it was not truly Trina committing those acts, Esme."

Easing back, I meet his gaze. "I know. I have no objections to caring for her. She'll need much care for some time. The things she's done and seen will stay with her all her life, and she'll need to learn to live with them and overcome them."

"Can you think of any other people in the coven who will offer to make her their family?" He lifts his brows, already knowing the answer.

"I don't know, and I can't say that I would trust her care to anyone else. Minerva is a fine healer, but I think she will be sent to Kent very soon." My stomach knots at the thought of my friend facing whatever danger lies in Kent.

William stiffens. "Is Minerva blessed with more than healing powers?"

"I suspect that she holds close her true abilities so as not to frighten the rest of us. Also, she is a strong shield. Dark magic will bounce off her."

"I really have so much to learn about magic and witchcraft. It's all so fascinating." He looks around the room at the remaining witches as if he's trying to decipher each one's gifts.

A long yawn pulls at me. "I think you must take me home, husband."

Grinning wide, he spins me once around the room. "It would be my greatest pleasure.

We gather our household, and William's mother, and make our way out to the two carriages and the cart that will carry us home.

Theodora rides with us. "You make a handsome couple. I'm very happy for you both."

"Thank you, Mother."

Smiling warmly at me, she says, "And I finally get the daughter I always wanted."

"I'm glad you aren't disappointed, Mrs. Meriwether. I'm sure a shopkeeper and a witch weren't the notions you had to wed your only son."

She shrugs. "One adapts when the shopkeeper and witch is so magnificent."

Heat flushes up my cheeks.

William kisses the back of my hand. "We will bring the young witch Katrina Davidson to live with us, Mother. She's been ill and needs care."

Theodora cocks her head. "The skinny girl who sat on the steps most of the night? She looks as if she could use a few good meals."

"Indeed," I say. Those meals couldn't hurt either.

"There was much talk of trouble despite the festivities tonight." Theodora pulls at the edge of her glove.

"Yes. We have much to do to protect Windsor." I brace myself as the carriage pulls to a stop.

The staff is sent to bed, and other than Theodora's maid, relieved of their duties for the night. William and I are capable of getting ourselves ready for bed. We climb the stairs, and my legs feel like they're full of stones.

We slide into our bed without a word. I love the feel of his body wrapped around mine. In the back of my mind, the oddity of marrying a man who has expectations of a society wife worries me. I shall never be such a wife. Perhaps I am not all that he needs.

"What is it?" he whispers against the back of my neck.

I roll to face him. The fire and the breaking dawn light the room. "I must return to my shop tomorrow. I cannot be a lady who keeps your house and stitches useless pillows or paints tea sets."

"I don't recall asking you to change." He brushes strands of hair away from my cheek and tucks them behind my ear.

"Men often have expectations of their wives. We should have had this conversation before we committed for all time." I don't know what could have gotten into me that I would leap into a marriage without laying down my own needs.

A deep frown and the ache of his disappointment settle hard in my heart. He takes a breath. "Esme, our vows to each other were made many lifetimes ago. Of that, I'm sure. However, let's address your concerns. I don't wish to change anything about you other than my being in your life. I never dreamed you would leave your shop, only your apartment above."

Simon jumps on the bed and stretches long between us.

"I hope you will wish to stay here, but if you dislike this house, I will give it to my mother and live with you above the shop. The only thing I'll not compromise about is our being together." He scratches Simon's ear, and the cat calms his growing worry.

"Then you don't want a wife to stay home and have babies while managing kitchens and nannies?" I lean forward and press my cheek against his chest. I know these fears are my mother's warnings and have nothing to do with us, but I need to hear him say it.

William pulls me in tight, displacing Simon, who curls up at the end of the bed. "If that were the kind of wife I wanted, I would not have fallen so thoroughly in love with you. I want a wife who drains a pond to save me from drowning, then breathes life back into my lungs. I want a wife who cares that Mrs. Bates' son has a rash and likes a certain skin cream. I want a wife who is so beautiful inside and out that she takes my breath away every time I see her."

"I want a husband who sees me as I am and loves me anyway." I breathe him in like a drug, and all my worries float away.

"Oh, sweet Esme, not anyway. I don't love you in spite of who and what you are. I love you because of all you are." His lips find mine, and I know the decision to marry William was the best of my life.

CHAPTER
TWENTY-FIVE

WILLIAM

It's midday before we rise, and even then, it's hunger that drags us from bed. After a hearty meal with Esme, I find Mother in the parlor, writing at her desk.

"May I interrupt you, Mother?"

She puts aside her letter and smiles at me. "Of course."

I sit in the leather chair with thick wooden arms at the side of her desk, and pull a bundle of papers from the pocket inside my coat. "I have made some arrangements should anything happen to me before a legal marriage can be arranged between Esme and myself. I would feel more at ease if you would assure me these things will be done."

Mother frowns but takes the papers. She reads for several minutes. "I will see to it should the need arise, but you must know I would have seen to Esme without this letter."

My heart is so full I don't know how to express it. For a moment, I stare at my hands in my lap. Finally, gathering my self-control, I'm able to look up. "Then this would only make it easier for you. Thank you, Mother." Rising, I kiss her cheek.

Simon runs into the room, screaming out a loud cry. His tail is fully puffed out, and the hair on his back is standing straight up. He jumps on the back of the sofa, looks at me, and cries again.

My heart pounds. Dark magic presses in, and I feel fear and pain that is not my own.

"William!" Esme rushes into the parlor. "Something is wrong."

"I feel it, too."

Henry rushes into the room. "Shall I get the carriage?"

I look at Esme for some course of action, but her eyes are wide and seem to be searching inward.

The panic flowing through me is neither Esme's nor my own. We have to move fast. "Just my horse. We'll ride to the coven house."

Nodding, Esme picks up Simon. "He feels it too, and will wish to follow. Mrs. Meriwether, try to keep him here, please."

Mother takes the cat and clutches him to her chest. Fear etches lines in her face. "Be careful."

Running out the front door, I take Esme's hand.

Henry leads a bay and my black to the front. No saddles, but he did take the time to put bridles on.

I jump onto the black's back, and taking Esme's hand, lift her up behind me. We ride hard through the streets with Henry on our heels. It feels as if time is speeding by, and we are moving too slow to stop it.

"I can't reach anyone mentally. It's as if only fear can escape." Esme grips my waist tight.

We're moving at a dangerous pace, but whatever has ignited the witches' fear is already happening, and we're late before we begin.

The coven house looks quiet, but the pressure in my chest that tells me something is drastically wrong has not eased. The blinds are drawn on the street, and I'm tempted to go around to the alley, but not willing to take any more time.

Esme slides to the ground and runs toward the door before I can dismount. "Wait, Esme."

She stops short at the door, giving me enough time to rush to her side. She conjures a ball of fire in her left hand.

I hold my magic close, but not knowing what's inside, I don't try to guess.

"Do come in. We've been waiting for you," a man calls from within, sounding calm and genteel as if he's been holding teatime for our arrival.

Opening the door, I grip Esme's arm, so she enters behind me. She doesn't like it, but I do it anyway.

Standing in the middle of the room is a tall, thin man with white-blond hair and pale skin. His eyes are the lightest blue. His breeches and shirt are both black, accentuating the stark difference between his complexion and his clothing. His lips are twisted into a cruel smile, and he's gripping Trina by her hair.

Eyes wide but empty, Trina hangs from his hand like a rag doll.

"We haven't met. Let me introduce myself." He drops Trina, who thuds to the floor. "I've been following your progress, Sir William. Impressive gifts you have. They'll be wasted with these lower witches. That would be a shame. You need a coven that can support you, not these kitchen witches."

Worry for Trina clouds my judgment. I need to stay calm, but if he's killed that child, I don't know what I'll do.

Esme's magic hums. She whispers in my head, "*Alive, but in some kind of trance.*"

Relief fills me. "You have me at a disadvantage, sir. You know about me, but I'm at a loss for who you are."

He rolls his eyes petulantly. "Orin Sallows, formerly of Windsor. I am High Priest of the Kent Coven. They have come a long way since I took control." Evil rolls off Orin like a sour smell.

It's hard to breathe in the wake of such darkness. "Took control. Does that mean you killed the high priestess who preceded you?"

"I relieved her of her duties. She was nothing. She thought to send me away. Of course, I'll not be thwarted again in this lifetime. I'm too powerful for that anymore." He glances at Sara Beth near the hearth.

"Was that your parlor trick that visited the other day?" I hurtle forward, keeping Esme behind me.

Minerva takes Sara Beth's hand.

Sylvia is in the doorway of the stillroom.

Prudence is above, I can feel her, but I don't think she's conscious. Not many witches, but still, they outnumber him. Why did they let him harm Trina?

Orin's laugh is disturbingly joyless. "Parlor trick? That was higher magic than a novice like you can possibly fathom. You think bringing about my temper will distract me. You are a typical gentleman."

"What makes you think I'm a gentleman, Mr. Sallows? We've hardly met." I think about the outcome I want. Sending Orin away and keeping these witches safe.

"You live in a gentleman's home. Your father was a gentleman. You were knighted. What more do I need to know? Your kind is predictable and simple of mind." He steps in front of Trina, a ball of gray light in his right hand.

Esme's magic bubbles behind me.

"Orin, you cannot win this," Sara Beth calls.

He grins, showing straight white teeth. "She worries for me. It's cute that after all these years, she still cares. Yet, she wouldn't come with me when her bitch of a mother banished me from my home." By the end of his recollection, the smile is gone, and he looks ferocious. Red flashes in his eyes. "I'll kill you last, Sara Beth. I want to make certain you see the deaths of everyone you care about. I'll take particular pleasure in tearing your 'great mother' to shreds. I thought she'd be easier to quell, but she took to the trance just like this peasant." He nudges Trina with his boot.

"So, you've come for revenge?" I ask.

"I've come to take this coven from her. I've come to gain what is my right. You could stand at my right hand, William." He opens his arms in a kind of welcome.

I circle to the right. Henry moves with me, keeping Esme between us. "I fail to see how this coven is your right, but that aside, let's go back to what you know of me. For example, did you know I was knighted for my deeds as a soldier?"

"I had heard you were injured, but you seem quite fit." His examination of me is uncomfortable.

"I wonder what pleasure you gain in harming a young girl like Trina or an old woman like Prudence. Was something lacking in your childhood that makes you prey on the helpless?" I keep edging toward the hearth.

A dark shadow falls over Orin's face, and his eyes narrow an instant before he hurls the ball of light at me. Esme throws fire back and the two magics collide, exploding in midair.

Minerva and Sara Beth throw magic.

Orin raises both hands.

Magic fills the room.

The hair on my arms stands as magic sets my skin tingling from every direction. Before it can happen, the carnage is in my mind, bodies lying about dead and injured in my mind. Unable to bear it, I call to my magic to stop the scene. Everything before me freezes.

Esme holds another ball of fire, and she's about to hurl it at Orin from over my right shoulder. I send her magic back to Goddess.

Aiming his pistol, Henry is midstride, moving to my left for a better position. I lift his arm so the shot will do no harm.

Blue, gold, and green magics fly in Orin's direction from the other three witches.

With a swirl of my magic, theirs rain down like fireflies and disappear.

Orin's magic is dark and murky, and it crackles in bolts of lightning from his fingertips.

I ask for strength to disperse his magic to the ashes in the hearth where it can hurt no one.

"Just for a few seconds, Goddess. Please," I pray.

I let loose my breath, and the room comes alive again.

Henry shoots the ceiling, and dust and wood rain down.

Everyone looks too shocked to breathe while they consider what happened to their magic.

I level my gaze on Orin. "No one will die today. Not here. If you are wise, you will pray Goddess saves you from whatever demon has seduced you."

Orin gives Trina's limp body a long look. "I am the demon that you should fear, William." His eyes lack the passion they held before as he flashes into black smoke and is gone.

Esme runs to Trina, who is crying as she recovers from the spell that entranced her.

Sylvia bounds up the steps. "Prudence?"

Minerva helps get Trina into a chair.

My legs feel like water. Kneeling on the floor, I draw a shuddering breath. "I thought I'd lose you all in one moment just like my men on the killing fields."

Esme turns and wraps her arms around me.

Henry squeezes my shoulder. "You did well, sir." He finds a chair near the door and sits. Sweat drips down his face despite the cool day.

On unsteady feet, and with Sylvia's help, Prudence descends the steps. "I never felt him coming. We will need better wards."

Sara Beth runs her fingers through her long dark hair. "I'm a fool. The spells that protect this house have changed little since Orin lived in Windsor. I never dreamed he could have become so dark."

Looking at me, she lets only one tear fall. "What did you do?"

"I removed the threat to life."

"I understand your desire for all to be spared, William, but that might not always be possible. Today, Orin had no notion you could do such a thing, but he will protect against it in the future." Sara Beth folds into a chair. "I wish it was as easy as scaring him, and he'll fly away for good."

"It worked today." Minerva sits between Sara Beth and Trina.

Trina's color is coming back. "He'll come back. He wants the crown. But you did scare him, Sir William. I've never seen Orin afraid before."

My heart begins to slow. "His fear will turn to anger. If he's poisoned the Kent Coven, he'll infect those witches with his rage. Trina is right. He will come back."

"We'll have to make ourselves ready." Sara Beth lifts her chin and pulls her shoulders back. "King George must be protected. Power like Orin's can be seductive, even to someone who has much."

Henry laughs, but there's no humor in the sound. "If

history is to be believed. The more power a man has, the more seductive the idea of gaining more becomes."

"Orin Sallows must never get close enough to tempt the king." Sara Beth stands.

Prudence goes to her and takes her hands. "I have some old friends in and around Kent. Some in the coven and some lone witches. I'll contact each one and see if I can denote changes. We'll gather information and then, it's likely, we'll have to send Minerva."

Esme grips Minerva's hand. "You cannot send her alone."

Smiling at her friend, Minerva says, "I cannot be turned. I can go to Kent with a glamor and not be noticed. I'll be safe enough. It would be nice if Great Mother could find me a witch in the light to stay with, but I can manage regardless."

"You might be impervious to dark magic, but you can still be killed." My pulse speeds up again.

"I'm more formidable than I look. Had you let my magic fly, you would have seen just how cruel my magic can be. Even a witch in the light is allowed to protect herself and those she loves. In fact, it's her duty. I'll be fine." Minerva presses her hand to Trina's forehead and the girl's worried eyes soften.

"I should go. It's me that Orin wants." I stand up.

Esme stands beside me. She doesn't want to go to Kent, but she'll never leave my side. I'm bolstered by that knowledge.

Prudence ambles across to me. She cups my cheek. "You have a wife with a child on the way."

Cheeks pinkening, Esme presses her hand to her abdomen. Wide-eyed, she stares from Prudence to me. "I think she's right."

Fear, joy, jubilation, and every other emotion known to man riot through me. "I...I still think I should go. Esme must protect the baby, and I must protect this coven. I have sworn to do so."

"And you will, but from Windsor." Prudence smiles. "You have Trina to heal and the shop. You have your own magic to gain training with. There is much for you here, William. This battle will return, and you must be ready."

I have no choice but to concede.

Once Esme and I have helped build new wards around the coven house, we go to the shop and do the same. By the time we get home, it's after midnight.

Rogers opens the door. "I'm glad to see you both safe, sir, madam. The staff was quite worried."

"Thank you, Rogers. You should get some sleep. Hopefully tomorrow will be a less interesting day."

"I pray so, sir." With a bow, Rogers goes down the hall toward the servants' stairs.

Having returned home earlier, Henry's waiting in the foyer. "Your mother is in the parlor."

He remains in the doorway as we pass.

Mother looks to have aged a few years since we left her this afternoon. Simon is sprawled across her lap, but raises his head when we enter. "If not for this ball of fluff, I'd have known nothing until Dove returned." She scratches Simon's head and is rewarded with a purr. "He knew the moment you were out of danger and relaxed as if none of it ever happened."

"He has a good sense of things." Esme says and sits beside Mother. "We sent Dove to you as soon as we could spare him."

Mother caresses Esme's Cheek. "I know, and I appreciate that more than I can say. However, I had to see you both for myself, or I'd never have found any rest."

I sit on the chair adjacent to the ladies on the sofa. "We are fine. It was not an easy day, but we are fine."

Mother looks from Esme to me. "But this ugly business isn't over yet, is it?"

It's the first time I can really see that Mother does have

some sense that is a kind of magic. "No. I couldn't bear to kill, so the threat remains. Perhaps I bought us a few months by showing him I'm more capable than he thought."

"Esme, you couldn't kill either? That Sara Beth looks formidable to me. Could she not do away with the man?" Mother's brows are high.

Henry chirps a short laugh from the doorway.

With the most beautiful smile and my child growing in her belly, Esme is everything. She shakes her head. "William could not bear it, so he removed the possibility. I've never seen magic like his. We have much work to do to really understand his gift."

"And a young woman to heal. She's had a terrible day as well. We shall bring Trina to live here tomorrow." I stand and offer Esme and Mother each a hand."

Esme takes it, but Mother waves me off. "You two go to bed. I shall sit a few more minutes and process everything you've told me."

"It's all going to be okay, Mother." I want to reassure her. "You could return to the country, where you'll be out of all this madness."

"Perhaps. Go to bed. You too, Dove. I'm fine."

Reluctantly, we leave Mother in the parlor.

In our own room, Esme kicks off her boots and shrugs out of her dress. "Will she go to the country?"

I shrug. "Probably. We can tell her about the baby in a few months. Then perhaps she'll return for the birth."

Esme sits on the edge of the bed. "Are you pleased about the baby, William?"

Kneeling in front of her, I take her hands and press my cheek to her flat abdomen. "I've never been happier about anything in my life." I kiss her fingers.

"A baby." She lets out a long breath. "I never dreamed any of this."

"Perhaps your dreams were too small, my love." Wrapping my arms around her, I stand and lift her to the center of the mattress before toeing off my boots and joining her.

"You may be right, but I could never have dreamed such a perfect life, with such a perfect man. One would think as a witch, I might have sensed you were for me." She runs her fingers through my hair where my head is pressed to her breasts.

"You told me you knew of me before I hobbled into your shop." My eyes are heavy with contentment and exhaustion.

"That seemed like a fantasy. The articles in the paper and your portrait. That was some perfect hero who could never be mine."

"Far from perfect, and I am yours for all our lifetimes." She's lulling me to sleep.

"Thank Goddess for that," Esme says on a yawn.

And I do.

EPILOGUE

ESME

I agreed to come to William's country estate for the final months before the baby arrives. I feel certain it's a girl. It shouldn't matter, but the idea of a daughter makes me exceedingly happy.

Laying on the chaise in the parlor is lovely. With the spring breeze wafting through the window, I doze. William rests his head gently against my round belly and reads some old tome he's found on a top shelf.

Poking her head in the door, Theodora smiles. "I'm going for a walk, if either of you would like to join me."

I'm content and tell William so silently.

"No, thank you, Mother. Take Henry with you for safety's sake, please," William says.

Henry appears an instant later, holding Theodora's wrap for her. "I'm already summoned, sir."

Once they've left, and their voices drift away, William sighs contentedly. He rolls to look up at me with his blue eyes brimming with mischief. "We are alone. Shall we away to the bedroom, or shall I ravage you here in the parlor?"

Laughing, I thread my fingers through his soft hair. "Trina is still at home. How you can find me desirable in my current shape, I shall never understand."

He caresses my full belly and growls. "You are stunning, my love."

Dozing on a chair in the corner, Simon responds to his growl with a hiss before settling back to his afternoon nap.

William snuggles against the baby and wedges himself between my legs. "Trina is in the back garden and likely won't come in until teatime."

With a girlish giggle, I nudge his shoulder. "I think you should read your book, and make love to me this evening when everyone is in bed, and there is no chance of us being interrupted."

"You could throw up a blocking spell and keep us hidden from the world for a few minutes," he suggests.

Mirth rises up in me and tumbles out as a loud laugh that is most unladylike. "A few minutes. Is that all you want? Well then, no need to even move from the chaise if your pleasure is that urgent."

With a laugh and a dramatic sigh, he shakes his head. "You're right. I'll never be satisfied with just a few minutes. I shall wait for dark to have you completely to myself and seduce you properly."

My flesh tingles wantonly. "I shall spend the afternoon looking forward to it, William."

The look he gives me is positively ravenous. "So shall I."

Being with child means that laying in one spot for too long is uncomfortable. I wiggle around him to sit up, then rise and stretch my aching back.

William rubs from the midpoint to the swell of my bottom and helps relieve the ache.

"What are you reading?" I take a turn around the room and admire all the blue and white furniture and dark woods. Outside the tall windows, the trees that wrap around the drive are full of sappy leaves and the warm scent of spring.

Trina helped me plant a fine garden in the back of the house, and I spend time tending it daily in hopes of a good crop for the shop. With Minerva in Kent, Sylvia and Ava are taking turns minding things while I'm away. Having a coven has its benefits.

"It's an old journal written in 1701 by an ancestor named Early Meriwether. He gives some indication that he knew he was a witch but hides all evidence from society. I found an interesting passage." He flips the pages back as he sits up.

Giving Simon a scratch on the chin, I smile at how the sweet feline always makes me feel content. I return to the chaise and sit next to William. "What does it say?"

"It speaks of an old enemy who has become a fiend or ghoul. I'm not sure what he means. He says the fiend came calling at his home and had to be spirited off." William studies the handwritten page.

"This Early is very cryptic. Fiend and ghoul then spirit. What else does he say?" My gut tightens.

William shrugs. "Only that he'd won the battle, but the war would rage on until forest burned."

"Forest?"

"That's what he says, though his spelling is poor." He holds up the book and shows me where it's spelled "forrest."

Finding it hard to draw breath, I read over what William just told me. "Could it be intentionally spelled wrong? Could he have been talking about destroying an old family foe whose name was Forrester, and over sixty years, the last two letters were lost to time?"

"But he calls him a ghoul and a spirit. Forrester was a witch as far as I can tell, and even with the length of our lives, would have been quite old by 1701."

An uncomfortable chill runs up my spine. "If a witch turns to darkness and becomes a master of the craft..."

"What?" William takes hold of my shoulders and turns me to face him. His eyes are full of worry.

I calm my breathing. "There are tales of witches turning to demons and extending their lives indefinitely by inhabiting other dark witches."

"Orin." William breathes the name softly. "Forrester is Orin. That's what he meant by his being the demon I should worry about."

My heart sinks. "You will have to go to Windsor and tell Sara Beth. This is too dangerous to be sent in the post."

"I'm not leaving you. I will try a fire spell. Sara Beth uses them to communicate, and I've been studying the skill. If I fail, then I'll send Henry to the coven with a note." He wraps his hand around mine and kisses my forehead.

It's silly, but I'm flooded with relief. "*Somehow, I know we must stay together until after the baby is born.*"

He nods and pulls me into his arms. "I know. I feel it, too. The demon would like to separate us and see if we can be defeated individually now that he's seen how powerful we are together. We'll not give him that chance."

Trina sashays in with a large vase filled with spring flowers. She looks at us and freezes. "What's wrong?"

It's a loss to separate, but I force a smile. "Nothing. We may have figured something out about Orin's power, and we had a little fear. All is well. Those flowers are beautiful."

The baby kicks, and I rub her little foot and tell her, "You should be more polite."

Simon sits up. He no longer hisses or scratches Trina, but he's still wary.

With haunted eyes, Trina places the flowers on the table near the window. "Do we have to leave here?"

William's smile is warm and reassuring. "No. We will remain in the country as a family until the baby is old enough to travel to Windsor. Be at ease, Trina."

She nods and offers a forced smile before heading for the door. "I'll go check on tea. Where is madam?"

"She went for a walk. I'm sure she'll return shortly." I push away the worry, and the baby calms inside me.

Once Trina has gone, I say, "She's finally coming around to find some joy. I hate the idea that battles are yet to be fought, and those will set her back."

"She must fight her demons both real and imagined, Esme. As must we all."

He's right, of course. I lean in and press my lips to his.

Deepening the kiss, William devours my mouth.

My body thrums with excitement that makes me wish I'd not turned down his earlier offer. I wrap my arms around his neck and toy with the hair at his collar.

His fingers skim up and down my back before he cups my bottom and pulls me close.

The tenderness is cut short by the sound of Theodora and Henry at the front door. He smiles and shrugs. "Later, my love."

"I will hold you to that promise." I attempt a wicked grin even as warmth fills my cheeks.

"I shall never break any of my vows to you." His whisper sends a tremor of desire between my legs.

"No. You never have, my sweet William."

As the family gathers for tea, I'm warmed by both having

such closeness here and in Windsor, and knowing that I'll have William to myself in a few short hours.

Perfect.

Thank you for reading Magic Touch. I hope you enjoyed book one of the Witches of Windsor. Keep an eye out for Magic Word, coming this fall. Better yet, subscribe to my newsletter and get all the information first.

www.asfenichel.com/newsletter

In the meantime, if you love the paranormal historical mix, you'll love Ascension for your next read.

ASCENSION
The Demon Hunters – Book 1

When demons threaten London, even ladies must answer the call...

Lord Gabriel Thurston returns home from war to find his fiancée much changed. She's grown from a sweet girl into a mysterious woman who guards her dark secrets well. When he sees her sneaking away from a ball, he's convinced it's for a lovers' rendezvous. Following her to London's slums, Gabriel watches in horror as his fiancée ruthlessly slays a man.

Lady Belinda Clayton's only concern was her dress for the next ball—until demons nearly killed her, and a group of Demon Hunters saved her life. Now, a lady by day, and a demon hunter by night, she knows where her duty lies. Ending her betrothal is the best way to protect Gabriel from death at a demon's hands.

Gabriel soon realizes, like him, Belinda has been fighting for her country. He joins in the fight, determined to show her that their love can endure—even at the gates of Hell.

Also by A.S. Fenichel

HISTORICAL PARANORMAL ROMANCE

Witches of Windsor Series

Magic Touch

Magic Word

The Demon Hunters Series

Ascension

Deception

Betrayal

Defiance

Vengeance

HISTORICAL ROMANCE

The Wallflowers of West Lane Series

The Earl Not Taken

Misleading A Duke

Capturing the Earl

Not Even For A Duke

The Everton Domestic Society Series

A Lady's Honor

A Lady's Escape

A Lady's Virtue

A Lady's Doubt

A Lady's Past

The Forever Brides Series

Tainted Bride

Foolish Bride

Desperate Bride

Single Title Books

Wishing Game

Christmas Bliss

Christmas Chase

CONTEMPORARY PARANORMAL EROTIC ROMANCE

The Psychic Mates Series

Kane's Bounty

Joshua's Mistake

Training Rain

The End of Days Series

Mayan Afterglow

Mayan Craving

Mayan Inferno

End of Days Trilogy

CONTEMPORARY EROTIC ROMANCE

Single Title Books

Alaskan Exposure

Revving Up the Holidays

SHORT CONTEMPORARY ROMANCE

WRITING AS ANDIE FENICHEL

Dad Bod Handyman

Carnival Lane

Lane to Fame

Changing Lanes

Heavy Petting

Mountain Lane

Summer Lane

Hero's Lane

Visit A.S. Fenichel's website for a complete and up-to-date list of her books.

www.asfenichel.com

About the Author

A.S. Fenichel gave up a successful IT career in New York City to follow her husband to Texas and pursue her life-long dream of being a professional writer. She's never looked back.

A.S. adores writing stories filled with love, passion, desire, magic and maybe a little mayhem tossed in for good measure. Books have always been her perfect escape and she still relishes diving into one and staying up all night to finish a good story.

Originally from New York, she grew up in New Jersey, and now lives in Missouri with her real-life hero, her wonderful husband. When not reading or writing she enjoys cooking, travel, history, and puttering in her garden. On the side, she is a master cat wrangler and her fur babies keep her very busy.

Connect with A.S. Fenichel
www.asfenichel.com